Also by Joyce Maynard

Looking Back

baby love

Joyce Maynard

baby love

New York   Alfred A. Knopf   1981

For Steve

This wee one, this wee one
This bonny winking wee one
The first night that I with him lay
Oh then hee got this wee one
I'de bin a maide amongst the rest
Were not I gott this wee one

SEVENTEENTH-CENTURY SCOTTISH POEM

baby love

Four girls sit on the steps outside the Laundromat. It's unusually hot for May, and they have just put three dimes in the dryer, which they are sharing. Sandy, who uses Pampers, doesn't need to do the wash, but she's here to keep the others company. Tara could have left her laundry another day too, but she has made a little pigtail with Sunshine's inch and a half of blond fluff and put a ribbon in it. She wants the others to see—particularly Wanda, whose baby, born with thick black hair, is now bald.

They are sixteen years old, except for Sandy, who is eighteen and married. They all wear size seven jeans except Wanda, who used to wear size five but gained sixty pounds when she was pregnant and still has forty to lose.

"I got this cocoa butter at the health food store," Sandy tells Jill, pulling up her India-print shirt to show her stomach. "See. No stretch marks." Jill has just told the others that her period is now six weeks and four days late. She's fairly sure that she's pregnant. If it's a boy she will name him Patrick, after her favorite actor on *Dallas*.

Across the street at the Gulf station, Sandy's husband, Mark, is looking under the hood of his car, which he has

brought in for an oil change. The car is a 1966 Valiant with
a slant-six engine and has only 32,000 miles on it. He is
about as proud of this car as Sandy is proud of Mark Junior,
who will be celebrating his five-month birthday next
Wednesday with a party to which Tara and Wanda and
their babies, Sunshine and Melissa, are also invited. Sandy is
going to make devil's food cake with coconut icing, and there
will be paper hats for the babies. Jill will be there too. Mark
plans to go trout fishing that afternoon.

"He's so cute, Sandy," says Jill, meaning Mark and not
Mark Junior. (At this moment Mark's rear end is all that can
be seen of him, leaning over the Valiant.) "You're real
lucky." Just then Ronnie Spaulding walks past—he is on his
way to the Rocket Sub and Pizza shop for a grinder—and
the girls stop talking. Wanda tosses her head so her hair falls
over her shoulders and shifts Melissa onto her stomach. The
girls are very busy for a moment, adjusting their babies'
shirts and kissing their heads. (For the first time in her life,
Tara never has to worry what to do with her hands.) When
Ronnie has gone, they all giggle quietly.

They do not talk a whole lot. For one thing, they have
covered most subjects by this time. They know, for instance,
that Virgil Rockwell is the one responsible for Jill's present
condition, though he doesn't believe she is really going to
have a baby and says she is just trying to get in good with her
friends. They know that Wanda is on the waiting list for a
job at Moonlight Acres Takeout this summer. They know
that Tara's mother is a bitch and refuses to call Sunshine
anything besides *it,* and says Tara should put her up for
adoption. They know that Mark and Sandy had a big fight
last night because Mark doesn't like still having Mark Junior
sleeping in their bed (Mark and Sandy bought a water bed
with the check Sandy's grandmother sent for her birthday),
but Sandy read an article in a magazine about the sudden
infant death syndrome and she doesn't want the baby alone
at night until he's past the danger age. Also—the others
thought this was pretty funny—one time she climbed into

Mark Junior's crib to see what it felt like to lie there and from flat on her back on the crackly rubber mattress the room looked very spooky. She noticed, among other things, that the clown mobile she had chosen so carefully, at the K-Mart, just looked like a bunch of flat disks floating around. She also thinks it is traumatic starting out your life behind bars. Mark said, "Don't you think it would be pretty traumatic to start out your life waking up in the middle of the night and seeing your parents screwing right next to you?" Sandy—who really wouldn't mind if they never did that anymore—said, "We can do it on the couch." Mark said, "What the hell did we get a water bed for?"

So the girls are just sitting in the sun. Wanda would like to get a tan. It's three months since Melissa was born, but she still looks fat and she thinks that a tan would make her face seem thinner. If she were in school she would be thinking about the prom around now—picking out a pattern at Martin's with her mother, probably, or even shopping for a dress store-bought. She has no regrets though. Now she has her own apartment, just above Rocket Subs. She can have chocolate ice cream for breakfast if she wants. She gets food stamps, and money from the baby's other grandmother, Mrs. Ramsay, whose husband is dead, whose son joined the navy six months ago, and who says, "I don't care about marriage licenses, just so I have a grandchild." Mrs. Ramsay has crocheted five different jacket-and-bootie sets for Melissa and baby-sits anytime Wanda goes on a date. Wanda was surprised that even when she was eight months pregnant, guys would take her out and not even necessarily do anything. One of them—Sam Pierce, who was older, thirty, and worked at the mill—was mostly just interested in seeing what she looked like with no clothes on, and she was actually sort of proud to show him. Nobody had seen her except the doctor at a clinic. She was never big on top before and then she was huge all of a sudden. Sam Pierce had wanted to suck on her breasts, which she didn't tell anybody. She thought this was weird but also she liked it. He grew up on a farm, so he knew—which she didn't—that what comes out wasn't milk, it was colostrum. The milk comes later, he said. Actually, Wanda had not breast-fed Melissa. A girl she knows said, "That will ruin your boobs and then for sure you'll never get anyone to marry you." So Sam Pierce was the only one who ever sucked on her breasts. He hasn't come around in a long time.

Sunshine wakes up crying. Tara's mother says Sunshine has colic and that it is because Tara breast-feeds the baby and it isn't getting enough milk. Tara has no intention of putting Sunshine on formula though. She has observed that Sandy's and Wanda's babies have splotchy rashes on their faces, while Sunshine's face is smooth as an apricot. Privately she also believes that Sandy's son is overweight. You can count three chins on Mark Junior, while Sunshine has a chin like Cheryl Tiegs. Tara plans to get her a bikini this summer, for the beach.

Tara had never gone all the way before. The boy was Sterling Lewis, who is on the basketball team and planning to go to Dartmouth like his father, the year after next. It was their second date and there has never been another. She has not discussed the baby with Sterling Lewis—though her mother has written many long letters to Mr. and Mrs. Lewis, late at night, when she is drunk. Tara is not sure whether her mother mails these letters or not. Anyway, Sterling Lewis goes with Leslie Dillon now, and is always deep in conversation when she passes him on the street. Tara does not really care. Going all the way did not seem to be a very big deal—it happened so fast she is still not too clear about the details but feels dumb asking, since obviously she is a mother, and should know. All that matters is she has Sunshine now, and soon she will find a job and get out of her mother's house and get her own apartment with a room for Sunshine, which she will decorate with a mural of *Sesame Street* characters. She was always good in art.

"Don't you feel weird doing that right in the open, with

guys around and everything?" asks Jill, as Tara unbuttons
her shirt.

"Some thrill," says Sandy, laughing. Even now, Tara
has very tiny breasts. Sunshine twists her mouth sideways,
trying to locate her mother's nipple. She makes tiny snorting
noises as she catches hold, curling her fist around the edge of
Tara's collar.

Ronnie Spaulding comes out of the Rocket Sub shop
and crumples an empty Coke can in his hand. Wanda picks
a piece of fluff out of Melissa's nostril. Ronnie stops in front
of the Laundromat, looks over his shoulder as if maybe he's
checking to see whether a train is coming. Not really, of
course—no trains run through this town.

"So, Wanda," he says, starting past the group on the
steps now, in the direction of the dryers, which have all
stopped spinning now. "I was wondering if you'd like to go
bowling Saturday."

Wanda says she guesses so. Ronnie says, "See you."
Sandy, noticing that Mark has slammed down the hood of
their car, gathers up her diaper bag and adjusts the visor of
Mark Junior's sun hat, which says "Little Slugger" on the
front. She shifts the baby onto her hip as she crosses the road.
"Stop over tonight," she calls to Jill. "I'll lend you some cute
tops."

Ann would feel better if it were raining. When the sun's
shining like this she feels guilty sitting in the house with the
TV set on, eating pancakes. She has been sitting here on the
couch for three soap operas and a quiz show. She had popcorn for breakfast—left over from last night—and then she
had a doughnut and it was stale, left her feeling that wasn't
what she really wanted. She should have something like oat-
meal for breakfast, or a little bowl of granola. High in cal-
ories, but filling. Eat something you really like and you
won't eat so much. So she had a bowl of granola and just as

she was getting to the bottom of the bowl she thought she'd put some honey yogurt on top and it was so good she had another bowl with more yogurt. There was a little yogurt left then, so she made herself another bowl to finish it off. Then she did fifteen sit-ups. Then an ad came on for maple syrup, with a family sitting around the table—father, mother, a boy about eleven and a girl around nine. Trina's age. That's when Ann got up and made herself some pancakes. Now she is undoing the top button on her jeans, pulling a blanket around her. In a minute she will fry up the rest of the batter. Soon she will turn off the TV set. Then she will eat another cup of yogurt, but only because that makes it easier to throw up. She will go into the bathroom and pull the shades. She will tie back her hair and run cold water over her index finger and stick it down her throat.

This is why she is not fat. She's not skinny anymore, but no one would call her fat. Just sort of puffy looking. She thinks about what Rupert would think if he walked in right now and saw her standing over a toilet full of vomit at two o'clock on a beautiful sunny afternoon. He's probably planting tomatoes right now. No, Trina must be home for vacation. They're probably traveling. Maybe they've taken a canoe up the Allagash River and built a tepee on a bank somewhere. Maybe they are sitting in a café in Vienna eating Black Forest cake. She pictures Rupert sitting at the corner table of the Copper Kettle waiting for her, because she has never been to Vienna and cannot picture that.

When Rupert told her she should move out she remembers thinking: Now I'm going to find out what it means to have a nervous breakdown. They were on vacation in Florida—Rupert got Trina on vacations—and Trina wanted Rupert to fly a kite with her and he had looked at Ann and said, "I'm too old to go through this all over again." She remembers bending to pick up her towel, trying to push her foot into her sandal without unbuckling the strap, thinking: In a minute something is going to happen, and waiting, almost curious, to see whether her legs would give out under her or whether she would walk into the water with all her clothes on or straight into the path of one of the cars that are always racing up and down the sand at Daytona. Maybe in a minute she would begin to scream.

But what happened was, she turned in the direction of the hotel, smiled when she passed the woman from Burlington whom she met in the lobby the day before, remembered her room number. Opened the top drawer, with her stack of T-shirts on one side and Trina's Old Maid deck and jacks on the other side. Packed. When Rupert and Trina came back to the room—not right away, because Trina had wanted to fly her kite some more—Ann said, "My mother's sick. I have to go home right away." Trina said, "You mean you can't come with us to Disney World?" and Ann said, "I guess not." There were no more planes that day, so they all had dinner together that night. Nothing special, just the hotel restaurant. Ann thought she would be unable to chew, or to swallow, or that Rupert might suddenly pull the cloth off the table with all the food on it and say, "Surprise, I didn't mean it." But they had a normal meal and then they went to the movies—*The Muppet Movie,* which they had seen twice before because it was Trina's favorite. Rupert still laughed at the part where Kermit rides a bicycle, with his little toothpick legs.

Then they went back to the hotel, put Trina to bed. Ann thought: Now something will happen. She had begun to cry—not uncontrollably, still—and Rupert said, "Trina will hear." She said, "Then come into the bathroom." So he sat on the edge of the bathtub and she sat on the toilet and couldn't think of any of the things she'd been saying to him, in her head, all through the movie. Just please let her stay and she would promise not to interfere with his work anymore, didn't need to have a baby if he didn't want one. Just please let her stay. She can remember him leaning toward her and how she thought: Now he's going to put his arms around me. What he did was, he tore a piece of toilet paper off the roll, folded it over three times and handed it to her.

He said, "I hope you didn't get a sunburn today. Put some aloe on it when you get home."

All this she can remember very clearly. She plays these scenes over in her head nearly every day, picking out different parts to focus on, saving them for nighttime, usually when she's in bed. Sometimes she thinks about the flight back to Vermont, dusting the snow off the car, having to empty her purse out in the snow to find his keys. Leaving a little pile of crumbs, a couple of dry roasted peanuts, a couple of seashells lying there for someone to wonder how there would get to be shells in the Burlington airport parking lot in March. Sometimes the scene she focuses on is her and Trina lying in the double bed that night—Rupert said Trina would feel left out if I sleep with you on our vacation. She remembers lying awake all night, just wishing she could be alone and cry, needing to cry the way sometimes, when she was little, she'd need to go to the bathroom during a test. Thinking she might burst. Watching Trina sleep, with her mouth open and a corner of her nightie wound around her thumb. Dreaming about Disney World probably.

What happened after is blurred. Clearing her clothes out of his closet, sorting out her records—Bob Dylan, the Rolling Stones, the song Trina thought was so funny, about a dead skunk—from his shelf full of Glenn Miller and Sinatra. She remembers drawing a picture of herself, naked, in the dust on her bedroom window, trying to picture him finding it, feeling sad.

What she did then was take the money that her father had left her out of the bank and open a checking account. She bought a new red car and a stereo tape player and sixteen cassettes that same afternoon. She drove the U-Haul with her clothes and records to her friend Patsy's house in Brattleboro, bought six newspapers and circled all the real estate listings that had old houses and land and didn't cost too much. She spent three weeks driving around Vermont and New Hampshire and upstate New York and then she found a Cape with four fireplaces and twenty-four acres with a brook running through at the end of a dirt road. The real estate agent—a man about Rupert's age, early fifties—said didn't she want to consult her parents about this, hire someone to check out the roof and the sills. "Of course I'd like to make the sale," he said, "but I've got a daughter about your age and I sure wouldn't want her taking on something like this." Ann had seen her mother only once in the two years since she left college and moved in with Rupert. She would have liked Rupert to see the house, know what she was doing, but she said no, I don't want to consult anyone, and bought it with cash.

This was a year and a half ago, when she was twenty. She thinks now that she does understand what it means to have a nervous breakdown. It's not something that happens like a heart attack—nothing so dramatic as walking into the ocean and disappearing. For her it has meant sitting on this couch watching soap operas for eleven months, driving into town every day to buy yogurt and bananas and cheese and raisins and movie magazines and Dolly Parton records and Kahlúa and a deluxe Golden Touch sewing machine she'll never learn how to use, and a loom and a .35-millimeter camera and a ten-speed bike and begonia bulbs and grape vines. She buys plants and then never gets around to planting them. They sit in the wheelbarrow she bought, dropping leaves. Sooner or later they die, and it depresses her, seeing them every day on her way out to the car. So finally she takes them to the dump and then she buys more, and pretty soon they die too.

Mark stands in front of the bathroom mirror holding an imaginary guitar. They're playing the new Grateful Dead album on the radio without commercials and he's pretending he's the bass player. He is not wearing a shirt. He's so involved in the fingering during this particular song that he doesn't even see Sandy—who has just put the baby down for a nap—standing in the doorway watching him. "Hamburgers or tuna casserole?" she says.

"Don't you ever cook something different?" he asks her. "Roast beef or pot roast or something?"

Sandy has in fact planned something different for dinner: harlequin parfaits, from a recipe she saw on the back of a Cool Whip package. She has bought candles and a bottle of Cella Lambrusco. This was supposed to be a surprise.

"Roast beef costs a dollar eighty-nine a pound in case you didn't notice," she says. "Your fly's unzipped. Gross." He is not wearing shorts. He has plenty in the drawer, of course—ironed. He just likes the way it feels, wearing none.

This isn't what he thought it was like, being married.

He has no idea when it was, the first time they met. Mark and Sandy were born in this town, their parents belong to the same church, they have simply always known each other. They were Mary and Joseph in the Congregational Christmas pageant one time, and lab partners, years later, in chemistry. Sandy had filled out by then: she was always cute, but around freshman year she also got a figure. Mark would think about lab session all week, worry because his hand trembled while he held the Bunsen burner, that he'd light the curled-under ends of her hair, which is honey blond.

They started dating at the end of sophomore year. The first time they went all the way was a few days after Christmas, junior year. They were baby-sitting for Mark's older sister Charlene, who has twins. She and Mark's brother-in-law left four beers in the fridge for them. "Don't do anything I wouldn't do," Mark's brother-in-law told Mark, at the door of his car just before they took off. Sandy was back in the house, waiting for one of the babies to burp.

She didn't hear him come back into the house. He had taken off his shoes so he wouldn't track in snow. Came up behind her very quietly, and she was singing to the baby.

She was only sixteen then, but already she looked like a mother.

The truth is (Mark doesn't like to think about this), Sandy has never turned Mark on as much as some other girls, though she's the only one he ever loved. When he would lie in bed alone and think about fucking he would picture one of the cheap girls in school, like Candy Patenaude, who didn't wear underpants, or Joyce Munson, who's pretty ugly. "Mouth like a cunt," one of the guys on the basketball team used to say.

But that time upstairs in his sister's house, with the Christmas tree lights blinking and the smell of fried chicken still in the air, some stupid TV show droning down in the family room—*Price Is Right,* it sounded like—and Sandy's off-key voice singing "Hush little baby, don't say a word," it was almost like they were married, and that was their bedroom across the hall with the chenille spread all smoothed out and the big jar of Vaseline next to it on the nightstand, the two pairs of slippers lined up on the floor. It was almost like that was their wedding picture, not his sister's, on the bureau, and the twins were theirs. Mark got this tremendous hard-on, just thinking about it, and when Sandy laid the baby down and turned around, he sort of fell into her arms.

Even then he can't say he was so anxious to go all the way exactly, he just knew he had to. It was like a responsibility, part of being a family man, and it went with those beers in the refrigerator, the eagle-design bedspread and the file box on the kitchen counter, filled with proof-of-purchase panels from cereal boxes. After it was over he was a little surprised there wasn't more to it. Later he bought a copy of *The Hite Report* to find out how many times a month most people did it. And when he and Sandy have done it three times in a week he sometimes feels like he has been let off the hook, knowing he can take a few nights off if he feels like it, or not take a few nights off, and be above average.

He always knew they'd be married sometime, though he wasn't expecting Sandy to get pregnant when she did, in

spring of junior year. He didn't like his mother thinking
Sandy was fast, thinking that was the only reason they got
married. He wished he could've taken his diploma, taken the
two-year auto mechanics course at the Manchester Techni-
cal Institute. He wished they could have had a real wedding
like his sister's, with Sandy in the long white gown.

But other than that, he was happy enough about the
baby. He loved doing all that stuff like putting his head
against her stomach and feeling it kick and making lists of
names. (He told Sandy if it's a boy what about George, for
your father, but of course he was secretly happy when she
said no, Mark Junior.) He loved fixing up their apartment.
(Sandy has a touch, and could be an interior decorator, in
his opinion, except of course she wants to stay home with the
baby.) He didn't mind how big her stomach got, even when
they couldn't make love anymore, by the ninth month. It
was worth it, to walk down the street with his hand pressed
against the small of her back and have everybody know he
was the reason she had this enormous belly sticking out a full
foot and a half in front, those (briefly) enormous breasts.

She made felt Christmas stockings with their names
stitched in sequins. (She left the baby's blank because he
wouldn't be born for another week.) Christmas morning she
gave Mark a Swiss Army knife and a box of White Owl
cigars to hand out after the baby was born, and a vest she'd
made from a kit, orange and green crochet. He wore it to
Christmas dinner at her folks', to please her.

He gave her a kitten, which got run over by a car three
weeks later. He also gave her a pressure cooker, which his
mother said was one of the five most important ingredients
to a good marriage, and a pink lacy nightgown to take with
her to the hospital, and for a joke, a copy of *Playgirl* magazine with a bookmarker in the page where the foldout was.
She didn't understand it was supposed to be a joke and said,
"Why would I want to look at that?" And even then she
wouldn't leave it alone. "That was a waste of a dollar-fifty,"

she said later in the day. "When there are so many things we need."

He came home one time (Mark Junior was born by now) and found her sitting around with her friends. They were all laughing in this high, hysterical way girls have when they get together. The minute he walked in they stopped.

The baby looks nothing like him. "Are you sure you're the father?" his brother-in-law said (kidding). More than one person has called Mark Junior Sandy's clone.

"Doesn't Sandy know it's more expensive to buy name brands?" his mother said one time when she stopped over with something for the baby. "The store brands taste just the same." Also, she should defrost the refrigerator.

"So how's the new man in your wife's life?" said his mother-in-law when he ran into her at the post office. Mark had to think for a minute before he understood what she meant.

"Has she bought you an apron yet?" said Virgil. He and Jill dropped over one night on their way to a Bob Seger concert in Boston. Sandy was already asleep in their bed, with Mark Junior in her arms. The six-week period when they weren't supposed to make love was over, but they still hadn't done it. Virgil kept nuzzling his head against Jill, burrowing his face in her hair. They started to arm wrestle, and then he pinned her on the floor, kneeling down between her spread legs in tight jeans. Mark was afraid his face might be turning red, and went to get a cigarette.

His sister called him an old married man. When he picked up his son the baby cried. People started asking when they were going to have another one.

Sandy must have told Jill they weren't doing it yet, because one day Virgil stopped him, said, "Must be getting pretty horny by now, huh?"

She left him with the baby for an afternoon, when she went for her postpartum checkup and to be fitted for a diaphragm. When she came home, with her mother—her mother was in on this—the two of them started that high-pitched laughing again. Evidently Mark had put the baby's diaper on wrong, though he couldn't see what was so humorous about that.

She still keeps the house very clean, though there are a few things she never remembers to do, like sponge off the part of the toilet underneath the seat, the part he uses. She's also a terrible cook.

And lately he has been thinking about sex more often, having these ideas that never occurred to him before. Things about tying her down, doing it standing up. Things that aren't about her at all. If he told anyone they would lock him up.

He hasn't forgotten why he wanted to get married, how good it feels to wake up in the morning curled around her, the warm safe feeling of their bed, even when Mark Junior has soaked through his diapers in the night, and there's a moist pissy spot under him. He liked buying an insurance policy and having Sandy's name to write on the line that said Beneficiary. He likes going to Howard Johnson's on Fish Fry Night— the three of them—and seeing the waitress come toward them with a high chair for his son. He still gets a kick out of saying "my wife," "my family," and tries to work them into the conversation when he can.

But instead of making him feel more like a man, Sandy sometimes makes him feel like a little boy. Twice he has called her Mom by mistake. And one time, for a couple of seconds there, he couldn't remember what his son's name was.

He just wishes he hadn't been in such a rush. It's like tearing down the highway to get to this party by seven-thirty, and then you get there and it's really kind of boring, and you think: How am I supposed to fill the time between now and midnight? Because even though it's not that great, you still don't want to go home.

* * *

Because the weather has finally turned nice, Reg Johnson has taken his Rototiller out of the garage, and is turning over the soil so he can get his lettuce in. He's also glad to get out of the house: eight days of rain, stuck listening to Doris gabbing on the phone, left him ready to dig ditches just so he could escape.

One day last fall, Reg's neighbor Pete Murphy stopped by on his way back from the mailbox when Reg was boarding up his dormer windows. He said, "I see you're shutting the dormers for the winter," and Reg had stopped in his tracks for a minute there, just looking at Pete. Reg thought he'd heard Pete say he was shutting Doris up for the winter. He figured Dr. Joyce Brothers would say that's what he must really have had on his mind.

What he's thinking about now is another neighbor, the girl down the road. He sees her driving past his house every day around noon, coming back a half hour or so later. She has a red car—foreign. He doesn't know her name. He can tell she's very young, and wonders what she's doing living by herself in the old Richards place. Doris says she's probably got some drug headquarters going. How else would you figure she'd get the money to buy a piece of property like that? (Reg and Doris had to take out a second mortgage on their own place, after Reg hurt his back and had to quit his job. Now most of Doris's conversation centers on how much everything costs.)

Reg wonders why the girl doesn't have a boyfriend. He never sees any cars heading down the road except hers. "She must get pretty lonely down there," he says to Doris, who answers that it takes all kinds. This is her response to most things he says to her, and to every night's Walter Cronkite broadcast. "Live and learn." "What can you expect?" "It takes all kinds."

This afternoon, he thinks, he will walk down the road and say hello. Neighbors should introduce themselves. She might want him to Rototill a garden patch. The Richardses used to have a beautiful garden.

He turns off the motor and reaches for his jacket, with "Ashford Bowling League" in maroon script on the back. No—no need of a jacket. Just a hat. He runs a comb through what is left of his hair and heads toward the girl's house.

If Sandy is ever reincarnated as a man, she will know just how to act. What it takes to make a woman happy is so simple it's hard to understand why so many men mess things up. It doesn't even cost money. Sandy knows there are those other kinds of women, who want jewels and fur coats and things, but she believes they're the minority. Flowers might be nice, but they don't even have to be roses. A bunch of violets and daisies would work just as well. Better.

Here is all Sandy needs, all most women need, she thinks. (And someday she's going to tell this to Mark Junior, and he will have a very happy marriage.)

A kiss on the cheek first thing in the morning, his hand brushing the hair away from her face. Good morning, darling.

Not just when he wants to make love. When she is cooking the eggs sometimes he might come up behind her and press his lips against the back of her neck. He might put his hands on the sides of her waist. When she comes out of the shower he tells her, "You sure look pretty."

He should be a little interested. When she mentions that she saw this hair clip at Felsen's that would go just right with her blue dress, he remembers, and that night at dinner there it is, all wrapped up in her napkin.

"What did you put in the chicken?" he asks her. "It's so good."

What does a candle cost? A card on their anniversary and occasionally on no particular day: "Just Thinking of You." He could take her dancing, or just some night in their living room he could say let's waltz.

Tell her what a wonderful job she's doing with the baby. Ask her if she's had any interesting dreams lately.

They could buy a bottle of wine some night, take out her old English books and read each other poetry.

He could want to see what she looks like when she was little, say—when her mother visits—"Tell me about Sandy's first day of school."

But the main thing is if he would just talk to her. If— instead of stretching out on the sofa after dinner, watching TV—he would tell her his hopes and fears, describe his day. I'm alone in the house all day long for goodness' sake, with a baby that only says four syllables. I need to hear about your life.

It wouldn't have to be just the good things. Why does he think he has to be a hero all the time? She could comfort him.

He comes home one night with a bag of fresh strawber- ries—remembering how she likes them—and a box of whip- ping cream. He says come outside for a second, I want to show you this fantastic sunset. He hugs his son close to his chest. Why do fathers think all they can do with their sons is wrestle them, tickle them, throw them in the air, make jokes about them having the hots for some ten-month-old girl who's having her diaper changed: "like father like son"?

"You know," he says, "the baby has your chin."

He takes her hand. He tells her his dream, that someday he can get a little piece of land a few miles outside town, build them an A-frame with his own two hands.

"I know you can do it, honey," she says. At this moment there is nothing she wouldn't do for him, absolutely nothing.

Carla and Greg's last stop, before getting onto the FDR Drive, was West Eighth Street for bagels. Dan and Sally have told them you can't find a decent bagel in the entire state of New Hampshire, and there will be plenty of room in the freezer for a couple dozen. Enough to last for a month anyway, and by that time someone is bound to pay them a visit from civilization.

baby love

Dan and Sally keep their place in Ashford for summers mostly, and vacations, but when Sally got a grant to teach a three-month photography workshop in Morocco, they offered the place to Carla and Greg. So now the Volkswagen's packed with three boxes of new paperbacks (a fresh copy of *Walden,* lots of poetry); Carla's cast-iron pots and the Cuisinart, with Marimekko floor pillows around it for protection; the stereo and Greg's jazz collection, his New Wave stuff, Carla's sixties folk and her complete ten-record set of Buddy Holly, the original first-release Patsy Cline album with "I Fall to Pieces." Carla's unsure what kind of clothes people wear in New Hampshire. She has bought a pair of purple overalls and some bright-green high-top Converse sneakers, a half-dozen new hundred-percent-cotton T-shirts and a patchwork skirt she pictures herself square dancing in. Greg has ordered hiking boots from L. L. Bean, a fishing pole and hip boots and a pound of the new sugar snap pea seeds he read about in *Organic Gardening.* Mostly, though, he's planning on making a lot of art this summer. Earlier this morning they stopped by Jaimie Canvas and bought ten gallons of Mars Black and twenty gallons of Titanium White and thirty yards of canvas. Color is too seductive, he told Carla last night, over their linguine. It seems appropriate that at the same time they are giving up their place on Duane Street, their membership in the Y, their 250-gallon saltwater aquarium and Szechuan cooking, Greg should also simplify his work.

Greg teaches art to eleventh- and twelfth-graders at the Walker School. He does his real work on Saturday afternoons and Sundays, and occasionally he shows his paintings at a cooperative gallery in SoHo, where members pay a quarterly fee and take turns waxing the floor in exchange for exhibition rights. What he would like, of course, is to live by his painting, to have a commercial gallery sign him on. Taking his slides around is very depressing though. The last time he made the rounds he was told "We aren't taking on new artists" (four times), "We're only into superrealists," "mini-malists," "younger women painters," "superminimalists."

There's a collector he met through his friend Nick at the Whitney, who has bought three of his paintings—two for his place in the Hamptons and one that hangs in his office at the Chemical Bank building. (Carla is annoyingly proud of this, as if that proves he must know what he's doing.) Greg visits this collector two or three times a year, and always gets his shoes shined on the man's electric shoeshine machine when he does. The collector always says, "You should have a show." When he buys a picture he pays in cash from a wall safe behind an original Stella. Greg puts the money—a thousand dollars last time—into his wallet. After he leaves the collector's office he takes the elevator down one floor, goes to the men's room there and transfers the bills to his shoe. Then he takes the bus home instead of the subway.

Greg has a friend, Turner, who has had a gallery on Fifty-seventh Street representing him for three years. Turner has never had to explain to a sixteen-year-old girl how Jackson Pollock's *Number One* is different from the linoleum floor in her aunt's summer place. Turner has a twenty-three-year-old art student working for him in his loft on Broome Street, stretching canvases—he's turning them out that fast. Greg, on the other hand, has gone through periods when he stopped using red in his work simply because he ran out of red paint and couldn't afford more.

Now, of course, with their two jobs, he and Carla don't have to worry much about money. What hasn't changed is the moment (usually at a party, meeting new people) when someone asks what he does and he says he paints, and then the question comes, "Are you represented by a gallery?" When it's Carla they ask, she'll give a long explanation about the directionlessness of the New York art scene, how gallery owners no longer take risks, how everyone is selling out, and that by paying for his own shows an artist remains pure. Greg tells them flat out, "No gallery." And for a long time he felt so confident about his work, his promise, that it wasn't even so bad when people—hearing that—stopped taking him seriously. But lately he has begun to wonder what the point is of making art almost nobody sees, and fewer understand. He has stopped assuming that someday soon something great will happen in his career. All the openings he attends, of friends' shows, have begun wearing him down.

So he's glad to be getting away from all of this for a while, feels lighthearted, tossing his quarter into the New Rochelle toll basket. The car is filled with the smell of poppy seed bagels, and one of Carla's favorite songs, "Lucille," has just come on the radio. She's harmonizing with Kenny Rogers on the chorus.

"I think I'm going into a heavy country music phase," she says. What she's thinking is, she'd like to have a baby.

Mark Junior can sit up on his own, but because Sandy's slicing the carrots for dinner she has put him in his infant seat on the counter beside her. Propped in front of him is a piece of stiff cardboard with photographs of babies glued to it: the baby from the Ivory Snow box and the baby from an old Pampers box and lots of pictures of babies from magazines. Mark Junior gets very excited when Sandy shows him these pictures—waves his fists and jerks his head forward, makes little bubbling noises. The cardboard is curled up at one corner where he has drooled on it.

Sandy thinks her son is cuter than any of these babies, and wishes she knew how they choose the babies that get to be on TV and in the ads. Before she got pregnant people used to tell her she should be a model, and in fact she had sent away for a brochure from a modeling school in Boston and was planning to enroll as soon as she saved up the money for photographs. Now what she dreams about is getting Mark Junior in one of those ads.

He's also very bright. She began cutting out pictures of

babies for him (she calls them his study boards) when he was just four weeks old and now the Ivory Snow baby is like an old friend. Most of the pictures show mothers and babies, but she's always on the lookout for pictures of fathers and babies because she believes this will help Mark Junior in his bonding. When she was pregnant Sandy read a great deal about infants, and one of the big things they talked about was bonding. The first hour after birth, for instance, is when the child and his parents lay the foundation for their future relationship, which is why Sandy was so anxious not to take any anesthetic and to have Mark stay right beside her the whole time.

They were watching *CHiPs* when her water broke. "Jesus, you got this stuff all over me," Mark said. She had to explain that it wasn't pee. He didn't know anything, he never read the books and skipped all but two of their natural childbirth classes. In the admitting room at the hospital, while he filled out the forms, she had watched another couple. The girl looked a little older than Sandy—maybe twenty-one or -two—and she wasn't very good-looking. But what got Sandy was the way her husband knelt down in front of her on the floor and took off the girl's shoes. It reminded Sandy—though the girl's belly was even bigger than hers—of some fairy tale with a prince and a princess, and afterwards—several weeks after—she had said to Mark during one of their fights, "You never took my shoes off for me when I was pregnant."

In the end Mark was not present for his son's birth. Sandy's labor lasted fourteen and a half hours before the doctor told her she was ten centimeters dilated and could start pushing anytime. She had planned that when this moment came she'd focus on Mark's eyes and that would give her strength, but Mark looked like a stranger to her in the green hospital mask, and also he looked scared, so she focused on a fluorescent bulb on the ceiling that was flickering very slightly. Then she remembers hearing Mark, as if he were far away, saying, "I think I'm going to be sick." When they put the baby on her stomach and cut the cord, the nurse brought him back in. The doctor was stitching her up. "Jesus," he said. "What a mess."

There were many reasons why Ann knew this was the house she wanted. The house came completely furnished, for one thing, and while it didn't contain any particularly valuable antiques, there were things like old tin canisters that said Bensdorp's Cocoa and goose-down pillows and a really solid-looking Mixmaster from the forties, and a waffle iron. Mrs. Richards had died and her daughter lived in Florida, in a mobile home, and didn't have room for anything. So except for a few pieces of silver plate and a couple of crystal candlesticks, everything was left in the house when Ann moved in. A pantry full of china: pale-green Depression glass, eight complete place settings of Fiesta ware, a Blue Willow tea set, a soup tureen with swans for handles. There were linen dish towels hand-embroidered with "R" in the corner and a purple martin house in the yard that was an exact replica of the real house. On the beds upstairs—under the mattresses, for some reason—Ann found a Dresden plate quilt and a Log Cabin quilt, both in pretty good condition. In the garage there was an old croquet set and a completely outfitted picnic basket with a huge silver thermos and blue enamel plates and cups and silverware with bone handles and a blue-and-white-checkered tablecloth. Ann found it the first time the real estate agent was taking her around. She imagined a picnic she would have, if Rupert and Trina came for a visit, with Cornish hens and homemade bread and Brie and chocolate chip cookies and watermelon. She couldn't get that picnic basket out of her mind, and when Cassie Richards turned down her first offer on the house—$35,000—it was the thought of that picnic basket that made her say, without thinking more than half a minute, "O.K. Forty thousand." That was nearly all the money she had—her funds are down pretty low now, and she will have to get a job soon—but Cassie Richards sent back a mailgram: Offer accepted.

Down the road from her house—less than half a mile—is the prettiest waterfall Ann has ever seen, even in a tourist brochure. People in Ashford seem to take Packers Falls for granted: it's never crowded, even on the hottest Saturdays in August. Somebody has built a summer house right next to the falls, but it's usually empty, the yard scattered with trash. Kids throw beer bottles against the rocks along the falls and shampoo their hair in the water, leaving empty tubes of Prell floating downstream. Even so, the water stays clear and full of trout. On a day like this the falls rush so fast Ann can hear them, standing in her driveway. She looks at her dog, asleep under the car, and feels guilty that she doesn't play with him more. "Come on, Simon," she says.

He's excited—runs ahead of her, then backs up, circles so close she almost trips over him. When they reach the falls he jumps onto a rock and takes a long drink. Ann is thinking: I should do this more often. Bring a book. She follows Simon out onto the rocks and cups her hands to taste the water. She spreads her jacket on a flat rock and lies on her back, studying the stone-arch bridge that runs over this section of the brook. It's very old, made without mortar, supported just by the tension of the stones.

She sees them then, in the shadows under the bridge: a boy and a girl on a blanket spread over the largest stone. His jeans are pushed down to his thighs and his buttocks are dead white. The girl lies still underneath him. He pulls away suddenly, his penis still erect. He holds it like a fishing pole.

Ann wishes she could leave, but she knows if she gets up Simon will come splashing toward her, and the boy and girl will see. She feels the way she used to at college, lying on the top bunk listening to Nona, her roommate, whispering to her boyfriend. Nona was very tiny and doll-like. She wore Villager skirts and Lady Manhattan blouses with only the top button undone and wrote to her parents twice a week. Ann could never believe the girl she saw getting out of bed in the morning to do her twenty-five jumping jacks was the same one she heard whispering "Fuck me" and "My cunt's on fire" over and over through the night.

"So he orders a cheeseburger and three pepperoni pizzas to go, with fries and Cokes, and two grinders, right?" the girl is saying. "And when I bring that he says, 'Make that three grinders and a couple side orders of cole slaw.' So I bring him that and he says, 'Do you have brownies?' And you know what he leaves me? Three pennies and some Green Stamps."

The boy has just urinated. Now he's zipping up his pants. The girl folds the blanket very neatly, redoing the folds when she doesn't get the corners just right. The boy brushes a leaf out of his hair. They will be gone in a minute. Ann closes her eyes. Then she hears a voice almost directly above her. The boy.

"Yeah, well, I guess that's how some people get off."

An engine starts, the radio comes on—it's some punk group she doesn't recognize. The car tears down the road, laying rubber.

No one has touched her in a year.

Carla and Greg have been together seven years now, since she was twenty-two and he was twenty-four, but they aren't married. Greg used to suggest, every six months or so, that they go ahead and do it. "Think of the great party we could have," he said. Carla can't imagine leaving him, or who she would rather be with, but she doesn't want to feel trapped either. More accurately, she doesn't want him to feel trapped. She asks him often, doesn't he sometimes fantasize about other women? Which of their friends, for instance? She tells him she could understand this perfectly. She tells him she would rather have him leave her than stay, anytime he starts feeling stuck.

But the truth is, they might as well be married. Greg always sleeps on the left-hand side of the bed. Carla knows not to talk to him until he has been awake twenty minutes. Greg does not pour her coffee until her English muffin is ready, and knows not to butter her muffin until it's cold.

Sometimes, when she's pushing her cart up and down the aisles at D'Agostino's, Carla observes a couple in the early stages of a love affair. She can always identify these couples—the very young ones, at least, the NYU students, young actresses and musicians, recent graduates of bank training programs. For one thing, it takes two of them to choose the groceries. (Greg has not accompanied Carla to D'Agostino's in six years.) They don't buy twenty-five-pound bags of flour or cleanser. They buy things like artichoke hearts and the ingredients for brownies, have comical discussions about whether to get creamy peanut butter or chunk style. The man may put his hand in the girl's back pocket as they move down the aisle—closer, even, than the crowds at D'Agostino's necessitate. They sometimes whisper, but also they tend to make most of the other shoppers aware of their presence in the store, and while Carla finds herself feeling annoyed by the young lovers, she can tell that the housewives—the ones with babies in the front of their carts and envelopes of store coupons in their purses and red plastic bill calculators—really hate these couples.

Carla met Greg at the Museum of Modern Art, in the sculpture garden. Her friend Joan, who used to spend many nights listening to Carla tell her how lonely she was, had said museums were the best place to meet "a preselected group of sensitive men," but that was not why Carla had come to the museum. She was just out of college and working as an assistant to an editor at a women's magazine, writing a play at night. She liked sitting in the sculpture garden and listening to people's conversations. They gave her ideas for dialogue.

Greg was standing in front of a very large Henry Moore of a naked woman. He was wearing neatly pressed corduroy pants but there were paint spatters on his shoes. She liked the fact that he wasn't wearing paint-spattered pants, the way some people did who wanted you to know they were painters. He also wasn't looking at anybody else in the sculpture garden, the way a lot of people were. He stood in front of the sculpture long enough to smoke one cigarette. When he put it out he stroked one of the naked woman's enormous breasts. He did this very slowly, and Carla thought it was an extremely erotic gesture. She tried to think what a character in her play might say, as a way of opening a conversation with this man. She pictured herself going over to the sculpture of a naked man that stood next to the Henry Moore and patting the buttocks or stroking the penis, looking meaningfully in the direction of the painter. She wished she were dressed in an artier way, but she was wearing the black gabardine suit she had bought for her job at the women's magazine and carrying the kind of purse her mother would use. Her mother had given it to her.

She thought she might send this man a message through extrasensory perception. She had tried this sometimes, mostly as a game, on buses—getting a man to talk to her, using just her eyes. One of these men had got off at her stop once and asked if she'd like to have a drink. A pleasant-looking man carrying a briefcase. She stared straight ahead. She is not brave or adventuresome.

Several years ago when she was coming back from Europe on the *Queen Elizabeth* (a package deal) she had met George Harrison. She was at the salad bar, trying to figure out which was the blue cheese dressing, and a thin man in an Indian shirt had leaned over and said, "I wonder if you'd like to join my friend and me for dinner." The friend—wearing a Nehru jacket, recently returned from India—was George Harrison. He asked what she'd been doing in France and she said junior year abroad, told him about getting a flat tire on her bicycle tour of the Loire Valley and the fourteen-year-old French boy in a red beret who had fixed her bike and tried to have an affair with her. George made up a song about *"Je voudrais parler à Carla"* which was pretty good. She asked him how things seemed in Bangladesh, but did not mention the Beatles. He asked her if she'd like to come back to his room and listen to some sitar tapes. She had said—her friend Joan still can't get over this—"I have to get up really early tomorrow" and went back to her cabin.

The painter was moving toward the door. The guard looked at her watch. In an hour Carla would be in her apartment on East Thirtieth Street stirring canned blueberries into a bowl of ricotta cheese, sitting on the floor by the TV set, watching the news. She would probably get a call from Michael, who was in his third year at Johns Hopkins medical school, was studying for his gastrointestinal exams and didn't want her to visit until the end of the term, because it might break his concentration.

She tapped the painter on the arm. He turned around, looked interested but not (as she would be, if it happened to her) startled. She wouldn't have done this if she had realized how handsome he was. She said, "Do you want to have dinner?"

Normally, if there was going to be a man coming over, Carla would take at least half an hour arranging things in her apartment. She would bury the magazines like *Family Circle* underneath a stack of *New Yorkers*, put something classical on the stereo, or a very unmelodic jazz album somebody once gave her that she doesn't really like. When she came back to the apartment with Greg there was a pair of underpants on the floor in the hall (she had been late for work, dressed in a hurry, hadn't remembered those were the ones that never stayed up). There was a three-quarters-eaten Mounds bar on the kitchen counter and a copy of the *National Enquirer*, bought for a story on Marlon Brando's life in Tahiti.

She was not embarrassed. She was surprised to realize that she wasn't asking a great many questions—where did he come from, what did he do, what brought him to New York, did he have brothers and sisters. He did not volunteer much, but she didn't find the silence with him uncomfortable. She said, "Like an omelet?" He said, "Sounds good." She put on the Rolling Stones' *Out of Our Heads* and turned on only one light. They sat on floor pillows across from each other. When he chewed she could see all the bones in his face. He smiled at her. She took off her shoes and pulled a couple of bobby pins out of her hair. He said, "Do you have any coffee?" She ground the beans while he chewed one. She put on Bob Dylan, "Lay Lady Lay," and didn't worry that it might seem too obvious. He put down his cigarette and moved beside her on the floor. She let the telephone ring for about a minute before it stopped. He unbuttoned her shirt and said, "How does this work?" when he couldn't undo her bra, which hooked in the front. She had never slept with someone right off like that.

"You know who that was back at the falls?" Virgil says to Jill, after a minute. The song on the radio is "Rock Lobster."

"Some woman that bought the house down the road from my parents," she says. "She comes into Sal's sometimes for a doughnut." They don't say anything for a minute, listening to the song.

"Why?" says Jill, grabbing at his crotch and tickling him. "Modest?"

"I've got to get the wheels on this thing realigned," says Virgil. "Damn potholes."

"You know," says Jill, "you don't have to pull out before you come anymore. I'm pregnant anyway."

"Are you going to start in on that again? You've been hanging around too much with crazy girlfriends."

"You'll see," she says, smiling.

It's five-thirty when Greg and Carla reach Ashford. Carla takes out the envelope that has Sally's instructions on the back. They turn onto Big Pine Road. "Now we're supposed to watch for a waterfall," says Carla.

A bright-orange truck tears past the Volkswagen, with a

couple of teenagers inside and music blaring. "So much for the peaceful bucolic existence," says Greg.

Then they see the brook, and up ahead, the falls and Dan and Sally's cottage. Greg shut off the engine. Except for a young woman and a dog, just heading up the hill maybe a quarter of a mile away, there is no one, and no other house, in sight. There's a piece of an old condom lying in the dirt. Greg gets a stick and pushes it into the woods. Carla has already gone on ahead with the bagels.

The red car is parked outside the girl's house, but no one answers when Reg knocks on the porch door. He thinks maybe she doesn't hear him, so he opens the door to the porch and tries again, on the kitchen door. On the porch table there are three yogurt containers and an empty granola box. Leaned up against the door is a rosebush that appears to be dead.

He's not the prying kind, but he looks inside the kitchen, in case maybe something is wrong. The place looks different from when old Mrs. Richards lived here, that's for sure. There's a mobile made out of shells hanging over the sink. There's a pan in the sink that has something burnt-looking in it—popcorn maybe. A cat is sitting on the counter eating butter off a plate. The stove has been painted bright red, but some of the paint has peeled off. There's a bookcase inside the kitchen fireplace, made out of cinder blocks and boards, with records stacked on it. She must have a couple hundred records. His daughter Jill would like that.

Still no answer. He guesses he should go. Maybe he will just write a note, ask if she'd like her garden tilled. Looks like the house could use some paint too, and a gutter is falling off the roof. One thing at a time.

There's a pad of yellow lined paper and a felt-tip pen, just inside the door. Shame to come all this way and not leave a note. He looks out to the field again—a perfect spot to grow corn. His own yard is too shady, and all granite besides. He dusts off his boots and steps into the house.

"Maybe you have forced yourself to forget what you and I felt," it says on the yellow pad. "As for me, I would rather be in agony than numb."

Two lines down the page: "I feel like an exile. I have lost your world, and can no longer enter what used to be mine."

"I'm working hard, planning a garden, taking walks. I am thinking about adopting a Cambodian orphan. I have a dog named Simon. I think you would like this place. I hope you would be proud of me."

"I would come back tomorrow if you wanted me."

"I think my heart is broken."

Reg didn't mean to read these things. He puts the pad down. He will try another day. Doris will be waiting supper.

He hears a door slam on the porch, then, and a dog yipping. She is scooping dog chow into a blue ceramic dish.

"Reg Johnson from down the road," he says, shifting his feet. "Thought with this old house and all, maybe you could use a man." She's still standing there, holding the dog dish. He is thinking: She's not that much older than Jill.

"To help out," he says. "I'm pretty handy."

"Yes," she says. "I guess I could."

Doris is surprised—this being Tuesday—that Reg has worn his shorts to bed. This is how she knows he would like to have relations, and they do not usually have relations on Tuesdays on account of *Rockford Files,* which is his favorite show. She finds the show confusing—impossible to follow, if you're also knitting—but she likes Jim Garner. He seems to have put on weight lately; in one of tonight's chase scenes, she thought he might actually split his pants. But there's no getting around it, Jim Garner is a very good-looking man. Kids today: her daughter Jill's idea of a man is this Rod Stewart, who wears eyeliner and a girl's hairdo. How could a young girl look at Jim Garner and not know that was a real man?

Doris has read that Jim Garner and his wife of twenty-three years, Lois, split up recently. What a shame. It doesn't seem fair to Lois, who stood by him during the lean years, before *Maverick*. Raised his children. Some thanks.

Still, Garner is a very attractive man, and if they are going to have relations tonight, Doris will pretend that Reg is Jim Garner. In fact, Reg is built something like Jim Garner. Not so much hair, of course. But he's also a big man.

What Reg is thinking about, as he slides the waistband of his shorts down his legs (he always waits until he is under the covers to do this), is that loose gutter. Tomorrow, when he goes back to the girl's house to till her garden, he will mention the gutter. No need to charge her: it will be a simple job.

Her name is Ann. Looks like an Ann—quiet type. What's she doing down there? What does she do at night? He wonders where her bedroom is. Downstairs probably—there would be no point heating the upstairs for just one person. That room in the front, most likely.

He imagines coming down her road very early one morning—3 or 4 a.m., the hour he leaves the house during hunting season, when he's after his deer. He pictures himself in his red plaid shirt, with his gun over his shoulder, opening the front door. Scuffing the dirt off his boots on the front hall rug. Hanging his orange cap on a hook by the door, walking through the doorway to her bedroom. He would have to duck his head, the ceilings are so low.

She would be wearing a long white nightgown and her hair—why does she tie it back?—would be spread out on the pillow like an angel.

He would just stand there for a few minutes, watching her sleep, the way he used to go into Jill and Timmy's room sometimes, when they were very little, just listening to them breathe. Then he would bend over and pull back the covers. He would see her nipples, pink under the nightgown, and her other hair, down below.

"Your hands are so rough," she says, in that sleepy voice

children have when you get them up in the middle of the night because you've got a long drive ahead, to the grand-parents'.

"I know," he says. He worked on a construction crew before his back gave out on him.

He leans his gun against the bed and bends to unlace his shoes. "Let me do it," she says. She sits up slowly and kneels at his feet. When she bends to untie the knots he can see the tops of her breasts. They're the kind that tilt up.

"I'm sorry," he says. "I have to take this off you."

"I know," she says, and stands in front of him, absolutely still, while he rips the long white gown from the lace at her neck to the hem. It falls to the floor. She's white as a birch.

Then he picks her up and carries her out to the field, the spot where corn would grow so well. He lays her down on a patch of moss and kisses her flat stomach just above where the hair starts. He lowers himself very slowly down over her. He is hard as the butt of a rifle. "Yes," she cries, as if she's wounded. "Shoot through to my heart. My heart is broken."

"Are you finished?" Doris asks him. "Can I get up now and wash?"

Her curlers have left little ridges on his cheek.

The baby's mother has left a can of Enfamil in the diaper bag and a pink terry-cloth sleeper suit, but Mrs. Ramsay does not need these items. As soon as Wanda leaves (she seems to be getting fatter and fatter), Mrs. Ramsay takes down the little jar of Blueberry Buckle that she picked up at the Grand Union last Tuesday. She props Melissa on the sofa next to her, supported by three crocheted pillows. She takes out the yellow duck sweater she has just finished, unties the ugly little sneakers the mother put on and replaces them with yellow booties. "How about some Blueberry Buckle?" she asks conversationally.

"Let's see what we have tonight," she says, opening *TV Week* to Thursday. *"Mork & Mindy.* 'Mork picks a fight with Mindy and she tosses him out of the apartment. Mork: Robin Williams. Mindy: Pam Dawber.' That sounds good.

"Now, at eight-thirty we have a choice. We have *Benson,* comedy. That's the show with the Negro and the little girl. Also *Family Feud,* game. I never cared for that one. And Dick Cavett. He is a strange man, Dick Cavett. Short.

"Nine p.m. 'Julia Child prepares a dinner that won't strain the pocketbook.' We can surely use that. 'Julia suggests stuffed hen, fresh asparagus and salad.' Mmm. Sounds good.

"But we also have *Quincy* and *Barney Miller* and *Hagen.* That's a new show. Hagen is Chad Everett. He used to be on *Medical Center,* before you were born. *That* was a good show.

"Ten o'clock, *Rockford Files. 20/20,* newsmagazine. Dick Cavett again. And I see Johnny has Suzanne Pleshette on to-night. It looks as if we're going to be busy."

Melissa has tipped over on her side, so that one of the crocheted pillows covers part of her face. She is making soft snorting sounds. Mrs. Ramsay has just remembered the little hat she made the other night during *High Plains Drifter.* There was a violent movie for you. She would never let Baby see a show like that.

"What are you doing lying down?" she says. "Don't you like Mork?" She sits the baby back up against the pillows and ties the hat under her chin. Then a bib. She does not in-tend to get Blueberry Buckle on the duck sweater.

"I don't want to upset you," she tells Baby. "But I do not think your mother is up to any good tonight. She is run-ning around with *m-e-n.*" A little trickle of puréed blueberry is dribbling out one side of Melissa's mouth. She has not had solid food before, and doesn't know how to swallow it. Mrs. Ramsay sticks another spoonful into her mouth.

"That is how you got here in the first place," says Mrs. Ramsay. Mork has just walked into a closet and stood on his head.

"She spread her legs. She made terrible noises in the

night. They thought I was asleep, but I heard them. She enjoyed it. She did it over and over again. She is a slut."

Now Bill Cosby is on, eating chocolate pudding. The Negros are everywhere.

"Don't worry," she tells Melissa, who looks as if she has a blue beard. There's Blueberry Buckle all over the duck sweater now, in spite of the bib. "You are coming to live with me soon."

Mark did not finish his harlequin parfait. After three beers (he didn't want the Cella Lambrusco either) he told Sandy, "I'm going for a drive." Most likely he has gone to Rocky's to play pinball. He will probably spend five dollars tonight on those stupid machines and the jukebox. Jill said when she was in there last Saturday he played "Blue Bayou" three times in a row.

She has finished the bottle of wine and wishes there was more. She turns on the TV, but it's just Mork making dumb faces. She turns it off. She takes out the scrapbook her mother gave her when Mark Junior was born—"The Golden Days." She has already filled in the pages concerning the baby's birth, of course. Weight: six pounds twelve ounces. Height: twenty inches. Eyes: blue. First activities: wets on his father, curls hand around mother's finger. Major events of Birth Day: Author of *Born Free* found dead, believed to have been mauled by a lion.

She tries to think of some new things she can write in the book. Mark Junior has been sucking on his fist a lot lately. She thinks he may be getting a tooth. His father gave him a sip of beer yesterday, out of a spoon. Mark Junior screwed up his face and sneezed. Much funnier than any TV character. Why do people sit around watching TV when they could be watching real babies? Sandy can't think of anything bigger or more important, except maybe finding a cure for cancer, than having babies. She still cannot get over the fact that she and Mark made a person. Just two teenagers in the backseat of a '66 Valiant parked in the clearing beside the town dump with the motor running, because it was March. They didn't even have their diplomas, and they made a person. When she marveled at this to Mark he said she was nuts.

She goes into their room, where Mark Junior is lying in the middle of the water bed with a stuffed platypus on one side of him and a plush panda bear Mark won at the Hopkinton fair, the September before the baby was born, on the other side, so he won't roll off the bed. "I'm going to win you the biggest stuffed animal they've got," Mark told her that day. He spent $4.75 at the skeet-shooting booth getting this panda, which was not the biggest stuffed animal they had, although it is pretty good-sized. Now the bear smells faintly of urine, but she doesn't wash it because she thinks it's probably just stuffed with sawdust and she worries that it might get wrecked. And she wants to always have a memento of that day at the fair, which was the best day she and Mark ever spent together. She was six months pregnant—big but not really awkward yet, more like the pregnant women you see in maternity shop ads than the way pregnant women really get to look. He was very proud and protective—kept his hand resting on the small of her back, just where she hurt, and bought her cotton candy, which they shared. He took her on the merry-go-round because most of the other rides were too rough, and she sat side-saddle on a green horse and he stood beside her and whispered "I love you" just as the ride was slowing down. They leaned on the railings by the boats and watched a young couple and their little girl, who looked about three, circling round and round very slowly, with each of the parents holding one of the little girl's hands and not seeming to mind that it was a baby ride. Mark put his arms around her and said, "That's going to be us soon."

Mark Junior sleeps on his stomach with his arms under his chest and his bottom sticking up in the air. His father sleeps absolutely flat on his back with his feet sticking straight out. Sometimes when she comes back to bed after the two o'clock feeding Sandy puts her head on Mark's chest or strokes his cheek, which is still almost as smooth as the baby's. He never wakes up but sometimes, in his sleep, he will say something like "Get back. It's going to blow up," or "Cylinder's misfiring. Timing off." She keeps hoping he'll say something about her, but so far he never has.

A knock at the door. Sandy forgot—Jill must be here for the maternity tops.

She's alone. "Virg dropped me off," she says. "I told him you were giving me some stuff for prom decorations. He'll be back in a half hour."

"I meant to iron these for you," says Sandy, pulling a box out of the closet. She shakes out a jersey with "Baby" written on the front and an arrow pointing down.

"Decent," says Jill. "You think I'll be showing soon?"

"Let's see what you look like."

Jill pulls her Erik Estrada T-shirt over her head and steps out of her jeans. She does not wear a bra. Her pants are bikinis that say "Tuesday" on one hip.

"My boobs feel funny," says Jill, inspecting one breast. "And I think I'm bigger."

Sandy cups a hand over Jill's stomach, just above her pubic hair.

"And last week in home ec I thought I was going to puke."

"You do look kind of swelled up here."

"I know just when it happened too. That day they let us out early, when Didi Hatfield spilled sulfur in the chem lab? And Virgil and me drove to Manchester because Bi-Rite had a sale on tires. And on the way home he said, 'I feel like a quick one,' and we pulled over right on 114 and he didn't think he was ready yet but then they played 'Tonight's the Night' on the radio. That part where Britt Eklund talks dirty in French always gets to him. Anyway, he was just going to pull out of me and then he said, 'It's too late.' And that was

just about ten days after my period. And you know the next
song they played? That one Stevie Wonder does about his
daughter, with the kid crying in the background. That's
when I knew. Boy, is my mom going to be pissed."

"Do you think you'll get married?" Sandy asks.

"Search me."

Jill is trying on a pair of white maternity pants. She examines the stretchy knit panel in the front, stuffing a pillow
inside. She's still naked on top. She begins walking around
Sandy's living room like Mia Farrow in *Rosemary's Baby*.
Sandy laughs, and Jill's walk becomes more exaggerated.
She rocks from side to side with her legs spread apart and her
breasts bouncing. The door opens. Virgil and Mark stand
there.

Early evening is a hard time for Ann. If she has been in
town, and she's driving back, she can see the lights on in
houses. Mothers fixing dinner. TV sets flickering. Babies sitting in high chairs, waving their spoons. She remembers evenings with Rupert, going down to the garden together to
pick squash and peas and tomatoes for dinner. Turning on
Lawrence Welk and dancing to that corny music. Sitting beside him while he read, making dirty pictures of the two of
them that she would stick in the pages of his book.

Late at night it's better. Ann feels she is coming close to
perfecting loneliness, putting together the most poignant
evenings possible. There's something almost delicious for her
about the hours between 11 and 3 a.m.

She turns out most of the lights, first of all, and lights
the oil lamps. She may write a letter to Rupert, though she
won't finish it. She paces the floor, sipping Kahlúa. She
pours some bubblebath in the tub, turns on the water, very
hot, and puts a little bamboo stool beside it with another
glass of Kahlúa and ice. She puts a stack of records on the
stereo. She doesn't care if this is bad for her records.

She does not play rock music on these nights. Rock-and-roll reminds her of her college dorm, mixers when she stood by the wall all night, or exchanged SAT scores with some boy from Amherst. Even then these boys seemed young to her.

Now she plays Tammy Wynette and George Jones: "Help Me Make It Through the Night" and "Nothing Ever Hurt Me Half as Bad as Loving You." She heard some organ music on a classical radio station once that made her cry. She called the station to ask what it was and got the record—the composer is Albinoni. It's a very lonely piece of music and she plays it a lot.

What she plays most are her Dolly Parton records. The old songs: "I Will Always Love You," "On My Mind Again," "Sometimes an Old Memory Gets in My Eye," "If I Cross Your Mind," "Lonely Comin' Down," "Living on Memories of You." She also likes the duets Dolly Parton used to record with Porter Wagoner. She has studied very carefully their photographs on the covers of these albums. On one—*Burning the Midnight Oil*—there are two pictures, juxtaposed. One shows Dolly in a long red dress sitting in front of a fireplace reading a letter. An oil lamp is burning. In the other picture is Porter, wearing a flashy shirt, sitting in a black leather chair. The ashtray next to him is full of cigarette butts and he is pulling his hand through his blond pompadour. Tearing at his hair, really. Ann has spent nights like that.

She thinks people completely miss the point when they focus on Dolly's breasts all the time, and the crazy blond wigs. Ann is not fooled. She knows Dolly could not have written these songs, could not sing them this way, if she had not experienced real heartbreak. She knows that Dolly has been married since she was eighteen to a man named Carl Dean, who is in the asphalt-paving business. She wonders if Dolly Parton was actually in love with Porter Wagoner, with whom she never records duets anymore. Porter Wagoner is thinner than ever now. One seldom sees him, now that Dolly has gone off on her own.

Last summer Dolly Parton came to Hanover to sing at Dartmouth. Ann drove an hour and a half to see her. She is singing more upbeat songs these days, trying for a broader appeal. She herself makes jokes about her bust—needing a fire department to put out the flames when she tries burning her bra. Her backup band nearly drowns out the guitar on "Coat of Many Colors." She doesn't even sing most of the old songs anymore. But Ann feels she understands: Dolly has made a decision to go on with her life, even though it means leaving the best part of herself behind. She will smile and make jokes, even if her heart is broken. She will be a bigger star than ever, and almost no one will ever know the real truth.

Ann pictures herself doing the same thing. She will find a kind, good man someday. He will be nothing like Rupert. She will never tell him about Rupert, although he will know that she can only care for him deeply—never precisely love him. They will not talk a great deal: he will tell her how things went at work; she'll ask him what he'd like for supper. They'll have several children.

Here's what all of this builds to, in her mind, as she lies in the tub—the water lukewarm by now and the bubbles gone, the Kahlúa glass empty, Dolly and Porter singing "Just Someone I Used to Know." Ann will be in the supermarket, standing at the checkout with her husband. She will have a baby on her hip and another child about Trina's age beside her, and she will be pregnant, although her face will be very thin. She hears a voice behind her, asking, "Do you have Birds Eye Tender Tiny Peas?" Rupert used to eat them for breakfast. Their eyes meet; he studies the baby's face, and he does that trick where he makes his ears wiggle, for her older child. Neither of them says anything. Ann's husband pushes their cart out to the car and she looks over her shoul-

der one last time. He's standing in the magnetic door holding his single box of peas with the saddest look on his face.
They never see each other again.

Carla has taken the top three drawers for her shirts and
jeans, just like at home. The bottom drawer's for Greg. He
puts his box of painting clothes in the wooden camp locker
Dan and Sally use for a coffee table. His paints, for now, sit
in boxes by the door. Tomorrow he'll set up a studio in the
little room overlooking the falls that Dan and Sally use for
guests.

Carla is putting the last of her cast-iron pots in a Hoo-
sier cabinet Sally refinished. It has a built-in flour sifter; you
open a little door at the bottom and crank out the flour.
Carla thinks she will learn how to bake bread this summer.
Maybe English muffins. There's a recipe in one of her Julia
Child books.

For dinner they had smoked salmon and cream cheese
omelets and wine that Greg chilled in the icy water at the
falls. The stove is from the thirties—pale-green enamel, on
legs, with a warming oven. The refrigerator has not been
plugged in yet, and they'll have to prime the pump (Dan has
left instructions) before they have water. There's also a wood
stove and a pile of dried ash, split, outside the door. Greg
doesn't have the hang of the stove yet. His fire went out. But
it's not a cold night. Carla's just as glad that they will have
to lie very close under the covers tonight.

On the walls of their sleeping loft is a series of photographs Sally must have taken. At first Carla thought they
must be pictures of hills, one behind the other, with long
shadows falling in the foreground and some kind of fuzzy
boulder in the distance. Then she realizes Sally must have
taken these pictures while she and Dan were making love.
Knees, one elbow, part of a breast, and Dan's testicles hover-
ing overhead like a bomber.

Greg stands at the window watching the falls. There is

an almost full moon. "I've got to learn how to fly cast," he says. "We can have trout for breakfast."

Carla finishes the last sip of her wine and leans against the sink, watching him. That almost flat ass, his pants hanging loose at the hips. The piece of hair that always stands up on the top of his head. (When they go out to a good restaurant he uses a dab of Vitalis. She used to make fun of him for that.) He looks so hopeful, excited. How she feels about him, sometimes, is almost maternal. She never thought she would ever want more for another person than for herself. "This is going to be great," he says.

Ronnie Spaulding is pleased. He bowled 144 tonight: three strikes and two spares. His date—Wanda something—threw mostly gutter balls. A couple so bad he thought they might end up in the next lane. She's not very coordinated: takes three steps, winds up like a pitcher, and then when she gets to the line she just stands there. Stops. Bends over (what a big ass) and lets it go more like she's launching a baby duck in a pond.

No point spending another dollar on a second string. "Want to get some pizza?" he asks her. Of course she will.

Wanda's just as glad to leave the bowling alley. She feels very self-conscious when she gets up to bowl. She knows she looks worst from the back. Wanda is actually a pretty good bowler, but she feels so uncomfortable that she can't concentrate. Just as she is about to let go of the ball, her brain flashes something like a picture of her rear end or the little roll of flesh that she can feel hanging over the top of her jeans. This makes her stop. Then all she wants is to get it over with so she can go sit down again, with her sweater across her lap. There are so many skinny girls here tonight. She's going to start on a diet very soon.

He asks her if she'd like to go for pizza. She says sure.

*   *   *

Jill cannot imagine what to do. She bends over to get a shirt
to cover her top. The Erik Estrada shirt has been buried in
the pile of maternity things. She rummages in the pile, can't
find it. She can feel her nipples getting hard, sticking out.
She must just cover herself up.

The shirt she pulls over her head turns out to be the one
that says "Baby." She's still wearing the pillow stuck in the
maternity pants. Mark is the first one to speak. His voice is
flat; he sounds dead.

"Congratulations," he says.

Wanda and Ronnie are sitting in the corner booth at
Rocky's. He has got them a large double cheese pizza and
two Cokes. "New Kid in Town" is playing on the jukebox.
" 'It's those restless hearts that never mend,' " Ronnie sings
along with the Eagles. He takes a bite of pizza. I'll just have
one piece, Wanda thinks.

" 'Johnny come lately, new kid in town,' " Ronnie sings.

"Are you in a league?" Wanda asks.

"Second in the division," he says.

Jill and Virgil pass by the door. She stands outside. He
comes in for a pack of cigarettes. Wanda waves to Jill, who
does not notice.

"Friend of yours?" Ronnie asks. "Cute."

They watch Virgil leave, Jill follow him to the car.

"Cops better not be around tonight," says Ronnie.
Virgil is driving very fast.

Wanda reaches for another slice of pizza. Ronnie looks
at the piece of cheese sticking to her chin. "You done?" he
says.

He parks outside the mill. He can see this spot out the window when he works the second shift. It's his private thing,

looking out the window while he's working, remembering the night before. He unzips his fly.

This is her first time since Melissa was born. The doctor said she could do it in six weeks, but no one asked before. She figures it will be safe.

She is thinking about her stomach. There's a dark black line from her navel to her pubic hair. The thing that's worse is the stretch marks. It's hard for her to believe now, when she takes out her bikini from last summer, that she ever fit into that thing. Now it's like she's carrying a wrinkled old parachute around her middle. Her skin is all covered with wavy lines with white spaces in between. Her belly, which was so hard when she was pregnant—like a rock—feels like one of those crocheted pillows of Mrs. Ramsay's that has lost half its stuffing. Her breasts are not so big as they were when her milk came in—before the pills the doctor gave her made them dry up—but they have stretch marks too, and her nipples have turned brown. She never used to wear a bra. Now, when Ronnie unhooks her, tugs the straps off (he is not gentle like Sam Pierce), her breasts drop heavily.

He is not interested in her breasts, does not kiss her. He sticks his penis in her right away and rams it in very deep. She remembers the feeling, as Melissa's head shot out, before they had time to cut her. She thought she could hear her skin rip. Her throat was too dry to scream.

She's dry now and it hurts. He is pounding her, back and forth. She can picture her skin—red and sore—being rubbed raw. She has not looked at herself yet, since Melissa was born, but in her mind she sees her baby daughter's pink, hairless genitals—surprisingly large, in proportion to the rest of her, and a tiny dot of bright red blood on the tip of that little piece of skin whose name she has forgotten. Melissa had a drop of blood on her like that, in fact, the day after she was born. Wanda got very scared when she saw it and rushed into the hall, dripping blood herself, to find a doctor. "She's having a little menstrual period," the nurse said. "Sometimes mother's hormones affect baby that way."

Ronnie groans, flinches, goes limp. He lies there for a minute, his breathing slowly coming back to normal. Then he rolls away from her, zips up his pants.

"You want me to drop you at the baby-sitter's?"

Carla takes her diaphragm out of her makeup case, squeezes out a little Koromex. She is careful not to get any on her hands because there is no water to wash it off.

She pulls off her shirt, her underpants. Naked, she climbs the ladder to the sleeping loft. Pulls back the goose-down quilt, thinking: Tonight I will take the left-hand side of the bed.

Greg is curled up, hugging the pillow. He's asleep.

It's a little past eight-thirty in the morning and Wayne is sitting in the sunroom on the fifth floor of the Good Samaritan Hospital, looking out the window. Actually, he is always on the fifth floor—has been for five and a half years—except when they have a field trip. Even then he is seldom allowed to go out, because forensic patients require one-to-one supervision and there are not often enough orderlies for that.

The TV set is on. It's always on, even when there's just a test pattern. The volume is turned up very loud, so that Jane Pauley, who's interviewing a collector of antique dolls—a great hedge against inflation—seems to be yelling. She is not really yelling, but a number of people on the fifth floor are. Not the forensic patients so much—they are the most normal-acting ones. But across the hall, in the Manchester unit. There is a man who has been hitting his head against the door since Tuesday. There's a kid who appears to have dropped too much acid, and now all he does is yell that Mick Jagger is trying to kill Karen Ann Quinlan. They are going to bomb the Bedford Groves Roller Rink on Memorial Day. His mother puts saltpeter in the food here. That's why Bo Derek stopped visiting him.

So far today, Wayne has done sixty push-ups, taken a shower, shampooed his hair, shaved. (All this he must do under supervision. There are no doors in the bathroom—a person can't even take a shit in private here. And of course they have to watch him with the razor in case he might want to murder someone or commit suicide.) He has asked Charles, the only orderly he will talk to, for one of his cigarettes. Only one, because this pack has to last until Sunday. He had to ask Charles to light the cigarette for him, naturally. No telling when he might try to set Mrs. Partlow's girdle on fire.

Then he got his breakfast tray. Forensics do not go to the dining hall. Breakfast today was fried eggs and hash browns. He does not eat that junk. He is watching his cholesterol. Most people here let their bodies get wrecked. Even the young ones are soft. But Wayne, though he will be thirty-eight this June, is hard as a football player.

Today's schedule is posted on the bulletin board outside the orderlies' station. Ten o'clock: shop. Not too much you can build without a hammer and saw. Eleven-thirty: current events. There will be a quiz on the days of the week. About half the class will flunk.

Lunch at noon. Fridays they have fish sticks and cole slaw. One o'clock: visiting hours. No one will come to see Wayne, of course. Still, he likes to change his shirt, slick his hair back with a little water, take the *Union-Leader* out into the sunroom. He will hold the paper open in front of his face but he will not read anything except the cars for sale. He has spotted some great deals. And he likes listening to the visitors.

Artie LeFleur, for example, who is in here for shooting his wife in the leg. She did not report his doing this for three days and by that time her leg was infected. Now she comes to visit him with their two kids, Norman and Marcelle. She has an artificial leg, which Artie refers to as her prosthetic device. One time he sneaked her into the shower stall while Wayne stood guard and Norman and Marcelle played pick-up sticks with Mrs. Partlow. Artie was too nervous to do anything, but his wife showed him her stump, which he hadn't seen before. You meet some weird people here.

Wayne picks up a magazine. *Woman's Day*, September 1976. Tips from the World's Most Expensive Beauty Spa. Why I Chose Sterilization. Help! My Hair Just Won't Hold a Set. Five Fantastic Meat Loaves. Are We Trying to Solve Too Many Problems with Sex?

Not likely.

He gets up, thinks he will take a stroll down the hall. They still haven't taken down the cardboard rabbits and chicks and the banner that says Happy Easter. Probably won't until the Memorial Day decorations go up. Mrs. Partlow's drawing of Snoopy, with the words "Five Steps to Mental Health" coming out of his mouth, has been there since 1978.

"Keep a disciplined schedule."

"Do not dwell on the past."

"Be outgoing. Make new friends." (Artie LeFleur)

"Avoid idleness. Keep busy."

"Think positive."

Back to the sunroom. He picks up the New Hampshire *Times*. Wayne does not have much use for the articles, which are mostly about very homey, backwoodsy things like maple sugaring and how to make your own horseshoes, which all the young kids are into who move here from places like New York. He would just like to check out the cars in the classifieds.

Nothing very good. He skims the page for something else that might be interesting. He has never noticed the personals column before.

Some make no sense.

"TO THE DANVILLE CAL. MONKEY BREEDERS. I've gone

bananas over your gift. My new little pal and I are real swingers. Love, Jim."

"WOOD BUTCHER: Two years have gone by in a minute. I've got love enough for hours. Augusta."

"CONCORD AREA WOMEN looking for two articulate, radicalized women to vent anger with us. Call Claudia."

"ANDROGYNOUS MAN, age 27, in open marriage, would like to meet female counterpart to share quality relationship. Interests include vegetarian dining, Judy Collins, solar energy, nonsmoking, intimacy, travel."

"FARMER. Shy, nice looking. Would like to meet serious woman into organic gardening and holistic medicine."

These men are a bunch of losers. Wayne feels he has much more to offer. He imagines what he would write. "INSATIABLE LOVER in search of same. THEY CALL ME CRAZY. Give me a call. SINGLE MAN. Not into travel."

Seriously. What does he have to lose? "Hey, Charles," he says. "Can I have an envelope and a stamp?"

Ann wakes up feeling better than usual. She will have just half a grapefruit for breakfast this morning and she will not turn on the Phil Donahue show. She is going to be busy today.

Things to do. Buy shoes for jogging. Vacuum house. Buy seeds and fertilizer, rosebushes, clematis vine. Fabric for curtains. Do one hour of exercise. Get newspaper, start looking for job.

Ann washes her hair. It is really getting long. After she moved out of Rupert's house—during one of those days when she was driving around looking at real estate and sleeping in motels—she took her nail clippers and really hacked herself up. She looked like the lead singer in a punk band. It was so terrible she had to do something, and there was nothing left to cut, so she bought some Nice'n Easy and dyed it red. After she'd been out in the sun for a few months it turned orange.

But now her hair touches her shoulders, and it's brown again. She blows it dry, turning under the ends, so it looks very fluffy. She puts on a little blusher and some eyeliner. "I am not going to throw up today," she says.

Today that man is coming to Rototill the vegetable garden. Reg. She will ask him to make some flower beds too. Maybe he can do something about the leak under the kitchen sink.

She has seen him in his yard, sawing up wood, and she remembers seeing a deer in his yard last fall. He was skinning it. She had to turn away. From the clothes she has seen hanging on their line—T-shirts with pictures of celebrities printed on the front—there must be a teen-aged daughter too. Sometimes she sees the wife bringing in the wash. She is a thin woman who wears curlers a lot. One time when Ann was walking past, the woman called out to her that she was the local Avon representative and would Ann be interested in any of their products. Ann said she guessed not. The woman said, "Just thought I'd ask," as if this was what she'd expected.

Ann doesn't know anybody in this town. The checkout girl at the Grand Union, of course. "You sure must like honey yogurt," she said a while back, when Ann came in for the second time during a really bad day of eating. After that she was careful to buy her yogurt at different places.

She wishes she had a friend here. Sometimes she stops in at Sal's for a doughnut and coffee. She does not really like coffee but she likes listening to the conversations of the people at Sal's, especially the high school kids. Ann has been out of high school only four years, but she can't remember what it was like being carefree and so unscarred. Her one big worry was getting into a good college. Her friends from those days will be graduating in a month or so. She hears from a few of them sometimes, but not much. Rupert never liked it when they called, and the one time when her friend Patsy came to visit was a disaster. Patsy brought a Talking Heads album and played it over and over, very loud. She was eating macrobiotic, trying to decide if it would be compromising her beliefs to take money from her parents for a trip to Japan that summer to study ceramics. The three of them went out to dinner together that night and Ann wore an outfit she had not worn since she moved in with Rupert—a green velvet jumpsuit with flat, Mary Jane–style Capezios. Rupert said, "You're trying to make me look like a dirty old man," and made a point of talking about how he was losing the hearing in one ear. Patsy did not visit them again.

Ann isn't sure who she could make friends with in this town. The high school kids would think she was very old— the boy who sometimes carries her groceries out at the Grand Union has called her Ma'am. She can't picture herself having tea with her neighbor the Avon lady, either. Even the women her age all seem to be married, with a couple of babies.

She'll get a job; that will help. She has not thought about a career in years because she assumed for so long that she would always live with Rupert and grow vegetables and make dollhouse furniture for Trina on vacations and have a baby of her own someday. Even after she left she was thinking: He will come rescue me soon. She still thinks that sometimes, but she must, in any case, be in good shape when he returns for her. She has to show him how well she's doing. She will start watching the help-wanted ads today.

And meanwhile she'll have a wonderful garden so that in August she can invite Rupert to drive down for a picnic. She'll wear her long antique dress with her blue-and-white-checked apron. She'll have a basket full of flowers over her arm, and there will be a table set up in the middle of the field, with a vase full of zinnias and the blue enamel plates, and soup with squash blossoms floating in it.

Maybe she'll invite a Fresh Air child to come stay for the summer. A little girl, six years old, would be good. Estrella. Corazon. Juanita. Some name like that.

She will be very small, very thin, when she gets off the bus. She will be carrying an A & P shopping bag, wearing

plastic shoes. Her hair is black and straight, long bangs over
large eyes. She will hesitate on the bottom step of the bus for
a second, scanning the crowd. Ann comes forward, takes her
hand. They will drive home very slowly because the little girl
feels carsick from all those hours on the bus.

She has never seen cows. They pull over at the side of
the road to look. Then at a produce stand for some fresh-
picked strawberries. She says is it O.K. to swallow the seeds?

Ann shows her the waterfall. The little girl gasps, says
this is how it looks in heaven. I'll buy you a bathing suit, says
Ann. I'll teach you how to swim.

They get up at sunrise every morning. Ann makes pancakes, and there is always fresh fruit on the table. A check-
ered cloth, maple syrup heated on the stove.

Then they go down to the garden, hoe up weeds. The
little girl says what if birds go to the bathroom on the lettuce? What if I eat a worm? Ann explains everything.

They ride bikes. They hike up Mount Monadnock. I
wish I lived here all the time, says the little girl. She's not so
skinny anymore. Ribs filled in.

Every afternoon they jump in the falls. Dinner is salad
from the garden, cheese, fruit, cookies they make together.
The little girl tells about her mother at home, who beats her.
I will protect you, says Ann (tucking a patchwork quilt
under her chin, plugging in the night light). You're safe now.

What if she's gone in the morning? And she has taken a pair
of pierced earrings, all the best animals from Ann's Steiff
collection, smashed every Fiesta plate in the pantry. Tram-
pled the beans, slashed the corn with a machete. There's
spray paint on the rosebud wallpaper. Ann doesn't know
Spanish, but she can guess what it says.

Jill is lying in bed trying to decide if she can make it to the
bathroom without throwing up in the hall. She can hear her

father outside in the yard, whistling "California, Here I Come." Her mother's watching Phil Donahue. "I don't want you to misconstrue my question," Donahue says, "but doesn't your wife think it's even a little bit kinky when you put on her brassiere?" The house stinks of bacon.

"What your viewers have got to understand, Phil," says a husky voice coming from the den, "is that we should all relate to one another as people, not men or women or husbands or wives. My wife views me as an individual who happens to enjoy dressing in women's clothing."

She's going to puke, it's just a question of where. There's a bowl of jelly beans on the dresser. If she empties them out, she could take the bowl into the closet and do it there.

"You up, Jill?" Doris calls. Because it's a school vacation week, she has been letting her daughter sleep until ten-thirty. Later than that she can't abide. She herself grew up on a farm, and she was milking cows by five o'clock. "I've got bacon and eggs ready."

"Coming, Mom," says Jill. She'll clean up later.

"Virgil brought you home at a respectable hour for once, I noticed." (If she had come home five minutes sooner, Jill would have heard the deep sighs her father always makes when he has just climaxed.)

"What was that big box I saw you taking up to your room?"

"Just some stuff for prom decorations that Sandy gave me." Jill was sure her mother would've been asleep.

"I wish you wouldn't hang around with that girl. Married and all. If you can call it that."

"She's just fourteen months older than me."

"Not so old I wouldn't take a belt to her if she were a child of mine." Phil Donahue has just been joined by a woman who has taken hormones to grow facial hair. Reg is whistling "Zip-A-Dee-Doo-Dah."

"Will you look at that?" says Doris. "It takes all kinds."

* * *

His back hurts some today, but Reg is feeling good. He has just come back from town with three flats of annuals. The flowers are Reg's project. With grocery prices going the way they have been, Doris says, it doesn't make sense to grow anything you can't eat. But Reg loves the sight of a vase full of marigolds and ageratum. When they bloom, he'll bring some down the road to the girl.

He has a few hours yet before it's time to till her garden. Looks like a good day to do some fishing. He gets his pole out of the shed, ties a couple of flies. It will be nice to sit in the sun by the falls anyway. He opens the kitchen door. "Think I'll see what's biting in the brook," he calls to his wife. She's watching her TV show and doesn't hear him. Jill is standing over the kitchen sink eating a piece of unbuttered toast. "You've got to put some meat on your bones," he says. "Or that boyfriend of yours is going to find somebody else."

Virgil likes to do it in a car. Naturally, sometimes the shift column gets in the way, or the seat belts. In winter it might feel a little chilly, even with the heater on. Also, you never know when some other car might pull up next to you. And one time Virgil's former girlfriend Denise got her tit caught in the space between the horn and rim of the steering wheel. Accidents will happen.

Still, in Virgil's opinion, a car is the best place to do it. He's even thinking about sending a letter to the *Playboy* Advisor, saying so. Listen, it's like your own personal, compact mobile love chamber. Built-in sound system, control panel, panoramic view through the windshield if you want one, cigarette lighter always handy. Virgil even likes the way things get a little tight, a little cramped. Kind of cozy. He likes fucking in a thunderstorm, the sound of rain on the metal roof. Pulling over to the side of the road at night—right on the highway, for Christ's sake—and hearing the cars whiz past while he's pounding her, watching the lights loom up on the two of them, light a strip of one tit or maybe her ass and then fade out, leave them in blackness again. In addition to his eight-track tape deck, Virgil has the buttons on his radio dial all set, tuned to his four favorite stations, so he doesn't even have to look up if all of a sudden he wants music. Just leave the key turned to Accessory and punch in.

Sometimes he likes to fuck in the backseat for variety. A little more spacious, a little more homey. He has this great line for the backseat. "Let's pretend we're married, on our honeymoon, and this is a big canopy bed. Wouldn't that be something." Like a charm.

Before his older brother got married, him and Virgil even shared the car a few times. Virg in the front seat, Buzz in the back, windows all steamed up. Most chicks wouldn't go for that kind of number, of course. We are sharing a beautiful private moment, just the two of us, et cetera, et cetera. But there were those kind of scaggy twins that really got off on it.

With Jill, Virg has been working on some of the fine points. Pressing her bare ass up against the dashboard, where it says IMPALA, making her look like she's branded. Driving around town when he picks her up after school, with his fly unzipped and his pecker out and Jill on the floor, jerking him off, never slowing down below forty-five. He has been thinking of maybe installing a bar in the back.

But now she keeps talking about this pregnant business, and it's one royal drag. A couple weeks ago, when they were over at Mark and Sandy's for some beers, Jill took him into the bedroom and showed him Mark and Sandy's water bed, made him sit down on it. Pretty wild, huh? Imagine no curfew. Imagine not having to get up and go home after. Imagine waking up together.

Imagining those things is just what makes Virgil love his car. Getaway car, zero to sixty in seven seconds flat. Lay rubber, I'm out of here. No hanging around staring into her eyes.

*　　*　　*

Tara wishes she had a guitar. She would like to learn some songs she could sing to Sunshine. She would make up her own songs. It would take a long time to learn how to play the guitar, of course. What would be good is an Autoharp. The music teacher used to bring one to their class every week when Tara was in elementary school. All you had to do was push a button and it would make a chord. Every week somebody got a turn playing it, but Tara never did. The week it was supposed to be her turn they had a snow day and the next day they moved on to someone else. Tara wanted to remind the teacher, but she has always been shy.

So she just hums to her baby. The only songs she can think of are "On Top of Old Smoky" and "Rock-a-Bye Baby" and "America." There's a song she heard on the radio she liked a lot—James Taylor and Carly Simon singing together. The only words she can remember are "devoted to you." Tara thinks James and Carly are a perfect couple. They must know a million songs to sing for their kids.

She's sitting outside the Laundromat again, although she's not doing the laundry this time. It's just a good place to sit. Sunshine can watch the other babies and their mothers who pass by on the way to the post office and the Grand Union. The important thing is to get her out of the house. This morning Tara's mother said, "When are you going to get rid of that baby?" Sunshine didn't understand, of course. But Tara doesn't want Sunshine picking up that kind of vibrations.

A woman bends to admire her. Tara thinks her name is Mrs. Ramsay. She takes care of Wanda's baby sometimes.

"What's your name?" she says. Tara's not sure if she is speaking to Sunshine or to her. "Sunshine," she answers. The woman seems to be talking to the baby.

"You're precious," she says.

"Thank you," says Tara. Sunshine kicks her feet and smiles.

"I have a granddaughter just your age," says the woman. "I bet you'd like her. Her name is Melissa."

"I know her mother," says Tara.

"Oh, really," says the woman. This is the first time she has addressed Tara. Tara notices that she's wearing just one earring, shaped like a basket of plastic fruit.

"I am surprised," says the woman. "You do not seem like the same type of person."

Tara doesn't know what to say.

"I think it's wonderful that you gave birth to this baby," says Mrs. Ramsay. "So many young people are going to clinics where they kill babies.

"Is this her natural color?" says Mrs. Ramsay. She examines Sunshine's hair, which Tara has put into a tiny ponytail tied with a piece of yarn.

Tara's not sure what the woman means. "When she was first born her hair was almost black and it grew right down her forehead," she says. There was also soft black down on Sunshine's back and shoulders and a soft little furry tuft on each of her ears. When people saw her—Tara's mother in particular—they seemed to think this was unattractive. Tara thought it was very cute, and she was sad when the black fuzz wore off. Probably from all those kisses. When Sunshine's new hair grew in it was blond. She explains all this to Mrs. Ramsay. It's the first time anyone has seemed so interested.

"I tint mine," says Mrs. Ramsay. Her hair is the color of Lucille Ball's.

Tara has begun to nurse Sunshine now. Mrs. Ramsay doesn't seem like the kind that would mind.

"I breast-fed my son too," she says. "They did not encourage it back then. I heard one of the nurses talking about me. She called me the Cow. But I didn't care. Why do you think God gave women that part of the body? He did not give women that part of the body so they could pose for pictures in magazines for men to read in the bathroom when they think their wife doesn't know. That was not what He had in mind."

Tara is having her usual problem. She doesn't know

what she's supposed to say. But Mrs. Ramsay seems to like her anyway. It's nice having someone talk to you.

"I wish my granddaughter could drink real breast milk," she says. "I worry about it all the time. Her mother never listens to me. I read an article that said even a grandmother can breast-feed a baby. I could get my milk back, if I could just get Melissa to suck long enough to activate my glands. They make a machine with tubes now that you hook up to your own nipples so the baby gets bottled milk while she sucks, until your own milk comes in. They designed it for women that adopt babies because they can't have their own. Of course, it is very hard for them to adopt babies now because so many of these girls are going to clinics where they have their babies killed instead of giving them to someone who could provide a wonderful home."

"Your mother would never have done that," says Mrs. Ramsay to Sunshine, who is curled against Tara's left breast, her eyes three-quarters closed.

She's right. Tara doesn't even like thinking about it. From the moment she went all the way with Sterling Lewis, she was hoping this would happen. It is the first time in her whole life she has had someone that loves her.

"What is your favorite color?" Mrs. Ramsay asks Sunshine. "I will knit you a duck sweater."

"Pink," says Tara. Speaking this way—as if she was Sunshine—does not even seem strange to her. Tara herself likes blue the best, but Sunshine has a different personality, and she thinks Sunshine would like pink.

"Then I will make you a pink duck sweater," says Mrs. Ramsay. "And booties to match."

Greg has been up since six. He has primed the pump—they've got water now, which tastes better than Perrier—and there's a good fire going in the wood stove. The day is warm enough that they could do without, but he's pleased to have mastered the system of dampers. The stove is black, a design of horses and trees and two woodsmen cast in the sides and a Norwegian saying cast in the front. He will have to find out what it means.

Now he's setting up his work space. He has brought several cartons of drawings with him from New York, and he's looking through them. One box is all abstracts. It's full of bull's-eyes and paintings that look like electrocardiograms.

He has a box full of drawings of bears. They're pretty realistic drawings, although the things the bears are doing aren't things bears actually do. There's a bear stuck in a subway turnstile, a bear studying a picture in a gallery, another making love with a beautiful young woman who resembles Greg's old girlfriend. Greg has saved these drawings through five moves, though they are like nothing else he has done.

Lately his work has been abstract again, and three-dimensional. Before they left New York he was working on very small, tight assemblages of sticks and nails and string. The last gallery owner to look at his slides called them "hostile."

But now, looking out the window at the falls, he's thinking about a different sort of piece. He would like to paint these falls, very large. He thinks he will put figures in the new painting. Not precisely representational ones, but not bears either. Right now, for instance, there is a man in a Ashford bowling jacket standing down on the rocks, fly casting. He would like to get some cadmium red for the jacket and put the man in his painting. He will put himself in the picture too, and Carla. He's not sure yet what they will be doing.

Carla is still asleep. Naked, he realizes with surprise. Her body has become so familiar that the sight of Carla there seems no different to him from the sight of her in her houndstooth jacket, hanging on to a subway strap or standing at a corner waiting for the light to change.

He reaches for the car keys—realizes there's no reason, up here, why he can't leave them in the ignition—and heads out the door. Probably the man out on the rocks can tell him where there's a lumberyard to buy the boards for a stretcher.

Ann buys the paper, reads it in the car outside Felsen's News. She's not sure what sort of job she has in mind, but nothing advertised (machinist, clerical worker, aide for senior citizen's home) seems possible.

She takes her laundry out of the backseat, carries her basket across Main Street. She recognizes the girl sitting on the steps by the Laundromat, talking to a red-haired woman. That girl is here nearly every morning. Ann wonders if the baby is her sister or her daughter. The girl puts the baby on her breast. She's the mother then. Ann puts her wash into the machine and goes to Sal's for a doughnut, then back to her car to wait for the laundry. Might as well see what Ann Landers has to say.

Melissa wakes at five-thirty these days. After Wanda changes her, they watch *Sunrise Semester* while Melissa has her bottle, and then they watch a rerun of *Leave It to Beaver*. (Beaver and Larry got sent to dancing school this morning, and had to wear gloves.) Wanda likes this show. She wishes she had a brother like Wally. In particular, she wishes she had parents like Ward and June. They're strict, of course, but understanding. Ward has long talks with Beaver, in the den. June leaves a plate of chocolate chip cookies waiting for Beaver on the kitchen table when he comes home from school. Wanda will bake chocolate chip cookies for Melissa when she's older.

Melissa seems to be a little sick this morning, and she has diarrhea again. Wanda wonders what the blue stain is on her new sweater. She didn't think to ask Mrs. Ramsay last night.

Now they're sitting in the kitchen watching *$20,000 Pyramid*. What would Wanda do if she had $20,000? She would buy a moped and a color TV. Join a health club, take skating lessons. She would get Melissa the Fisher-Price Ferris wheel music box and one of those Strawberry Shortcake dolls that smells like real strawberries. Put some money away for Melissa's education, of course. Get a puppy. There was a little white miniature poodle she saw at the New Hampshire mall a couple of weeks ago. She would name it Marshmallow Fluff, or Jennifer.

She will check today to see if they have any openings yet at Moonlight Acres. The welfare money is really not enough for the rent here. Also, waitressing would be a good way to meet some new guys. Wanda's trying not to think about last night. She stands in front of the mirror and pulls up her shirt, looking at her stomach. She shivers.

She goes to the refrigerator. There's some macaroni from the day before yesterday. Jell-O. A jar of peanut butter. She opens that and eats some off the spoon.

Down below, at Rocky's, she can hear the lunchtime crowd. They're playing Donna Summer on the jukebox— "MacArthur Park." She hears that song about twenty-five times a day. "Someone left a cake out in the rain. I don't think that I can take it 'cause it took so long to bake it, and I'll never have that recipe again." What a crazy song.

She goes back to the refrigerator, gets out a couple of blueberry Pop-Tarts, sticks them in the oven. Melissa has messed in her suit again. Wanda can see it dripping down her leg. There are no sleeper suits left. She will have to wear the pink organdy dress Mrs. Ramsay gave her—that's all there is—and Wanda will have to wash more diapers today. She wets a rag and cleans off Melissa's bottom. The stuff is all over the place. Melissa's screaming. Just as Wanda pins on the fresh diaper, there's another explosion of shit. "MacArthur Park" again, the smell of grinders and something burning. The Pop-Tarts are black.

She smacks the baby, hard.

* * *

Mark told Sandy this morning that he had to be at work an hour early, noon. The truth is he just had to get out of there. The baby was crying. His mother-in-law came over, talking about a woman she knows who's just had a colostomy. She calls Mark "Daddy."

Mark works at the Norelco plant, second shift. He puts filaments in the light bulbs they use in glove compartments. He has been doing this for almost a year now, since he and Sandy got married. "I give you another five years on this job before you're wearing bifocals," his foreman told him the other day.

But right now everything's cool. He's leaning against the wall outside Felsen's News, smoking a ten-cent cigar. He has bought the new issue of *Rolling Stone,* with Linda Ronstadt on the cover. Would he ever like to lay her.

There's a girl sitting in a red Fiat parked against the curb. She's looking through a newspaper and eating a doughnut. She looks a little like Linda Ronstadt, in fact. He wonders who she is.

He's going to think up some things he would like to do to this girl. Fuck her without having to worry about squashing a sleeping baby, for openers. She will take his cock in her mouth—something that Sandy has never done. She says it sounds very unhygienic. But this girl will do it, and he will come in her mouth and she will swallow it.

He tries to think up more things—the kind of stuff Mick Jagger might do. Mark has not even told Sandy this, but she's the only girl he ever laid, and he wishes he knew more about sex. He has bought some magazines, which he keeps under the carpeting in his Valiant. Virgil owns a copy of *More Joy of Sex,* which Mark looks at sometimes. He has tried, when he and Sandy fuck, getting into some of the positions they show in the pictures, but Sandy is nothing like the woman in the book, who does not shave her underarms or look embarrassed when the man sticks his cock in her asshole. He can't imagine Sandy in a black lace garter belt. She wears panty hose anyway.

The girl in the red car appears to be a little older than he. She doesn't look like she comes from around here—the foreign car and all. From the city probably. College girl.

What if her car wouldn't start? He would come over to her window. She would roll it down, look up at him. He would lay his right arm on the roof of her car, with his left thumb hooked through his belt loop, and lean his head inside. Need help?

She says, "I don't know anything about cars." He nods his head in the direction of the passenger seat. She knows that means move over. He slides in, adjusts the choke, presses his foot lightly on the gas, turns the key back and forth like a guitarist making a vibrato. He knows just how to touch a car.

Still no response. "Wait here," he says. She doesn't ask why. It's clear he's boss. He steps out (patting the hood in that sort of intimate, familiar way he has), crosses the street without checking traffic, because of course cars will stop for him. He ducks into Rocky's, says, "Give me a Coke," and ambles back to the Fiat. No need to rush. Sandy's always telling him, "Hurry up with that bottle," like it's the baby who's in charge. Not here.

He lifts the hood, pops the Coke can open, pours some over the battery terminals, which are all caked up, like he knew they'd be. A girl like this never knows how to take care of a car. She's standing behind his shoulder watching as the fizz dissolves all the crud and trickles down over the engine. "Fantastic," she says. He takes a rag from his back pocket (one of his son's cloth diapers, bought before they switched to Pampers) and wipes the battery dry. He's always neat like that, takes his time.

"She should be fine now," he says, clicking the hood shut.

"Let me pay you something." He shakes his head. "At least for the Coke."

"No sweat," he says.

"Still," she says. "There should be something."

She's wearing a strapless dress—white, like the one Linda Ronstadt wears on the cover of *Hasten Down the Wind*. Her nipples show through the fabric. He looks at them like he's looking into her eyes, makes no effort to pretend he isn't doing it. Strokes the hood of the car, says nothing. She doesn't move. About sixty seconds pass like this.

"See that car over there?" he says. He points to the Valiant. "I treat her just like a woman."

The trout's a small one—seven inches maybe. Reg leaves it on the porch. Doris hates the smell and can't stand seeing the eyes. He'll clean it later.

She has just got off the phone. She's still wearing her curlers. He tries to remember what the occasions are that she curls her hair for. He can't picture her with curls, only curlers.

"New people moved in down at the falls," he says. "From New York City. An artist and his wife." (Greg did not explain that they aren't married.)

"It's getting to be like a commune down our road," says Doris.

"He seemed like a nice fellow," says Reg. "Said he wants to learn how to fly cast. Maybe the wife would be interested in some Avon."

She perks up a little.

"I asked for black coffee," says the customer. This is Jill's third mistake today, and she has only been on duty an hour. Sal gives her a funny look. She pours another cup, apologizes. Her tips are going to be crummy today.

She's not concentrating. The reason is, on the way to work she bought a home pregnancy test ($9.95 at Rexall). She put four drops of pee in the glass tube (it's tucked behind the coffee filters, in the back room) and she has to leave it two hours to see if a red ring shows up on the paper. She has fifty-five minutes left to wait.

She looks out the window. Sandy's husband is standing outside Felsen's, reading a newspaper. She's embarrassed, thinking about how he saw her bare tits last night. She has always thought that Mark is very cute. So's Virgil, of course.

Virgil did not French-kiss her good night after their date. He's acting more upset about their baby than she thought he would. She tried to cheer him up by telling him that as a result of her pregnancy, she's getting bigger on top. He didn't seem interested.

She asked how he felt about the name Patrick. That was when he put his hand over his eyes and said he had a headache. She said do you want me to give you a neck rub. He said forget it.

The girl who lives in the Richards's old house comes in for a doughnut to go. Jill wonders if the girl recognizes her from the falls.

Ann is almost sure of it. That waitress is the girl she saw yesterday. Everybody in the world is having sex except her. Even sixteen-year-old kids have boyfriends making love to them in the woods, and babies. Even that skinny girl outside the Laundromat had someone make love to her. Ann sleeps with a hot-water bottle.

She feels as if someone's looking at her. There's a boy around eighteen standing there holding a copy of *Rolling Stone*. He's having an erection. On his way to the waterfall probably.

Reg arrives with his Rototiller at half-past two. Ann leads him down to the field where she would like the garden to be. Just the spot he had in mind.

After she goes back to the house he stands there a minute, looking at the soil. It's black as coffee grounds. He bends to pick up a few sticks. He can hear a record playing back in the house. Some country singer. Ann must be playing the music very loud, because he can hear the words plainly even out here. "Through the sleepless nights I cry for you, and wonder who is kissing you. Oh these sleepless nights will break my heart in two."

"They're trying to get the Pope to declare it's an official miracle," says Mrs. Jakowski. She's telling her son Steve about a woman in Italy who woke up one morning to find a perfect image of Christ's face on her palm. Mrs. Jakowski is extremely religious. She usually reads to Steve from the Bible during these visits. She will open the New Testament in a minute, in fact, at which point Wayne will go back to his room. Steve does not appear to be very interested in the New Testament either. He's drawing a tattoo of a naked woman on his arm with a ballpoint pen Mrs. Jakowski has lent him. But it's impossible to know for sure what he is thinking, because he has not spoken in three years, since he stabbed Mr. Jakowski in the heart twenty-four times and cut off his testicles.

Mike Douglas is talking to his guest, Bert Convy. Mike is asking Bert what he will be doing in the next few weeks. Bert says he'll be in Vegas, opening for Lola Falana. Mike says that sounds exciting and asks Bert if he would be willing to sing something. Bert sings "Feelings." This makes Wayne start laughing very loud, which makes two of the orderlies and Mrs. Partlow look up nervously. Sudden outbursts like this are always a source of concern here. The orderlies don't understand that Wayne's laughter makes perfect sense. Last time he had his session with Dr. Poster, the psychiatrist for the fifth floor, and Dr. Poster asked (as he does every week), "What are you feeling?" Wayne had recited the lyrics of "Feelings." "Feeling like I never knew you. Feeling like I never lost you." It was the first time Wayne had ever seen

Dr. Poster write anything down on his pad. He had to ask Wayne to slow down so he could get it all. When Dr. Poster was done, Wayne had said, "I think you've got a hit on your hands." Dr. Poster wrote that down too.

Wayne decided it would take too long, sending his ad through the mail. So he has called the newspaper and they've told him they will send him the bill. He has simply given his address as 125 Prospect Street. Which it is, although on the rare occasions when he sends someone a letter (mostly President Carter and Mike Wallace), the return address he prefers is 125 No Prospect Street. In any case, his ad will run in the personals column tomorrow. He's in such a good mood that he offers to play Aggravation with Norman and Marcelle, who are here with their mother again today, on account of spring vacation. He lets Marcelle win.

Carla has made a list of things she needs to buy. When she woke up, Greg had already gone into town, so she'll have to make another trip. She would have liked to go with him to explore. But it's good that he's feeling so eager to get started.

Coffee filters. Sweet butter. Eggs. They probably have the brown kind up here. Vegetables for salad. Maybe a nice potted plant to put in the window.

She has hooked up the stereo and now she's playing an album of Carter Family classics: Mother Maybelle singing "Wildwood Flower" and strumming the Autoharp. Carla does some steps she remembers from her jazz class and sings, " 'Oh, he taught me to love him and called me his flower, that was blooming to cheer him through life's gloomy hour.' " This is what she is doing when she hears Doris's knock at the door.

Before she has even reached the house, Doris can hear music playing. It's as she suspected. These new neighbors are hip-

pie types. Doris wishes she hadn't bothered to take out her
curlers. The woman here probably doesn't even wear a brassiere, much less cosmetics. Still, Doris figures she has come
this far, and it was heavy lugging the sample case up the hill.
She might as well give her introductory speech.

The woman who answers the door looks around
thirty—tall, with frizzy blond hair. Wearing the kind of outfit Jill would buy: overalls and a T-shirt. No shoes. She's not
wearing lipstick or mascara or even foundation. If she wears
perfume at all, it will be musk oil or something. At least she's
smiling pleasantly.

"I'm Doris Johnson from up the road," she says, patting
her own hair. Hard to believe anyone would think that frizz
was attractive.

"And I was wondering if you'd be interested in a dem-
onstration of our spring line of Avon products. We have
some very exciting specials this month."

Much to Doris's surprise, this woman says yes. They sit
at the kitchen table while the woman—her name is Carla—
makes tea. Doris has never had tea like this. It's called Red
Zinger and it tastes like grass clippings. Carla's teapot has
two feet coming out the bottom with striped socks on them
and the kind of shoes Jill used to wear to birthday parties
when she was little. Carla apologizes for not having sugar.
Doris says, "It's delicious just like this, very unique.

"I wonder if you're aware of the fact that the Avon company is our nation's number-one cosmetics manufacturer,"
says Doris.

Carla says she had no idea. That's very surprising. She's
thinking: I would like to get along with the people here.

"You know, we got to be number one by providing de-
pendable products at reasonable prices," says Doris. "You
don't get to the top with an inferior product." Carla says
that makes sense and rummages in the packing boxes for her
tin of Italian biscuits.

"Our moisturizer, for instance," Doris says. "I've been
using it six years and I bet you'd be surprised to know I'm

forty-two." Carla says she would not have guessed. She notices that Doris is studying Sally's photograph of breasts and testicles. Where are those biscuits?

"I hear your husband is an artist," says Doris, still studying the photograph. She's trying to figure out if it is hills or valleys or what.

"That's right," says Carla. "Tell me more about this moisturizer. I should probably get some of that."

"Well, the secret ingredient is collagen." This is when she's supposed to take out her sample and let Carla put some on her cheek and compare it to her present brand. These off-key singers are distracting her.

"I've heard that's good," says Carla.

"Do you have children?" Doris asks. "I have two myself."

Carla says no. Then—later it will amaze her that she said this—she tells Doris that they're expecting one. Why did she say that?

"What wonderful news," says Doris. She's genuinely pleased. This woman's not as bad as she thought. "When are you due?"

"Not for a long while," Carla says. "We may have to go back to New York before then."

Doris hopes that won't happen. Her son Timmy, who's twenty-three, is still not married. She thought she might have a grandchild by now. It would be nice to have a baby nearby.

"Well, don't mention I told you," says Carla.

Doris says she knows how to keep a secret. Who is Carla's doctor? Is she having trouble with morning sickness? Doris used to be so sick in the mornings she had to keep a box of Saltines and a bowl under the bed. She couldn't keep anything down.

"Getting back on the subject," Doris says, noticing that Carla looks uneasy, "I can see it's going to be doubly important during the next few months to look your best."

"I guess for now I'll just take a bottle of the moisturizer," Carla says. She reaches for her wallet, to end this quickly.

Doris says she can deliver it in a few days. She'll come back then. And she would like Carla to take a complimentary sample of Perpetual Pink nail color. Carla says that's very nice.

It's not until Doris is halfway home that she realizes what those things were in the photograph.

Tonight Sandy's making pigs in a blanket and creamed corn and celery sticks with cream cheese dip for an appetizer. She's not sure, but she thinks Mark was mad when he left this morning. She wants to have something special waiting for him when he gets off work.

After her mother left (a depressing visit because Sandy wanted to tell about Mark Junior and her mother wanted to talk about Pauline Fisher's colon cancer), Sandy washed her hair and set it with hot rollers. She also gave Mark Junior a bath and a shampoo. (Mark Junior has so little hair he doesn't really need this, but Sandy likes the way the shampoo makes his head smell. It's called Gee, Your Hair Smells Terrific.) Then she dressed him in his best outfit, which is a shirt and pants that look like a baseball uniform, and the shirt says New York Wets. Then she put on her best outfit—the dress she got when they went to the justice of the peace to get married. White. Not full length, of course, or really formal. But it has a princess bodice and a ruffle. Mark really likes her in that dress.

The reason she did all this is that they had a photographer coming to the K-Mart today and the ad said a portrait would cost 88¢. She wanted to get their picture taken to surprise Mark on his birthday, which is ten days away.

It turned out the cost of these portraits was 88¢ for each person in the picture, meaning $1.76 for the two of them, and more if you order large prints. But Sandy only had about ten pictures of Mark Junior (she and Mark don't own a camera), and none of those is good of her. She figured it would be worth the money, getting a professional to take the photograph. And if she ever got the name of a modeling agency for children in Boston, she could send them a print.

There were five backdrops to choose from: a mountain scene, the ocean, a forest, snow in a field and an orange sunset. Sandy wished she could have had more time to think about it, but there was a very long line of children and mothers waiting to have their pictures taken and the photographer was getting impatient. She chose the mountain scene because Mark said one time that he would like to go to Colorado.

She didn't have enough time to get Mark Junior ready. He was so happy, the whole time they were waiting in line, and then when it was their time he started to cry. If she could have had a minute to do her choo-choo dance with him, she's sure she could have got him to quiet down. But the photographer was rushing her, sticking a teddy bear in her son's face, which only made him worse. When he snapped the pictures, Mark's mouth was open and his face was all red. She didn't realize until it was over that she hadn't even taken her coat off.

But they're going to have a nice dinner. She had to take off the white dress because Mark Junior peed on her during the photography session. But she has put on her black velveteen pants and a black blouse with nothing on underneath. After the baby's asleep she will let Mark do whatever he wants.

Wanda wishes Melissa would cry. All morning, since Wanda hit her, she did nothing but sleep. Wanda has tried all her favorite things—taking Melissa downstairs to Rocky's to look at the lights on the pinball machine, giving her a bath. She opens her eyes partway and then her head rolls over to one side and she's asleep again. Now one of her eyes is a little puffed up and there's a purple spot on her cheek and Wanda cannot keep her hand from shaking. This has only happened one other time, only the other time Melissa hollered very loud, instead of being quiet the way she is now.

She will say Melissa rolled off the changing table. That happened to Tara's baby one time. It could happen to anyone.

Wanda goes downstairs. She could use a candy bar.

After he has bought the boards for his stretcher, Greg decides to look around Ashford. Not very much to see, really. He likes that. He has lived in the city all his life.

There's a bowling alley. He'll take Carla some night. Just like a regular all-American date. They can go out for hamburgers after, at the place he saw down the road. Moonlight Acres. Maybe play miniature golf.

The Grand Union supermarket. K-Mart. Webster's Clothing, with a dusty mannequin in the window wearing an imitation-leather skirt and vest. A display of work boots. Clearance sale on long johns.

A couple of antique shops, for the summer tourists, he figures. He already finds himself feeling vaguely superior to those people.

Just-like-nu Shop. Good Used Clothing. He sees a pretty faded cotton dress hanging outside. It looks like something from the forties. Carla's type of outfit. He stops the car.

A woman comes out on the porch. Probably about forty and very thin, short brown hair, razor cut in the back. Her arms are folded across her chest. He says he'd like the dress. She looks a little surprised. "For your wife?"

"Girlfriend." It's the first time he has called Carla that.

"Only thing my husband ever bought me was a Waring blender and a hysterectomy," she says. "Nicest thing he ever did was leave."

She's bringing out more clothes. A long double-knit lounge outfit in pink and orange paisley. A velour minidress.

He says this is enough for now, gives the woman a dollar and two quarters.

He sees the girl in the back of the shop. She's sitting on a wooden stool sipping a Coke. She has the same face as the older woman, and she is very thin too, but not stringy like the mother. Her shirt is pulled up over one breast and she is nursing a yellow-haired baby. He has never seen such white skin—even the baby is less fair. The girl does not notice Greg watching her. She is humming "On Top of Old Smokey." She has a very pure soprano.

"Do yourself a favor and never have kids," says the older woman. "They'll cause you nothing but grief."

The baby jerks away from the girl, and for a moment Greg can see her small white breast very plainly. A thin stream of milk shoots out from her nipple. She notices him looking then and pulls down her shirt. The baby makes a surprisingly loud burp. Greg reaches down for his bag.

"Come again," says the woman in a flat voice. "I hope it fits."

When he gets home he's still thinking about that girl.

Sitting in the back of the shop, next to misses' coats, Tara switches breasts. Sunshine has been sucking on the right side almost an hour, but Tara is in no rush to finish. This is her favorite thing in the world.

At the hospital they told her she wouldn't be able to nurse her baby. Inverted nipples, nothing Sunshine could hold on to. The nurses put her on formula and sugar water without even asking, so when they brought Tara her daughter, the baby was already full, wouldn't suck. "Forget it," one of the nurses said. "Breast-feed a kid and you're trapped. Can't ever leave her with a sitter." As if she'd want to.

At night, under the sheet, she worked on her nipples, pulling them, rolling the skin between her fingers. "Suck," she whispered to Sunshine when they brought her in. "Please suck." Sunshine would just sneeze every time Tara put her flat nipple up against the baby's mouth.

On the third day her milk came in. She had a dream of being buried in the sand, woke to find her breasts huge and dripping, aching. Still Sunshine wouldn't suck, and the milk seemed to solidify, as if there was gelatin inside. By night-time her breasts were hard and lumpy. The nurses told her she'd better take the drugs soon, to make her dry up. No. Tara's mother came to see her that night, after she closed the shop. "Jesus," she said. "You look like you're full of tumors." Mrs. Farley has had (in addition to her hysterectomy) two radical mastectomies, and knows the look.

All that night she lay awake in her hospital bed, pulling on her nipples. At twelve, two and four, she could hear the woman in the next bed nursing her day-old son, whispering to him, big boy, take it easy, little man, go to it. The infant's lips smacking, slurping. Just the sound, even somebody else's baby, made Tara drip. Two wet spots on her nightgown.

The next morning her nipples stood out and Sunshine took hold, wouldn't let go, gained two ounces. From then, that was where she lived, at Tara's breasts. They didn't stay big very long—two weeks maybe—but Tara knew from her book that size has nothing to do with how much milk you've got.

She has tasted it, squeezed a little out with her fingers, licked it off the corners of Sun's mouth when she's taking a break. It's watery and sweet, very different from the formula Sandy and Wanda give their babies. My body makes milk, she thinks, over and over. She can't get over it, that she can create something they sell at the Grand Union. Her body works.

Sandy has her son on a feeding schedule. A bottle every four hours, a pacifier in between. Wanda feeds Melissa when she cries. Tara just holds Sunshine always, and when Sun begins to root around in the fabric of her shirt, when she makes this little kissing sound, Tara gives her a breast. She has no idea (Sandy asked her this) how many ounces it all

adds up to. Tara drinks two quarts of milk a day, never eats
any chocolate or onions or potato chips or TV dinners, anything like that. She tries not to get upset, because when she
does (when her mother talks about putting Sunshine up for
adoption, for instance) she can feel her glands tightening up,
feel the milk stop and the hard little lumps begin to form
again. Tara just walks out of the room now, when her
mother begins to talk like that. She's not about to expose her
milk to harmful vibrations.

She has read about milk banks—places where nursing
mothers donate extra milk, expressed with a suction
pump—for mothers who can't breast-feed. If there were one
of those milk banks around here, Tara would like to contrib-
ute. Everybody always said how skinny she was, how pale.
Now she knows how powerful she is, really. She forgets,
sometimes, that she doesn't have milk actually coursing
through her veins, pumping through her heart. That's what
it feels like. That could be why she's so white.

Here is something wonderful. There is some kind of
brain in her breasts that knows just when to open the dam,
let the milk flow. It's so sensitive that Tara can be flipping
through a magazine and come to a Gerber's ad or something,
and her milk will begin to drip. One time when she was sitting by the Laundromat, some woman's toddler got her
hand caught in the door of the dryer and began to scream.
And Tara's breasts—both at once—shot out twin fountains.
Sunshine was asleep in the laundry basket at the time, so
there was no mouth to catch it, and the milk just dripped
down the front of Tara's shirt, some of it making a wet place
on the sidewalk. Tara didn't care if people saw her (as they
often do) walking home with two round wet circles on the
cloth over her breasts. She's proud.

Sal has been in the back room five minutes, taking inven-
tory, and Jill is getting impatient because it's time to check
her pregnancy test. Tara came in for a Coke a few minutes

ago and Sandy stopped by to find out what happened. Wanda has been in too, getting something out of the candy machine. One thing's for sure—if Jill is pregnant, she will never get fat like that.

They will have a June wedding. She would like to have it in a church. She thinks of Virgil in the lavender tuxedo he wore when he took her to last year's prom, with a ruffled shirt and cuff links. Sandy will be matron of honor and Ricky Edwards, whom she used to baby-sit for, can be ring bearer. Jill will carry sweetheart roses and baby's breath.

They'll get an apartment in the new development out by the lake, with wall-to-wall carpeting and color TV. She'll work for another three months or so, to save up money for the layette. Sandy will probably give her a shower. Mark will give Virgil a bachelor party before the wedding too. The guys will tell jokes like the ones she has seen in Virgil's copy of *Playboy*. She doesn't mind.

She wishes Virgil would grow a beard. It would make him look older. Also his chin sort of blends into his neck more than it should. Unlike Mark's, for instance. In Jill's opinion, Mark is better looking than Erik Estrada.

She has only seen one naked man in her whole life. In June she will make a vow in the sight of God that she will never be with any other man ever. She wonders what it might be like with someone different. She thinks about the noises Donna Summer makes on that record "Love to Love You, Baby." She can't imagine making noises like that with Virgil. Sometimes she has heard her father, in the night. But her mother never makes a sound except afterwards, when she runs the water.

Jill and Virg will be nothing like Jill's parents, of course. They'll still smoke grass, go roller skating. Jill will do crazy things like draw a face on the tip of his penis with Magic Marker. They'll let their kids stay up late if they want to, teach them the words to all the top forty songs. Sometimes—even though they have a double bed—they'll still go down to Packers Falls and screw. Jill will never look like her mother. She would kill herself first.

But she knows Doris and Reg were not always the way they are now. She has seen pictures of her mother as a teenager—never pretty, but always grinning, in spite of her buckteeth, with curly blond hair that always looked a little out of control. There's one picture of Doris and her two girlfriends dressed up like boys for Halloween. The other girls look pretty flat on top, but Doris was really busty in the picture, and she's looking down at her chest, making this funny, surprised expression. Jill wonders what happened, because now Doris is all withered-up-looking on top, and the only expression she ever makes looks like a prune.

Jill has seen pictures of her father too, when he was just Virgil's age. You couldn't call him cute, like Mark or Virgil, but there's something about him in those pictures—Jill feels a littly funny admitting this—that's very sexy. He never smiles and he always stands straight in front of the camera, looking like something important is going on. In most of the pictures he's wearing a checked coat and a bow tie—always the same clothes—and the occasion is almost always Easter Sunday, with the family heading off to church. But there's one (Jill's favorite) of Reg wearing baggy work pants and a sleeveless undershirt, holding a giant pumpkin with a ribbon taped to it. First prize in the 4-H fair. When you look close you can read the names "Doris" and "Reginald" carved in the pumpkin, with a heart around them. When she was little Jill thought that was some type of magic pumpkin, like in Cinderella, but then her father explained that what you do is, when the pumpkin's very little, just forming on the vine, you scratch the words in the skin, and by the time it's ready to pick there's a deep scar forming the letters. He wrote "Jill" on a baby acorn squash one time, but it got killed by frost before it was ready to eat.

Her parents had to get married. They don't know she knows that, but she figured it out. First of all, her mother was always so vague about their wedding date. When she was little, Jill loved making greeting cards for every special occasion, even things like Arbor Day and Richard Nixon's birthday. "So when is your anniversary?" she kept asking. "Sometime in the spring," Doris said. "I've stopped keeping track." And then Jill looked in the family Bible her uncle had, and sure enough, the date was just six months before Timmy's birthday.

She can't imagine her mother lying on pine needles with her knees apart, or in the backseat of some old jalopy, her father telling her (the way Virgil used to), "Honey, I have to or my dick could get petrified." She was fourteen years old, and she actually believed him.

Her mother was probably asleep when it happened. She's sure her mother never felt the way Jill does, which is very horny sometimes. Not just with Virg, but at all sorts of odd moments, like when one of the lifeguards at Green Lake threw her in the water one time after junior lifesaving class, and when her biology teacher showed this film strip about primates and explained what it means when a baboon's rear end turns bright red. Sometimes she gets that way all by herself, even, lying in bed, thinking about Rod Stewart, pretending she's his wife, Alana, or looking at the picture she has on her wall of John Travolta with his shirt unbuttoned and his mouth partway open.

Of course, once you're married you aren't supposed to think about those people anymore. And there will be lots of good things to make up for it, like all the wedding presents and taking showers together and not having any more curfews. Jill wonders if everybody's penis looks like Virgil's.

She feels sad for her father, that the only woman he ever got to screw was her mother. She thinks about that time last summer when Reg picked her and Wanda up at the beach and all they had on was their bikinis (Wanda was pregnant then, but not enough to show). They all had to squeeze in the front of the truck, along with some groceries he'd got, with Wanda in the middle. He had this look on his face.

Of course it will be wonderful having a little baby, Virgil Junior. Jill's mother can take care of it sometimes.

If by any chance she isn't pregnant after all, Jill is going to get some birth control pills. So what if they make her gain a few pounds?

She imagines that her tongue is in John Travolta's mouth. She inhales when he exhales. They are breathing the same air.

Let me taste you, he says. Virgil would never do that, in a million years.

"We need more plastic straws and ketchup," says Sal, tying on a fresh apron. Jill says she will be back in a second and opens the door to the kitchen.

Three meat patties on the griddle and a piece of apple pie in the microwave. Steam rising from the dishwasher. Toni Tennille singing "Do It to Me One More Time" on the radio. Jill pushes aside the box of coffee filters and reaches for her vial of pee.

There is a red ring on the paper, plain as a bull's-eye.

At three o'clock the garden is finished. It was a slow job because the soil has not been cultivated for ten years at least and the weeds were pretty thick. Reg's shirt is wet under the arms and there's a damp V-shaped patch on his back. But he likes this kind of work. As he pushed the tiller, he was picturing eight rows of Golden Bantam corn. A row of yellow wax beans maybe, and a hill of Kentucky Wonder. Half a dozen Big Boy tomato plants, with marigolds and nasturtiums in between to keep the pests away. Watermelon.

He's always had a touch with plants. People used to tell him he could never get good melons this far north, but he grew them the color of raspberries inside, so juicy you'd tie a towel around your neck or get soaked eating one.

His father was a farmer. They only had thirty acres— the Johnsons were always hard up—but it was good land, southern exposure, clear of stones. Reg used to take a blue ribbon at the 4-H booth in the Deerfield fair every September, for his corn.

By the time he married Doris—she was three months along with Timmy, they were both eighteen years old—his father was dead and the farm belonged to Reg.

Doris said sell the land, I don't want to spend my whole life smelling cow manure. She signed him up to sell *World Book* encyclopedias, door to door. Bought him a suit. She loved it when he wore that suit.

But he's no kind of salesman, and the only one who ever bought an encyclopedia was Reg himself. Doris said it would be a good thing to have, for the baby. Not that he ever saw Timmy open any volume except *R,* which Timmy and his friend Skipper used to look at all the time for Reproduction. That was about it.

He joined the service for a while—didn't like being so far from the kids. When his tour of duty was over he took a job on a construction crew and left his farming to the one patch of their yard—thirty feet square—that got any kind of sun, and not much at that. He has always felt ashamed of the produce that comes out of the garden. Yellowish tomatoes, cauliflowers you have to cut hunks out of, where the cabbage moths have got to them. His son and daughter have never been interested in growing things. He would like them to know he can do better than that.

Ann could have a gem of a garden here. He could help. Show her how to pinch the tomato plants. Build supports for the pole beans and peas. Maybe bring over some fish heads to put in the corn hills. He'd plant a row of zinnias, to surprise her. Maybe build a scarecrow. He won't mention it to Doris yet.

Ann hears the machine stop and looks out the kitchen window toward the field. Reg is pacing the length of the garden patch, heel to toe. He has hung his cap on one of the handles of his Rototiller and she can see the sun glinting on a round bald patch at the back of his head. He rubs the base of his spine. He looks tired. She takes one of the beers out of the refrigerator and slips on her sandals. She walks toward him.

Wanda and Melissa are having a picnic. The grinders and the Diet Pepsi in the bag are for Wanda, of course, not Melissa. But Wanda has put some grape Kool-Aid in Melissa's bottle, for a special treat, and set her infant seat on the sand facing Green Lake so she can watch the older kids splashing around. She has put a bandanna over Melissa's head—tied in the back like a gypsy's so the bald patches won't get burned. Now she's rubbing suntan lotion over Melissa's legs. Melissa likes this. She has opened her eyes, finally.

They're going to have fun. Wanda looks around at the other mothers, watching what they do. The woman a couple of towels over from her, for instance. She's probably ten years older than Wanda, but Wanda feels like the old one. This woman has three kids, plus the older boy has brought a friend. She has a homemade picnic in her cooler—roast chicken and bananas, little boxes of raisins and individually wrapped brownies. She has on a white bikini and her stomach is flat and tanned. A minute ago she was building sand castles with the little girl. Now she's pulling the littlest boy around in the water, which is still very cold, but just bearable. Doesn't she ever get tired?

Wanda is the only one on the whole beach that doesn't have a bathing suit on. She's wearing one of her maternity tops, no bra on account of the heat. The waistband of her cut-offs is too tight, so a roll of skin is pushed up over the edge and Wanda notices for the first time that the flesh on her upper arms is getting saggy too. She studies the woman in the white bikini, running out of the water, her breasts bouncing just a little, like on *Charlie's Angels,* watches as the woman bends over her little boy with a fluffy blue towel. Wanda knows she will never have a rear end like that again.

A little kid, maybe three or four, rushes past, leaving a

few drips from his watering can on Melissa's leg. "Aku," says Melissa. She always chews on her fist like this when she's happy.

Wanda is thinking about last winter, when she was pregnant. Expecting, is how Mrs. Ramsay used to put it. Back when it seemed exciting to step on the scale and find out she'd gained another two pounds. Of course she loves Melissa more than anything in the world and she wouldn't trade her for any other baby or even change the little red birthmark on her forehead. Of course having a real baby you can cuddle and wash and put outfits on is better than just imagining. But back in January it was like carrying around this fancy package, looking at it every day, wondering what's inside. As long as you don't open it you can always pretend it might be a diamond ring or the keys to a moped or something. Once you open it, there will always be a million things that won't be inside, even if what's there is what you wanted the most. You've got it. You just aren't *expecting* anymore, that's all.

Wanda wanted to be a skater. In the Olympics, in the Ice Capades, like Peggy Fleming and Dorothy Hamill. Not Linda Fratianne, although Wanda watched her in the winter Olympics on TV and realizes that she is very good. Her triple toe loops and a couple of her double salchows were perfect, Dick Button said. She just isn't a dancer the way Peggy Fleming is, in Wanda's opinion. Of course people would laugh if she told them this—now especially—but Wanda thinks she could have been a better skater than Linda Fratianne, if she just had someone to show her the moves.

There was a thaw, back in January, when the temperature went up to fifty and all the snow melted. The crocuses even thought it was spring, started pushing through the dirt. Everybody was going around with no coats on, sitting outside Sal's eating ice creams.

Then came the full moon and a cold snap. All of a sudden the thermometer went down to zero and stayed there. In two days Green Lake was glass, the way you almost never get it because there will usually be snow to mess up the surface or winds to make it all ripply. Wanda was eight months pregnant, feeling like she was carrying around a lead ball, sitting in front of the TV watching all those skaters spinning around on Lake Placid, wishing it was her. She just wanted to feel light and free again. She didn't even care if people saw her walking down Route 9 at midnight with her stomach out to here and figure skates hanging over her shoulder, or that it was a mile walk, and still bitter cold, or that her skates were so tight, because she had this problem with fluid retention in her feet.

Nobody ever needed to show her how to do a figure eight. Also, Wanda made up some movements she never saw anybody else try. A half turn backward, then a half step forward, then a little turning jump—it's hard to explain. There's more to it than the feet anyway. Wanda likes to pretend, when she's skating, that she's a deaf person, and the way she moves her arms is like her sign language, instead of talking.

The woman in the white bathing suit has been swimming across the lake. (Her friend, in a red one-piece, is watching the kids.) She has been swimming for about ten minutes now, and she's still not over to the other side. Last January Wanda, eight months pregnant, on her skates, made it across like an arrow. Then she threw her parka down on the ice, also her sweater, so all she had on, on top, was a short-sleeved T-shirt, and still she wasn't cold. If she told someone like Sandy about that, Wanda's sure they'd be shocked, say, "What if you fell? You could've hurt the baby." But Wanda never falls when she's skating, and knows if things were always how they were that night, she and Melissa would be safe.

Suddenly—this has never happened before—Melissa is laughing. The little boy with the watering can is back, sprinkling one of Melissa's feet. "Want me to do your piggies?" he says.

"Aku," says Melissa. "Ku, ku."

"This little piggy went to market. This little piggy stayed home. This little piggy had . . . had . . ." He looks over at Wanda. She can't help him. Her mother never told her nursery rhymes, that's for sure.

He gives up, runs back to his towel. Melissa begins to make her little hurt-puppy noise.

"Be a good girl and I'll take you in the water," says Wanda. Melissa doesn't pay any attention. Wanda looks around at the other mothers, wishes the little boy could come back. She never knows what she's supposed to do at times like this. Melissa is not interested in the grape Kool-Aid.

"Mommy take you swimming," says Wanda. She wades in, with Melissa, still whimpering, in her arms. Realizes, just as the water laps up over her waist, that when her shirt gets wet it's going to stick to her breasts and she'll look gross. The woman in the white bikini is standing a few feet away, tossing her son in the air, catching him, raising him high over her head again. Wanda thinks she'll try that.

They're in pretty deep. If Wanda didn't catch Melissa she would just sink. She might sputter around for a minute—the bandanna would come off, float to the top—but that would be all. Everybody's so busy watching their own kids, nobody would even notice.

I'm going nuts, Wanda thinks, catching hold of Melissa by both arms, tight. I am a terrible person.

Everybody must be looking at her now. What kind of a mother doesn't even know how to make her own baby stop screaming? But what kind of a kid doesn't appreciate a picnic at the beach? Wanda tries her best. Who wouldn't go a little crazy, putting up with this racket?

One good swat and the baby's quiet.

Only a minute ago Ron Guidry looked unhittable and now this. Long fly ball to center field, going going gone. See you later. Number ten for Jimmy Rice. Pandemonium in the stands.

"Way to go, Rice," says Mark, taking a large bite of his pig in a blanket. His dinner is sitting on a TV tray. The Red Sox have just taken over the lead.

"I don't believe that guy," he yells.

"Shh, honey," says Sandy, coming over from the sink, where she's washing the supper dishes. "You'll wake the baby."

Mark says nothing. Fred Lynn is up. Solid hit.

"Way to be," Mark yells. Louder.

Sandy dries the bowl she used for dip. She sits down next to Mark, snuggles against his chest. She can remember watching him play basketball back in high school. She would be so nervous when he was going to make a foul shot, her hands got all wet. She was so proud when he scored.

"Remember that forward that used to play for Sanborn High?" says Sandy. "And he tried to pick me up that time, during the half?"

"Not now, O.K.?" Ken Harrelson is reminiscing about Carl Yaztremski's golden sixty-seven season. Mark lights up a thirty-five-cent cigar he has bought for the game. Sandy clears away his plate.

She should be glad. So many nights he wants to have sex and all she wants to do is go to sleep. While he's doing it she's thinking what will she make for his dinner tomorrow? did she remember to put Vaseline on Mark Junior's bottom?

It's not that she's so horny tonight. She doesn't even understand why, but she feels scared about something. She's not sure if it has to do with the article she read today that said ages seventeen to twenty-four are the sexual prime of men. When their appetite's the strongest. She's not sure if it has to do with the look on Mark's face when he saw Jill's breasts last night, or Jill's mentioning that she saw Mark outside Felsen's this morning, when he said he was going straight to work. Jill saying he's so sexy, your husband. Her mother, right in the middle of telling her about Pauline

Fisher, looking up and saying, "If they aren't getting it at home, you know, they start looking for it somewhere else." Scrubbing Mark Junior in his blue plastic tub, being particularly careful with his little penis and his scrotum, on account of the rash. When she rubbed the soap around the rim of his foreskin he got an erection. Thinking I wish there wasn't such a thing as sex. I wish there could just be hugging and kissing and having Christmas and going places like the Hopkinton fair. She's scared of the things sex makes people do. It seems like something out of her control. It's like having a gun in the house that's loaded and you never know when somebody might pick it up and blow their brains out.

Bottom of the ninth, Yankees with one out. Sox ahead by one, but there are two men on base. The fans are going crazy. Reggie's up next.

Sandy rises from the couch. It's like she's hypnotized. She walks over to the set. Not in front of it—she knows not to do that. Next to it. She unbuttons her black blouse and lays it on the floor beside her. She unzips her black velveteen pants and slides them down her legs. Pulls off her socks. What is she doing? What would those girls do that work in nightclubs? She turns around and wiggles her rear end, peeling down her panties partway. She faces him again and cups her hands under her breasts, does a jump from one of her old cheering routines. Then she takes her panties off and brings them to him, twirling them in one hand. She should have thought to wear newer ones. This pair is stretched out of shape from when she was pregnant.

She stands over him, lowering herself into a split. Not sure if she can still do it. He's just staring ahead; partly at her, partly at the game. The cigar's still in his mouth.

"Here comes the pitch," the announcer is saying. "Burleson scoops it up, flips to second. Remy takes the throw, fires to first. Pretty double play."

"Fuck me," she says. She has never said the *f* word before.

"Perfect timing," says Mark. The Red Sox win.

*   *   *

Mrs. Ramsay has bought four skeins of two-ply pink Sport Yarn and taken out her number-five needles. Now she is casting on eighty-eight stitches. She is making another duck sweater.

Merv's guest this afternoon is Susan Anton. Poor girl. Mrs. Ramsay knows (although Susan Anton is not talking about this) that she's in love with Sylvester Stallone, who has left her. Of course, it is good that Sylvester— Sly, they call him that—has gone back to his wife, Sasha. And most important, their two sons. The youngest is just a year old. What kind of a father would leave a baby like that? He does not deserve to have a baby at all. If he and Sasha get married again and then they get divorced, Sasha had better get custody, that's all. None of this Dustin Hoffman business. Babies belong with a woman. Not necessarily the mother, if she is a slut. But babies need the woman's touch.

Tonight she called the mother and invited her and Baby for dinner tomorrow. She will serve cream of mushroom soup and she will make it with heavy cream, not milk. She will serve stuffed pork chops and rolls with butter and baked potatoes with sour cream and asparagus with cheese sauce and blueberry pie à la mode. The mother is going to get very fat; she will get sores on the inside of her thighs where they rub together. Her fingers will get so puffy she won't be able to get off that class ring she wears. Fake emerald. They will have to cut it. If her son Dwight could see her now, he would wonder why he ever wanted to do those things with her. Although she has not heard from her son Dwight in a while.

After the blueberry pie Mrs. Ramsay will explain her plan to the mother. She will remove the eighteen hundred and twenty-six dollars from page 200 of *Joy of Cooking*. Mrs. Ramsay will put this money in the mother's fat hands and take out the paper she typed, that she had notarized, that says the mother admits she is a slut and Mrs. Ramsay should take care of Baby from now on. After the mother signs it Mrs. Ramsay will tell her to leave and never come back. She is not worried that someday the mother might return like that mother in the Dustin Hoffman movie. She will do it with so many men that she will have lots more babies. She will get fatter and fatter. Before long she'll be paying people to take them.

Mrs. Ramsay will not even go back to the mother's apartment to get Baby's things, although it is a shame to think of those beautiful sweaters. Never mind; she can make lots more.

She would like to find out more about that machine with the tubes you hook up to your nipples.

She will call the baby Susan.

The dress makes Carla look a little like the mother on *Lassie*. Greg had pictured her as more like one of those stark black-and-white Dorothea Lange photographs from the Depression, but Carla has attached a plastic pin of The Incredible Hulk to the collar. She likes the dress a lot. "This would have cost thirty dollars in SoHo," she said.

For dinner they had snow peas and water chestnuts and shrimp with lobster sauce, made in the electric wok. They have almost finished a bottle of *soave* and now Greg is rolling a joint. From the kitchen Carla is telling him she will grow lots of basil this summer and make pesto sauce in the Cuisinart. Enough to freeze some and bring it back to New York in the fall. Greg does not say that he has been thinking he would like to stay on through the winter here, tell the Walker School to find another art teacher. He imagines Packers Falls encrusted with ice.

"Didn't think I'd believe she was forty-two years old," Carla is saying. "When the truth is, she looks fifty." She has been telling him something about a woman who stopped by today selling makeup.

Carla does not mention that she told Doris Johnson she was pregnant.

"I didn't think they even made hair spray anymore," she says. He lets out his breath, watches the smoke disappear. He wonders how old that girl was at the secondhand store. Sixteen or seventeen probably. But nothing like his students in the city, with their punk outfits from Fiorucci and Caribbean tans. She was so pale.

He puts on an old Van Morrison album. Carla sits on the floor next to him with a plateful of Pepperidge Farm cookies. She puts her arms around his chest, under his shirt. He can feel her fingers moving along his ribs, his nipples, under his arms, inside the sleeves of his shirt. He knows they will make love tonight.

"What are you thinking about?" she says. She's always asking him that, although his answer is almost always the same.

"Artworks." The pale girl standing on the large flat rock at the base of the waterfall. An arc of milk shooting out of one breast.

"Hungry for your love," Van Morrison is singing. "I love you in buckskin."

"Do you ever think about a baby?" Carla asks.

He's startled. He sees the blond-haired baby in the secondhand store. Wearing a little ribbon in her hair.

"Because I've been thinking about it," says Carla. They have not talked about this for years.

Greg can't picture Carla holding a baby. His brother's kids visit them sometimes. They are five and seven and they love taking sips of Carla's Tab and riding in the first subway car with Greg holding them up to look out the window. Carla always takes her collection of Japanese robot toys down off the shelf for them to look at. Last time Alex lost the little airplane that used to shoot out of Gojira's stomach, and Greg could tell Carla was upset, although she said it was all right. Alex thinks Carla is terrific. "Not like other mothers," he says. That's true.

"I wonder what it would look like," says Carla. She's smoothing down his hair in the place where it sticks out. This always makes him feel like a little boy being cleaned up for church. He runs his hand through his hair to mess it up again.

"What would we do with a baby?" Greg asks. "I thought you didn't want to be tied down."

"I could get one of those backpacks they make. We could take it around with us."

"A baby's a big commitment," he says. This is not the sort of comment he usually makes.

Actually, he has always assumed he would have kids. It suddenly occurs to him that he simply hasn't been picturing himself having them with Carla. Not that he has thought about leaving her.

She got pregnant once, four months after they met. He had come home with a pair of mannequin legs he found in some trash outside a factory on West Twentieth Street. Carla was crying but when she told Greg he felt happy. This was before the teaching job and the only money they had was what they got from Carla's women's magazine, which wasn't very much, and some house painting he did once in a while. Still, Greg had hugged Carla. Then he did a funny little dance around the apartment with the mannequin legs, holding them high, with his cheek against the mannequin's flat, almost concave stomach. He was very surprised when she had said. "How are we ever going to pay for the abortion?" For that one minute he'd thought they were going to have the baby.

Now Carla's kissing his eyelids. He strokes her spine, feeling her hipbones, moving his hand over her stomach, down inside her underpants. He's remembering that first night—Carla in her expensive black suit. They hardly said a word to each other all night, except that afterwards he said, "I want to marry you." She said, "You're crazy, it's too soon to say something like that."

And it's true, he probably wouldn't say that to her now, seven years later, although he really meant it at the time. What Greg believes is that there's one right time in the universe for things to happen, and if you hedge around, it passes. Carla always says, "I don't like risks." In Greg's opinion, there's no way to avoid them. It's just a matter of whether you choose dangerous action or dangerous inaction. If Carla hadn't tapped him on the shoulder when she did they would never have seen each other again, and if they hadn't slept together that first night it might never have happened. And even though it was impractical, and a study conducted by her own magazine indicated that having a child in the first year puts undue stress on a relationship, their time to have a baby was six years ago.

His head is on her left breast, the one he likes best because he can hear her heart beating. Her breasts—though she is quite slim—are much larger than that girl's he saw today. When she lies over him they almost bury his face. He lifts his head up a few inches, just looking at her. Her dress is open to the waist and her eyes are closed. He's looking at her the way he would if she were one of the models they used to have at art school. Studying the perspective.

She pulls his head down so her nipple is in his mouth. "I feel like a mother," she says.

It's almost as if he's standing about ten feet back; he can see the whole scene that precisely. Carla gripping the neck of his shirt so tight that when he takes it off tomorrow she'll notice it has been stretched out of shape. The blue vein running along the underside of her breast. Two lemon nut cookies spilled onto the floor, where, in a minute, his shoe will crush them. Van Morrison singing "Put on your pretty summer dress. I want to make love to you, yes, yes." The toilet draining. (They haven't learned yet to jiggle the handle when they flush it.) Greg's hand sliding Carla's pants down her legs—a little black paint on his palm from the canvas he started today. His penis stiffening, pointing down toward her, following the movements of her hips without actually touching her yet, like one of those overhead microphones they use on *Saturday Night Live* that move back and forth between Gilda and Laraine. Lowering now, brushing against her pubic hair. Carla guiding his mouth to her other breast. Greg sinking down. Carla whispering, "I feel so soft and moist." Greg focusing on a piece of a feather that is coming out of one of their floor pillows. Greg pushing down, inside her now. The record player clicking off. Water rushing over the falls.

What Greg sees now is the pale girl, standing on the rocks. She is wearing the dress he bought, unbuttoned, and there is milk shooting from both nipples, splashing on the rocks. Like that painting *Origin of the Milky Way*. It is at just this moment—just as he feels his semen rising, shooting out—that he realizes Carla did not get up to put in her diaphragm.

Jill and Virg are parked at their favorite spot, the miniature golf course next to Moonlight Acres, which won't be open for another two weeks. Jill likes looking out the window at the little wooden windmill and the miniature bridge and the imitation brick schoolhouse, hole number five. Her favorite is the church, which is also a very difficult hole, although one time she got through it with just one stroke.

Normally they would be making out right now in the backseat. Virgil would have a cassette in the tape player—Fleetwood Mac or The Cars or Donna Summer—and there would be beer in the cooler in the front, and some chips. What they usually do is, they make out for one side of a tape, but they don't go all the way. Then they have a snack and sometimes they'll do something weird like drive right through the middle of town with Jill wearing her shirt and her jacket, but bare-assed. Or Virg will put her bra on over his down vest and stuff it with Kleenex or something. Then they make out some more and Jill lets Virg go all the way.

Then he drops her off at home. She's supposed to be back by twelve-thirty, but she's usually late.

Tonight when they got to their spot Jill explained that they had to talk. "I'm going to have a baby," she said. Then she told him about the pregnancy test. "It's ninety-seven percent accurate," she said. "And besides, I know I am anyway."

Virgil said, "Jesus Christ." Then he did this thing he sometimes does, where he starts pulling hairs out of his scalp and looking at the root, although it's really too dark in the car to see much. Then he cracked his knuckles. He said "Jesus Christ" again. Now he's sort of slumped on the seat, leaning against the door. He's staring in the direction of the miniature golf course, at the windmill, whose blades are turning very slowly in the breeze.

Jill was not expecting him to be pleased, but she thinks the least he could do is say something like "Are you feeling all right, honey?" On TV, when the wife tells the husband she's expecting, he tells her to sit down and brings her a pillow. Then he holds her hand and kisses her very gently. He wants to know when it happened, when the baby is due. Jill would like to tell Virgil about how she had to throw up in her closet in the jelly bean bowl. And of course she wants to discuss her plans for the wedding. She wishes Virg would say something besides Jesus. He has just said it again.

"This morning I had to go into my closet to throw up and it got all over my clogs," she says. Then she wishes she had said something different.

"I happen to know," says Virgil, finally, "that I'm sterile. I had this disease in my balls when I was a kid and it killed all the sperm. My doctor told me."

Jill is about to argue with this. Why, if he's sterile, did he always pull out before he came? She has also never heard of people getting a disease in their balls. Why didn't he ever mention this before? She's about to raise these questions and then all of a sudden she thinks maybe she's going to faint. Virgil is looking better. Jill feels sick.

"Sure is a bummer," says Virgil. He starts the engine, even though they haven't opened the chips yet. "Your mom'll kill you."

They're silent for most of the ride home, except one time when Virg turns off the tape for a second so he can listen to the transmission. He thought he heard something funny, but then it went away.

When they get to her house Jill begins to cry. "I never did it with anybody else," she says. She does not say this argumentatively. It's just a statement. She understands now that she will not be a June bride, and probably won't even have a date for the prom.

"See you," he says as she gets out. He guns the motor so hard the tires screech.

Upstairs in their bedroom, Doris turns to Reg, who's lying on his side thinking about the corn selections in the Burpee catalogue. "That boyfriend of Jill's," she says.

Tara is sitting by the front window of the Just-like-nu Shop working on Sunshine's baby quilt when she sees the school bus pull up. The bus doesn't usually stop here, not at this hour of night, and not only that—she realizes this isn't the regular town bus. There are paisley curtains in some of the windows and a rainbow over one of the wheels. Also, it's a very old model. The license plates say Georgia.

A woman around twenty-five gets out. She's wearing a long Mexican dress and a crocheted shawl. She must be nine months pregnant. Not until she's almost at the door does Tara see there is a little girl with her, half wrapped up in the swirl of the woman's skirt. The little girl is about four. She wears a halter top and a long white skirt that looks like a petticoat and sunglasses that have a white plastic Snoopy spanning the part that sits on the bridge of her nose.

Tara opens the door. "I guess you're probably closed," the woman says, tilting her head to see inside. The little girl chews on the fringe of her shawl.

"But we're traveling through town and my daughter just wet her last pair of underpants. I was wondering if you sold them. We could probably use some other stuff too. I haven't gotten to a Laundromat in a couple of weeks."

"I guess you could take a look," says Tara. Another little girl, about seven, and three little boys have now piled out of the bus.

"Hey, Denver," the woman calls out from the front hall. "It looks like you might fit some of these shirts in here." A tall, bearded man, about thirty, comes down the steps of the bus. Then a girl about Tara's age, also pregnant, and a slightly older girl, carrying a baby. The baby has just spit up on the girl's black velvet jacket. He isn't wearing diapers, and his penis has not been circumcised.

"We don't have too much underwear," says Tara. "Most people like to buy it new." She brings out a stack that has a couple of grayish bras, some men's shorts and a few pairs of pants.

"These are great," says the woman. She has picked out a red see-through pair. They are meant for a woman. "Look at these, Dakota. All we need is a couple of safety pins."

"Can I get a pocketbook?" asks the smallest boy, who's around four. The woman looks at the price tag on the patent leather bag he's holding up. Seventy-five cents.

"I guess so."

The man steps into a pair of work pants. The pregnant girl is unfolding baby undershirts. Another of the little boys stands in front of the try-on mirror, twisting up his face. Sunshine, lying on a mat on the floor, is waving her arms and making a noise that sounds like "tuna." Tara knows that means she's very excited.

"Traveling north?" says Tara to the woman.

"Just traveling," the woman says. "We're a spiritual community."

"Aren't you going to have your baby soon?"

The woman smiles broadly, circling her arms around her belly as if she's carrying an apron full of fruit. She is

slightly bucktoothed, but very beautiful. "I'm three centimeters dilated," she says.

Tara never learned much about the stages of birth, but
she knows this means the woman's baby will be born soon.

"Do you know how to get to the hospital?"

"We won't be going," says the woman. "My man and I
are midwives. We're just on the lookout for a campground."

"Hey, Kalima," says one of the little boys to the pregnant woman. "Look at the baby." He has noticed Sunshine,
lying in the corner.

"Juicy kid," Kalima says to Tara. "Yours?"

Tara nods.

Kalima lowers herself, bending at the knees instead of
the spine, until she's almost level with Sunshine. She swings
her hair over Sunshine's face and strikes one baby toe. The
girl in the black velvet jacket and the pregnant girl gather
around. "This is Boletus," says the girl in black velvet, holding her baby under the arms and making him dance.

"Her name's Sunshine," says Tara.

"Fits," says the man, who is also bending over now. Kalima begins to sing "You are my sunshine, my only sunshine.
You make me happy when I feel blue."

"I never heard that song," says Tara. She would like to
ask Kalima to write down the words. Sunshine is saying
"tuna, tuna."

Denver picks up Sunshine and dances around the store
with her, still wearing the baggy pants over his jeans.

"How'd your birth go?" Kalima asks Tara.

"O.K., I guess. The stitches were the worst."

Kalima looks sad. "At our farm in Georgia we never cut
a woman, and they almost never tear. It's all a matter of
good juice and perineal massage."

The little girl called Dakota has put on the red pants
now. The seven-year-old is holding Boletus, bouncing him
hard. Kalima sits down suddenly. "Denver, I'm getting a
rush."

Tara is frozen, watching them. The woman's eyes are

closed as she breathes in, lets the air out very slowly, breathes in again. The man breathes with her and so does the girl in the black velvet jacket. The seven-year-old girl is giving Kalima a back rub.

When it's over, Denver kisses Kalima. They do this with their mouths open, and he also strokes her breasts. It almost looks as if they will start making love. Tara thinks they look very beautiful, squatting there on the floor together.

"Getting it on like that helps her dilate," says the girl in black velvet. "Denver did it for me too, at my birthing. The real father wasn't around."

Tara asks the girl if her baby was born on the bus. The girl says they only travel like this once in a while, to give their birthing rap and to let people know about the farm. That's how she found out.

"I was six months pregnant. Thought I'd give the baby up for adoption. The doctor said I was going to need a Caesarean. Denver came into the health food store where I was getting vitamins and said why don't you come hear us tonight. So I did, mostly because he's so cute. And when it was over I went home, packed one suitcase and got on the bus. Boletus was born naturally, back in Georgia on Buckminster Fuller's birthday, the night of a full moon. Very juicy. The first thing he did was pee all over me. He took my tit right away. Man, could he suck."

Kalima has just finished another contraction. "You're really steaming along on this one," says Denver. He pulls Kalima's skirt up around her knees, breaks open a paper packet containing a surgical glove, eases the glove over his hand and puts two fingers into her vagina. He doesn't seem to notice anything else going on in the room: Dakota trying to put the red pants back on, with both legs in the same hole. The littlest boy (he's called Stanley) tugging at one of Kalima's breasts, saying "Milkie." Boletus lying on his stomach a few inches away, trying to lift his head off the floor, looking a little drunk. Tara just standing there.

"Five centimeters," he says. "Far out."

Tara is trying to think what to do. It's dark out now, and drizzling. The second shift at Sylvania will be out in a few hours, and then her mother will be home. Tara was supposed to have a whole stack of used Girl Scout uniforms ironed, ready to sell for next week, when all the Brownies fly up. She has not even started cooking dinner, and Sunshine needs a change. The young pregnant girl wants to know if they have any dried apricots.

Kalima, between contractions, smiles and rubs her hands on her belly in slow circular motions. "The baby has hiccups," she says.

Tara thinks about when Sunshine was born. She did not want her mother to drive to the hospital (didn't want her to know it was time, even), so she called her tenth-grade English teacher, Mrs. Koch, who had always liked her. Mrs. Koch sounded quite surprised. She had to get out of bed. In the car on the way to Concord, Tara had felt she should think of something to talk about. She asked how *Moby Dick* had turned out. She left school before they finished it. She wondered if the whale died.

Tara doesn't remember much about the hospital. She didn't want them to shave her but she was too embarrassed to say that, so they did. They also gave her an enema, which she didn't think she needed because all she ate that day was one cup of Dannon's coffee yogurt. She remembers a young married couple that came in while she was in labor. The man was carrying a painting of the ocean and a John Denver album. The nurse explained that they were going to the special birthing room, which had a record player and homey furniture. Tara wished there could be music playing for her baby when it came out. She wondered how they found out about that room.

She was in labor for fifteen hours. The doctor said she was taking too long and hooked her up to an IV with a drug called Pitocin. After that it felt as if her insides were having convulsions. She did not think it could be good for the baby, being wrung out of her that way.

In the end they gave her Demerol, which didn't keep her from hurting, just made her too drunk-feeling to do anything about it. Then they cut her. (Afterwards it occurred to her that no one except the doctor had ever seen her body the old way, and now no one ever would. With Sterling Lewis it had been just that one time, in the dark.) Then Sunshine shot out. One of the nurses said, "This one's for the state, right?" The other one said, "No, the girl's keeping it." Tara could hear the doctor smacking Sunshine's bottom, then a sort of sniffly crying. "She'll be more alert when the Demerol wears off," said the nurse.

"Hairy little devil," said the doctor. Then he began to stitch.

Kalima has got down on all fours now. The oldest child—her name's Jasmine—is stroking her hair and Stanley has agreed to nurse at the black velvet girl's breast. Denver is pushing his palm hard against the base of Kalima's spine. "It's posterior," he says. One of the little boys has fallen asleep in the seven-year-old's lap. They all seem very relaxed.

"You could have the baby here," says Tara.

"Incredible," says the girl in black velvet, wincing a little because she isn't used to nursing a child with a full set of teeth. "It was incredible vibrations that made us stop here."

Dakota appears in the doorway with a handful of Mrs. Farley's pansies, snapped off with about a half inch of stem on every blossom. She arranges them in Kalima's thick golden hair, like a crown.

Eight-thirty. Sal has just put a fresh batch of doughnuts in the window. Ann decides on honey dip and orders coffee. She spreads her newspaper on the table of the corner booth and turns to the classifieds.

Veterinarian seeks assistant, weekday mornings. Must like all types of animals. Opening for an experienced beautician. Key punch operator. Librarian.

Her glance shifts to the next column. Under personals there is a single item. "HELP I AM BEING HELD PRISONER." Underneath, in smaller type: "Somewhere out there is one person who will know this is meant for her. The rest will be too frightened—say they want love, but opt for light conversation, gourmet food, new dance steps. I have only one thing to offer. Total passionate devotion. My heart."

A nut, a real nut. Ann turns back to the help wanteds.

Sales route opened up. Good territory, great potential for advancement. Prestigious employer looking for vibrant personalities, career types. Meet exciting people. Unequaled retirement program. Fabulous benefits.

Total passionate devotion.

These ads are for losers, of course. Desperate lonely people. (As opposed to her? As opposed to vibrant personalities. Career types. Prestigious employers.)

She thinks about the one night she spent in Rupert's house, alone, after she came back from Florida, before she moved out. It was March but there was still a foot of snow on the ground. She had finished packing her clothes and taped up the carton of record albums. She put on her long flannel nightgown and stepped out on the front step. She was barefoot. Then she just started walking. Out behind Trina's tree house, into the woods. She lay down in the snow. She remembers thinking, as she lay there: Anytime something happens in my life that hurts a lot, I can think about this and it won't seem so hard. Someday when I'm having a baby I'll come back to this moment. Nothing else will ever hurt so much.

She never imagined she would kill herself. The reason is not, she thinks, because she was so unwilling to let go of her life. She was unwilling to end her total passionate devotion, and she is still unwilling. Whoever she may someday find, marry, have children with, she will always love Rupert. If she lives to be eighty, that will be so. Anybody can just die. She will walk around for sixty years, loving him, carrying around her broken heart. It's the kind of thing most people wouldn't understand. They think it only happens in Dolly Parton songs. Opt for light conversation, gourmet food. She has chosen total passionate devotion. The man who put this ad in the newspaper would understand.

She doesn't even hesitate then. She takes a three-by-five card out of her purse and addresses it with the post office box number from the ad. On the other side she writes: "This is one person who doesn't think you're crazy." And puts her full name in the upper-left-hand corner, along with a return address. Just, she tells herself later, out of habit.

When he lived in Boston, back in '68, Wayne drove a cab for a couple of months. He kept a box of five-cent cigars in the front seat and when someone who looked like a good candidate got in, he'd hand them one through the change window and say, "My wife just gave birth to a son. Seven pounds eight ounces. Our first." He could usually count on a two-dollar tip. Sometimes a five. Once, when his wife gave birth to twin daughters, a man gave him a twenty-dollar bill and told him to go buy a dozen roses.

He reads his ad again and laughs. Strokes his biceps, which have never been in better shape. Maybe today his new *Oxford English Dictionary* will arrive—free introductory gift from the Book-of-the-Month Club, his fourth membership. He has also signed Dr. Poster up for a year's subscription to *True Confessions*.

The secret of Mrs. Ramsay's pie is the filling. She grates a little lemon in with the blueberries. Also, she sprinkles tapioca on the bottom crust to thicken it. Today she will use double the sugar too.

Phil Donahue is talking to Suzanne Somers. She's

reading some poetry she has written, about her son. It sounds as if Suzanne must be a very good mother. She is so moved, reciting one poem, that she has to stop for a second and start again. Mrs. Ramsay can almost forgive her for posing naked in *Playboy*. A lot of the women in Donahue's studio audience are pretty shocked about that, but Suzanne explains that the pictures were taken a long time ago, when her son was a baby, and she had recently left her husband and she wasn't a celebrity yet. "We had to get money or we'd starve," she says.

Mrs. Ramsay wonders if her hair is naturally that blond.

It was not what Wanda needed today—an invitation to dinner over at Mrs. Ramsay's. For one thing, she was planning to start a diet this morning. Now she might as well wait until tomorrow. Also, though Melissa seems better now, she has a purplish mark on her cheek. Wanda will put a little Erace on it and maybe some blush-on. If Mrs. Ramsay asks, she will explain about the changing table, how she fell.

She is just getting ready to leave—she's heading over to Moonlight Acres to ask about that job—when she hears the knock at her door. Jill stands there in a pair of cut-offs and an Eagles T-shirt. Wanda notices for the first time that her waist is a little thicker than it used to be.

"I don't know what to do," she says. "I need to get an abortion."

Tara has cleaned all the stuff off her bed, but Kalima prefers the floor. She's down on all fours again and the breathing she does now is much faster than before. Her face is damp. Every couple of minutes, Jasmine wipes Kalima's forehead with a diaper that has been soaking in ice water. Between contractions, everybody except Boletus gathers around her, singing "Amazing Grace" or "Keep on the Sunny Side of

Life." Up until around midnight Kalima sang too, but now she just closes her eyes.

It is 2 a.m. Sunshine and Boletus are asleep in Sunshine's crib and Stanley is sitting on the floor, waving around Tara's blow dryer, which he has turned on, saying, "Windy, windy." Kalima has already checked to make sure it isn't one of the models with asbestos.

But now Denver explains she's in transition, and she isn't saying anything except chanting some words in another language between contractions. Denver examines her again. "Heat up a couple of towels on the stove," he says to the black velvet girl. "She's fully dilated."

Then he tells the pregnant girl to kneel down behind Kalima's head and lift her up partway. He spreads the warm towels on the floor next to him. Kalima's face is completely changed as she pushes. Denver makes the same face with her. Tara thinks it's incredible, how tuned in to each other they all are.

She's sitting behind Denver, just trying not to get in the way. Kalima is so red and stretched, where the baby's head is pushing out, that it looks as if the two halves of her will rip away from each other any second. The little patch of the baby's head that shows, that was the size of a penny, is the size of a silver dollar now, and sort of wrinkled up and folded over on itself like a walnut meat. Denver tells Kalima to pant. "Come on," he says, "blow out all the candles."

The baby's head seems to inflate as it shoots out. Kalima pushes one more time—making a noise like someone on a TV show who has just been wounded. The rest of the baby pops out, corkscrewing as it comes. "Take a look at that dink," says Denver. Then he puts the baby on Kalima's stomach, with the cord still throbbing.

The baby is making sounds like a puppy at Kalima's breast now. Jasmine puts her head down next to him. Stanley kisses his bottom. "One more push for the placenta," says Denver. He's still squatting between Kalima's knees, wearing the trousers he tried on the night before.

The girl in black velvet takes some of the white creamy stuff that covers the baby's skin and puts it on her face. "Want some vernix?" she calls to Tara. "It's fantastic for your complexion."

Tara is in the bathroom, holding Dakota steady on the toilet seat because Dakota is afraid of getting flushed away. Dakota has wound a little piece of toilet paper around her neck, which is part of a game she made up called Prolapsed Umbilical Cord. The bathroom door is open, so Tara can see into the bedroom, where Denver has just lifted a large slippery red mass from between Kalima's legs. Tara can also see into the hall, hear her mother's footsteps on the stairs.

"O.K., everybody," says Denver. "Who wants sautéed afterbirth for breakfast?"

"Guess what," says Dakota to Mrs. Farley, as she comes toward them. "I pooped in the potty."

Reg is at the feed store when it opens. It's too early for planting the tomatoes, of course, but he's anxious to get the spinach and peas in the ground today. Work some nitrogen into the soil. Start some flats of peppers. He would also like to haul a few loads of manure over to the garden, from Jim Bunting's farm. He has no time to waste.

What kind of corn? Silver Queen. A late variety with truly great flavor and tenderness well worth waiting for. Risky if we get early frost, but worth a try.

Country Gentleman. Sweet, pure white, slender kernels with tender skin. She might like that. Golden Cross is always good too. Honey and Cream. Early Sunglow. If he tills up another thirty feet or so he can plant two or three varieties.

Beans. Doris is always after him to plant more beans. Why bother with all those other things when beans freeze so well, she says. Don't pick them so young. Leave them longer on the plant, they'll be bigger, we'll get more meals out of them. All his wife wants to do is fill their stomachs, she doesn't care how.

"Planning a big garden this year, Reg?" Tom Murphy, who owns the feed store, knows Reg has only a small piece of land.

"Going in on a plot with my neighbor."

Murphy looks puzzled. "What neighbor is that?"

"Girl that moved into the Richards' old place. Has a nice clear field with a southern exposure."

"Doris must be happy about that. What with food prices."

Reg says nothing. He's looking at a little wooden windmill. When the blades turn they move a gear that makes a wooden figure of a man swing his ax, chopping a log. The man's shirt is painted bright red, like the girl's stove. Six ninety-five doesn't seem so bad. A thing like that might keep the crows away.

Murphy has already figured out the total when Reg goes back for one more item. Flower-print garden gloves in the smallest size.

Mark and Virgil stand a little ways above Packers Falls, casting for trout. They've been here since 6 a.m., caught two, threw one back in the water. Mark is smoking a cigar. Virgil is just thinking. They are not talking much.

"I heard the salmon are coming back," says Mark. "Now that they cleaned up the river."

"Man, would I like to catch one of them."

"Crazy buggers. Swim upstream and bash their brains out."

Virg is not happy about Jill having a baby, of course. He sure doesn't plan to get married like Mark. Still, he feels like a real man today. He would like to tell Mark what he said, about all his sperm being dead. That was a good one. The truth is, he's got so many he could stock the brook.

Mark is thinking about last night. "I don't like being on top," Sandy said. "I feel like a boy."

He would like to know what it's like with Jill.

*   *   *

Greg sits at his worktable, looking out the window. There are two guys fishing in the brook. Ten years younger than he is, probably, but he will probably never learn to cast a line the way they do. He knows other things, of course. Floor plans of medieval cathedrals. The New York subway map. None of it seems all that vital.

He's using charcoal to sketch out the forms on his canvas for the picture of the falls. He puts in the stones, a dead birch leaning across the water, downstream, this house. It surprises him to see how realistic he's making this one.

Carla gets out of bed, comes down the ladder cautiously. "There's coffee on the stove," he calls to her, over the sound of running water.

"I don't feel like any," she says. He looks up to see her standing behind him, wearing just her underpants. He has never seen her smile like that.

Jill has eighty-two dollars. She would have more, but last week she bought the new Pink Floyd double album and a pair of those jeans they've been advertising on TV. Wanda says they charge you $135 at the Women's Health Clinic in Concord if you go in the first trimester.

Wanda has put out a plate of Mystic Mints and fixed them each a glass of Kool-Aid. She and Jill are sitting at the kitchen table smoking cigarettes. She feels like one of the characters on *All My Children* that's always sitting around the kitchen table talking over her problems. She hasn't felt this important since the day Melissa was born, and even then it only lasted half an hour. As soon as she was out of the delivery room no one gave a shit about her anymore. Now she's saying, "We'll figure out something." It's like back in school when some kid got leukemia and the class would have a big meeting and hold a car wash. They made her secretary of the fund-raising committee one time—when Dennis Coutreau's house burned down and he needed plastic surgery for the burns. Her committee raised two hundred and thirty-eight dollars. The truth is, she has been wondering where she was going to get the money for this month's rent. But now she puts her arm around Jill (who, it suddenly occurs to her, looks a lot like Laura on *General Hospital*) and says, again, "We'll figure out something."

Doris likes listening to *Hollywood Squares* while she irons. That Paul Lynde is something else.

The clothes these kids wear. The shirt she's ironing now for Jill has a pair of fat red lips on the pocket, with a big red tongue sticking out. Sickening.

The contestant is kissing the host. She must have won the Secret Square. Doris hasn't been paying attention. She's been thinking about Jill, thinking that she has not been looking well. This morning her skin looked practically green.

Doris puts the tongue shirt on a hanger along with the three other blouses she has ironed and takes them upstairs. She's just putting them on the rack in Jill's closet when she sees it—a plastic bowl pushed in the corner behind the shoes, filled with vomit.

Down on his knees, Reg is patting the soil over the last row of spinach. He has also planted three rows of Little Marvel peas and one of sugar snaps. With luck they'll be ready by the Fourth of July.

He puts his hoe in the shed. Then he will just stop by the house to give Ann the gloves. Let the little wooden windmill be a surprise, when she goes down to look at the garden.

She's standing there at the porch holding a Miller. "I thought you'd be thirsty," she says. She's wearing a blue dress that's much too big. It's an old woman's dress. In some ways she doesn't seem like a young person at all.

He says a beer would hit the spot and sits down. The chair is wicker, hanging by a chain from a beam on the ceiling. He feels as if he's sitting inside an egg. She sits across from him in an old Boston rocker. She is not drinking beer herself.

"This hits the spot," he says. Did he already tell her that?

"It must be hard work, breaking up all those weeds."

He says he wouldn't know what to do with himself if he wasn't working hard. Those six months he had to lie in bed, after he hurt his back, nearly killed him. Listening to Doris's shows and to her talking to her friends on the phone about all the doctor bills.

She is looking for a job, she tells him. It's hard being cooped up in the house all day.

"It sounds like you're a music lover," he says. He could hear the records she was playing way down in the field.

She asks what kind of music he likes.

"Some of the stuff my daughter Jill plays," he tells her, "makes my hair fall out. I didn't used to be this bald."

She laughs. He's surprised. He never tells jokes.

"My idea of good music is the Mills Brothers and the Glenn Miller orchestra. They were way before your time."

She says she likes Glenn Miller too.

"Peggy Lee. There's a voice."

She asks if he ever listens to Dolly Parton. He says he's not that familiar with her. He thinks he's heard a song she does on the radio.

"Not the songs she does now." Ann explains that she has gotten very commercial. But she used to write some of the most beautiful songs. "Let me play you something," she says.

She puts on "Tennessee Mountain Home. Life was as peaceful as a baby's sigh." It reminds him a little of his father's farm, which has been made into a trailer park. Neither of them says anything during the song. Ann rocks in her chair. Reg tries to find a comfortable position for his legs in the basket seat and gives up. When the song is over he says, "That's pretty."

Ann asks if he has lived here long.

"All my life. So far."

Does he ever think about leaving?

Well, he went overseas when he was in the service. There was a layover in Tokyo, three days. They had these bathhouses there with men and women all together. Nothing happens, you just get clean. A buddy took him to a teahouse where they had geisha girls. Very beautiful girls. They treat you like a king. He has never told his wife about that—she would think something went on. But they just drank tea. He brought back a tiny kimono for his daughter Jill (she was just a baby then) and a tea set for Doris. She hasn't ever used it.

Why is he saying all this?

Leaving. No, he doesn't suppose they will ever leave. Doris thinks traveling is a waste of good money.

He would like to ask Ann what about yourself? But he knows that would not be a good idea. "I was thinking we could get some mulch hay for the tomatoes," he says. "With a garden like this that hasn't been cultivated for a while, weeds can be a problem."

She says that sounds like a good idea.

Just as he is leaving, he remembers the garden gloves. "You don't want your hands to end up like mine," he tells her. Then he says thanks for the beer.

After he has gone she walks down to the garden. There is a windmill turning slowly in the breeze. The wood-chopper swings his ax and lowers it. He swings again.

Because she chose this town as a good place to be invisible, Ann can't imagine what it would be like to have grown up here, lived here always, walked down the street and have everybody say hello. Can't take a step in this town that somebody isn't watching, Reg told her. But here in the woods you can consume a quart of ice cream daily, stick your finger down your throat after every meal and no one will know. You can spend a night pacing up and down the driveway, sobbing. Watch every TV game show between nine and three-thirty for a month. Encase your entire naked body in tightly wound Saran Wrap (she did that the night the scale read 140, to sweat it off) and stay that way for two days straight. But no one knows these things, knows her name, even, or looks up when she passes.

She would like to have no history, or a very tragic one. Fugitive, war widow. Weatherman gone underground. Amnesia victim, hair dyed blond, only the roots to remind her maybe she used to be somebody else. As it is, there are few telephone calls, seldom a letter. But there's her mother, of course, calling person-to-person from Seattle (as if there would be anyone else here to answer) to say please come home for a visit. I will send you a ticket. I would pay for a therapist. What did I do?

Her life was ordinary. They lived in Connecticut then. (Seattle came later, after the divorce.) Her father sold Prudential, made the million-dollar club four straight years. Her mother belonged to the board of trustees of the Hartford Symphony. (And would hate the music Ann plays now.) There is also a younger sister, Carol, but she and Ann have never been close.

Her father wanted to be a poet, talked about Wallace Stevens, quoted to Ann (when drunk) somebody's line about children being hostages to fortune. She was his favorite, and blamed her mother for tying him down, making him get a regular job. She thought then he must have been, could have been, an important poet. She believed a person should be willing to give up absolutely everything in pursuit of his great dream. What else mattered? Not a house in Fairfield and symphony tickets every weekend, certainly. "You don't understand what it's like when you have children," her mother said. "Everything changes." (Mostly they just didn't talk about this at all, but one night in Seattle, in her stepfather's house, the month after the funeral, they did.) "I am not interested in your excuses," Ann said. "I will never compromise, or force anyone I love to compromise either. I would rather just let them go." (Which is just what she ended up doing, with Rupert. Of course it could be said that Rupert was the one who let go, but Ann knows she made it possible for him to do it. She loved him that much.)

He was her freshman English teacher. When she fell in love with him, persuaded him to quit his job and move with her to Vermont, finally write full time the novel he'd been working on since 1968, she thought her father would be happy. Who should understand better the importance of freedom to pursue one's work, with a loving and supportive person at one's side? If Rupert was only three years younger than her father, so what. They would have more in common. They could even talk about the war.

The three of them had dinner together in Cambridge. There was a too-loud jazz band playing in the restaurant and Ann's father sat on Rupert's bad side, so Rupert couldn't hear much. When Ann suggested that her father show Rupert some of his old poems—started to recite one— her father said, "For God's sake shut up," and then looked surprised and upset, that he had talked to her that way. When he asked Rupert what he imagined the two of them would live on, up in Burlington, he sounded like her mother.

He had a minor heart attack six months later. Ann was meaning to go see him and then he had the second one, and after that he never regained consciousness. When she drove down to Hartford the next day, for the funeral, and to clean out his apatment, the first thing she did was find his folder of poems, which she hadn't looked at since high school. She realized they weren't very good, but didn't tell anybody this.

Particularly her mother, when she went out to Washington State for a visit, at Christmas. She wanted to make her mother feel bad and guilty, and the trip was a success.

But Rupert really was brilliant, and she knows that someday he will finish his novel, and imagines that there will be a character in it—not the main character, who is really Rupert—that resembles Ann. Sometimes she imagines the book will be dedicated to her. She is sure, anyway, that Rupert is living alone now. If he were going to live with anybody, it would be her.

So what could she tell this therapist her mother wants her to visit? That she sacrificed her whole happiness, her life, practically, so the man she loves could be free, which is the truest kind of love there is, because you don't do it to get anything back, and in fact, you do it even when the person wouldn't do it for you. If knowing how to love like that is sick, Ann doesn't want the cure. It is her one real and extraordinary talent.

And there's no point going to Seattle for holidays either, or seeing her sister, getting her mother's recipe for pie crust or going sailing in Puget Sound on her stepfather's boat. Ann is sure those things would be enjoyable, that she could have a good time, but having a good time is not her goal anymore. She doesn't want those kinds of good times to make her forget, either, what is real and important, which is her great love and her great loss. It's out of kindness to her mother that Ann never gives an answer when her mother asks what she did to make her daughter never call and never write, never visit, or even send a picture of the house. Because the answer is, her mother has nothing to do with the life she leads now, is not important enough to Ann to be responsible for grief of the magnitude she is experiencing. Ann likes to feel that her life began that first day in Rupert's class. Nothing in her history before then matters anymore.

*   *   *

Doris knows what it must be. That mental problem where teenage girls go on diets and make themselves throw up. Donahue had a show about it.

And Jill has been eating so little lately. She was never heavy, but now her cheeks are all sunk in. She is probably having trouble with her boyfriend.

What to do about that bowl in the closet? If she empties it Jill will know. She doesn't know what she would say to Jill. Better to leave it. Tonight she will make Jill's favorite dinner. She'll see to it that Jill eats. No daughter of hers is going to be mental.

Carla was hoping to stop by the secondhand clothing shop Greg told her about, where he bought her the dress, but the sign says "Closed." There's an old school bus parked in the yard, with a lot of stuff tied to the roof. She hopes they aren't going out of business.

She should buy vitamins. Take care of herself. She thinks she will also get back into yoga. Nothing too strenuous—just to keep her body flexible.

There's a very pretty girl in the drugstore—she can't be more than eighteen—holding a baby. She's trying to carry the baby and three boxes of Pampers, which are on sale. One of the Pampers boxes keeps slipping and the baby has begun to cry.

"Do you need a hand?" asks Carla. When this girl is my age, she's thinking, her child will be nine or ten.

"Could I," says the girl. "I should've waited till my husband could pick these up, but I was afraid they'd be sold out. It's such a good buy."

"I've got my car outside," says Carla. "I'll give you a lift home if you want."

The girl says that would be great.

Her name is Sandy. She lives across from the Laundromat. Carla says she's new in town, doesn't know where that is.

Sandy asks where Carla comes from. New York.

Wow, she would love to see New York City. All the beautiful clothes. Are the women there really wearing those spandex pants and things? Has Carla ever been mugged?

"Somebody broke into our loft once but we weren't home. There were a lot of junkies in our neighborhood."

"I was going to take my senior class trip to New York City," says Sandy. Only she didn't graduate.

"You probably didn't miss much," says Carla. "You never get the real feeling for a place on one of those trips."

That's what Mark said. What he wanted to do most was get passes for *Saturday Night Live* or go to one of those rock music clubs. Their adviser got everybody tickets for *Chapter Two*.

Sandy asks what Carla did in New York. She says she was an editor on a women's magazine and now she's trying to write a play. Her husband (she has been calling Greg that since they moved here) is an artist.

"A magazine editor." Sandy says that's where she gets all her recipes. Also those magazines are very helpful when you're raising a baby. Just today she cut out an article about exercises for babies to do to improve their coordination. She is wondering if Carla had anything to do with choosing the babies they use to model the baby clothes in those craft sections. Carla has just been saying how cute Mark Junior is.

They have reached Sandy's apartment building. "Do you want to come upstairs for a cup of tea?" she asks. Carla says sure.

There's a plaque on the door with two robins putting their wings around each other and the words "Love Nest" underneath. Inside, the place is immaculate. Flower-print café curtains, an African violet on the windowsill, a prism hanging above. There's a mug tree on the kitchen counter with two yellow mugs—"Mom" and "Dad." A cookie jar shaped like a giant apple. A framed reproduction of Picasso's *Don Quixote* and a piece of parchmentlike paper with a poem printed on it titled "Desiderata." A portable stereo, about fifteen records, a few rubber baby toys in a basket on a hand-braided rug.

Carla puts the Pampers boxes down beside the door and picks up the framed photograph of Mark and Sandy that's propped on top of the TV set. "Your husband's a good-looking man," she says.

"Thank you," says Sandy.

"How long have you been married?"

Sandy says fourteen months. Actually, their first anniversary's next month, but Sandy doesn't want people to think they just got married because she was pregnant.

"Having the baby right away—doesn't it sometimes make you feel tied down?"

Sandy puts the milk in a creamer and sets out the sugar bowl. "What would I be doing with my freedom anyway?" she says. She's pouring apple juice into a Fred Flintstone bottle for the baby, who's smiling and waving his arms.

Carla has an image, then, of the roomful of men and women in her Szechuan cooking class, back in the city. Standing over their cutting boards, cleavers poised. Chopping bamboo shoots into the shape of evergreen trees, sculpting mushrooms. Freedom: That's what she has been doing with hers.

Frank Pineo, who runs Moonlight Acres, is standing over the deep fryer, trying to decide if he can leave the oil another couple of days without changing it. The clams have begun tasting a little funny. Well, he will just serve a little more tartar sauce on the side.

"You said to come back this week and see about a job," says the girl. She has a baby with her, in a stroller, but Frank can tell this one doesn't have a husband. She's plump, the way he likes them.

"Uh huh." He turns back to the griddle. Checks the pilot light. Let her work for this.

"So I was wondering if there was an opening now."

He looks at his watch. He walks slowly to the other end of the counter and squeezes out a jumbo Softee Freeze cone, a Maraschino cherry on top. He looks back at the girl and licks it.

"You think you could handle this machine?" he says.

She says she is sure she could.

"Looks kind of like a woman's nipple, doesn't it?" he says, holding out the cone.

Wanda says she guesses so.

"Yours look like that?"

She doesn't say anything.

"When you're really hot for it?"

Wanda looks down at Melissa, slumped in her umbrella stroller. She is like an old man, all hunched over, with her head bobbing.

"So are you really hot for it?" He puts one hand down the front of his pants. He is about forty and quite fat. "The job, I mean."

Wanda says she needs the money pretty badly.

"One-eighty an hour," he says. "Hairnet. White shoes. No free eats."

Wanda says fine.

"You know what I always wanted to do?" he says, making a swirling motion on the ice cream with his tongue. "Lick this right off some chick's fat tit."

The pork chops are all set to bake. The pie is cooling. Nothing left for Mrs. Ramsay to do but the vegetables. That can wait until they get here.

She is working on that other baby's duck sweater. The mother seemed like a nice girl. It will be important for Susan to have a friend her age. They will go to Benson's Animal Farm and the Shriners Circus, when it comes to Manchester this summer.

And to church, of course. That is the first thing, to get Baby baptized. Mrs. Ramsay will take her to prayer meeting and Bible study. They will pray together every night. Susan will need that, born so sinfully. But she will renounce her mother. Her father too. He has been a thankless son. Just last week was Mrs. Ramsay's birthday. Did Dwight send a card? He used to write her such beautiful little poems and now he does not even send a card. It's too late for him, he has gone to the devil. But she will have an angel for a daughter.

Right after Boletus urinated in Mrs. Farley's Alka-Seltzer (his mother never did get around to putting a diaper on him, and, by what Denver said was a really karmic coincidence, her glass was in direct line with his penis)—right after that was when Mrs. Farley told Dakota she was going to put her in the oven and have her for breakfast. Kalima had explained to Dakota that Tara's mother was only making a funny joke, but since Kalima herself was munching on placenta when she said this, Dakota was not entirely convinced, and began to scream. Denver said this was not good for the introductory earth experience of the new baby, who had just been named Mountain, and took him outside. So he did not see Mrs. Farley pull the somewhat bloody monogrammed towel out from under Kalima, grab the patent leather pocketbook out of Stanley's hands, point the blow dryer in his ear and say, surprisingly quietly, to Tara, "If these people are not out of here in two minutes I am going to spray this room full of Raid." Which showed a pretty good understanding of the farm members' priorities, because if there was anything that could get them to move fast, during a period that is supposed to be very mellow and laid back, it would be the introduction into the birthing atmosphere of a petroleum distillate product.

So they packed up the truck, paid for Dakota's see-through red panties and Denver's new bloodstained work pants, hugged Tara and Sunshine, said, "If you're ever in Georgia," and left.

Now Mrs. Farley is setting up the ironing board, spilling

the pile of Girl Scout uniforms onto the floor beside it, lighting a Kool. Tara can't believe how quickly everything has gone from incredibly beautiful to incredibly awful. She has to get out of here.

And not just to the Laundromat either. She knows now that very soon she is going to leave this town and never come back.

Greg has been trying to paint the girl all morning. He wants her sitting on the flat rock at the base of the falls, nursing her baby. He can't get the positions right. It just looks as if she's holding a doll.

He wishes she were sitting right there in front of him. How was it she held the baby? He feels a rush of love, thinking about her. Carla would say you can't love someone you don't know. But he loved *her* right away, didn't he?

Then the idea comes to him. Find that girl, hire her as a model. She will certainly be able to use the money.

Carla has taken the VW, but he doesn't care. He can walk into town.

"Looks like someone's moved in the house over there," says Mark to Virgil. He has just observed Greg stepping out the door. The two of them watch him disappear down the road.

"Most likely summer people, roughing it," says Virgil. "They're probably loaded." He's irked because the yard outside that house has always been one of his favorite spots to get laid. He goes toward the house.

"Damn black flies," says Mark.

"Take a look at this," Virg calls to him. He's standing on a rock, staring in the window. From where he stands he can see Greg's painting of the falls, with him and Mark in it. There sure wasn't any girl sitting naked on any rock this morning though. What is she supposed to be holding, a bag of groceries?

"That's us, man," says Virg. Mark has come over beside him. "Guy didn't even ask permission."

"He must have a million albums," says Mark. Also, a Marantz amplifier and a Technics turntable.

"I bet he's got dope," says Virg. The door is open.

"You're crazy," says Mark. He is thinking: What I would give for a stereo system like that. Virg has gone ahead on in.

"Must be a chick living here too," Virgil calls to him. He's inside the house now, holding a pair of Carla's black bikini pants. She has never broken the habit of leaving them on the floor, wherever it is she steps out of them.

"I don't believe it," says Virgil. He is laughing almost hysterically. "They've got a picture of some guy's prick and balls hanging on the wall. Some people are weird."

Mark hesitates, steps inside.

"Cup of tea?" says Virgil in a sort of English accent. He's holding the pot with feet on it. He has hung the black panties on the pouring spout.

Mark is looking at the records. A six-record set of Buddy Holly. *Yesterday and Today* with the original banned photograph of the Beatles dressed as butchers. Every album Dylan ever made, including a bootleg copy of the Basement tapes. Two or three Brian Enos on an obscure label. The original master Audiophile version of *Dark Side of the Moon*. Graham Parker, The Roches, Elvis Costello, old Supremes. Everything's here. He would like to get to know this guy and ask if he could come over and listen to albums sometime.

Virgil has just found the marijuana in a wooden box with birds painted on the lid. Must be at least a pound. He can't decide whether to roll a joint now or just take it for later. Might as well have some for the road.

Mark has come to the Linda Ronstadts. They're all here. That old album when Linda was kind of overweight— not fat, just nice and soft looking, sitting barefoot in some dirt next to a couple of pigs. A couple from back when she was with the Stone Ponies. It takes him a minute to figure out how to work the turntable. Suddenly the music blasts out. He didn't know it would be so loud.

"Whenever I'm with him/Something inside/Starts to burning/And I'm filled with desire. . . ."

Virg is squeezing black paint out of a tube onto the window overlooking the falls. "Look at me, I'm creative," he says. He has to talk very loud because of the music.

"It's like a heat wave/Burning in my heart. . . ."

"Fuck you sucker," he writes in acrylic.

"Virg, we've got to get out of here."

"Don't talk to me, man. I'm an artist." He reaches for another tube that's lying on the floor. Carla's Koromex. He squeezes out a long stripe. Stuff smells awful.

"Love is like a heat wave/Heat wave. . . ."

"I'm splitting," says Mark. He has never done anything like this before. Might as well take some albums, now that he's here.

"Crummy dope's giving me a headache," says Virg. "I'm out of here." He tosses the bag of grass to Mark, who stuffs it into his pocket. Mark wonders if maybe he should neaten things up a little.

They are just about to walk on home when Virg remembers his trout. Mark says he will wait at the edge of the road. "Hurry up," he calls.

Virgil clambers down the rocks. His head is splitting. Damn line slips out of his hand. He leans over the water to pick up the fish, puts one boot on a dead birch tree leaning over the brook. Mark sees the tree give under the weight, but it's too late to do anything about it. His friend is in the water.

Reg's presents have left Ann feeling sad. It seems to her as if the people who are kind and loving to you are never the same ones you are kind and loving to. She has a neighbor whose hand trembles when she offers him a beer, and he brings her a windmill, and what is she doing? Thinking how she would lie down in front of a train for Rupert, who never even got it straight when her birthday was. And who does Rupert worry about? Trina, whose trip to Disney World should not be interrupted by Ann's life being wrecked. As for Trina, the only person she might lie down on a train track for is Jaclyn Smith from *Charlie's Angels.* Ann wonders if there is ever such a thing as two people both loving each other equally and being happy always. To her it feels as if misery is just built into love. Things aren't meant to work out.

She doesn't usually fix her Kahlúa drink this early in the day. (It's a few minutes after two.) She's just so low. She puts on a George Jones record. Nobody else, besides Dolly, can sound so totally hopeless. Then she takes out Rupert's letters. They were written during the period when she was still unsure about leaving school and moving in with him, and it was Rupert who didn't think he could live without her. It figures.

She saves these letters for special occasions. She's afraid if she reads them too often they'll be used up. So she hasn't taken them out in a month.

"Take me," says George Jones. "Take me to your darkest room/Close every window and bolt every door/The very first moment I heard your voice/I'd be in darkness no more."

She has gotten to the part in Rupert's first letter where he says how he thought about her while he was having his root canal surgery, and the dentist said he had never seen such a stoic patient. "Just to think about you makes me grin," he said.

"Take me to your most barren desert," George Jones sings.

"You say we will end up making each other miserable," he said. "How can that be? You make my gray old heart fly up."

She is crying by this time, of course. She gets up to pour another inch of Kahlúa and begins to pace the floor, singing along with the record.

"Take me, oh, take me to Siberia." George Jones is practically moaning.

The Just-like-nu Shop is closed, but Greg decided he will knock on the door anyway. He is just about to leave—he has waited a couple of minutes—when the mother opens the door.

"What now?" There is a bloody dish towel draped over the banister behind her. What's going on here? She has killed her daughter. Murdered the baby. He just stands there.

"We're closed."

"The girl" is all he can say. "The one with the baby."

"There's plenty fit that description," says the woman. "We have girls with babies crawling around all over the place here. They are reproducing faster than rabbits. Aren't even housebroken."

"I'm looking for your daughter," says Greg. "I might have a job for her."

"I bet."

He's wondering if he should call the police.

"Well, she doesn't tell me much. But you can usually find her over by the Laundromat."

He doesn't say good-bye. He just leaves.

Carla and Sandy are on their second pot of tea. Sandy's telling Carla about the time Mark Junior got constipated and she stuck a little chip of soap up his rear end. Carla seems to be very interested in pregnancy and babies.

"After that it just popped right out," she says.

"Didn't you feel scared in the beginning?" Carla asks. "A baby's so tiny. I'd be afraid I'd break it."

Sandy says she is always scared of something happening to Mark Junior. "I never had so much to lose before," she says.

She tells Carla her terrible dream. In this dream she's making love with Mark and she hears a knock at the door. Mark says never mind, they'll go away. He keeps kissing her, stroking her, rocking back and forth on top of her, and the knocking keeps on getting louder. Finally Mark is done and she gets up, wraps her robe around herself and opens the door. There's a little bundle on the doormat. She says, "Oh, look, a birthday present for the baby," and bends to pick it up. It's not wrapped in paper, it is bound up, sort of like bandages. She unwinds yards and yards of fabric. It seems to go on forever. Then she sees her son's face. She unwinds the cloth faster and faster, until he is lying there stiff and naked in her arms. He is cold as stone.

Virgil sits at the edge of the water, cursing. Shit, why did he leave his car back home? Why did he have to go back for that puny fish. Now he's soaking wet and frozen and it feels like his ankle's broken. Twenty feet away, on the window of the summer people's house, he can read the words "Fuck you sucker," backward. The guy is bound to come home soon. Virg can't even stand up.

"I think there's another house up the road," says Mark. "I'll go for help." He will say they were fishing, that's all.

He stashes the albums under some leaves and heads up the hill.

Tara watches the man walk along Main Street, knowing she has seen him someplace. He has a face like a statue in an art book. She also likes the way he walks. His back is very straight. He doesn't bounce exactly, but he looks sort of determined. Tara doesn't walk anything like that.

"This will probably sound odd." He has stopped right in front of her, outside the Laundromat. Denver and Kalima would say it was karmic.

"My name is Greg. I've been looking for you."

She tosses her hair the way she has seen Wanda and Jill do when a boy talks to them. Not that anyone like this has ever talked to them.

He's an artist. He wants to paint her. Also Sunshine. He mentions something about paying her, but she doesn't even concentrate on that. She just knows without having to think about it that he's going to rescue her.

He says if it's O.K. with her, then he'll pick the two of them up tomorrow here at the Laundromat, around noon.

She tells him her name. "Like in *Gone with the Wind.*"

After he leaves she remembers where she saw him, remembers he was buying a dress for his girlfriend. This doesn't bother her one bit.

Carla wants to know about breast-feeding. Did Sandy try it? Why did she choose the bottle instead?

"Mark didn't like the idea," says Sandy. "He said my chest was his." She wishes she hadn't told that. Now she's embarrassed.

"A friend of mine is doing it though," she adds. "Her baby's about the same age as Mark Junior." She glances out the window, thinking she will point Tara out if she's at her usual spot by the Laundromat.

"There she is," says Sandy. "Talking to some guy."

Carla comes to see.

As the house comes into view, Mark hears music. He doesn't mean to look in any more windows, but there she is. Holding a wineglass and sort of hugging herself with the other hand. She's barefoot, pacing back and forth, singing. Not in the quiet, mouthing way that most people do when they play records. She is belting it out like she's giving a concert.

So loud she doesn't hear his knock. Finally he has to put his head in the door and yell, "Excuse me."

She jumps.

"Sorry to bother you," he says. She turns down the music and puts her glass on the arm of a chair.

He explains about his friend. Can't walk, no car. Afraid his ankle may be broken.

"Just a second," she says. "I'll put on my shoes."

She screws the top back on the bottle and puts the ice cubes back in the freezer. Mark follows her out the door.

She turns her key in the ignition and opens the passenger door for him. He slides in.

"Nice little car," he says. "Get good mileage?"

"We've got a problem with Jill," says Doris. She and Reg are cleaning the creosote out of their stovepipe. It looks as if they won't be burning any more wood until September.

Reg knows he's supposed to ask, What do you mean? But if he waits she will just tell him.

"She's depressed. She's got mental problems. Doesn't have any appetite."

Reg had not noticed. He feels guilty and foolish. He's a middle-aged man with a wife and teenaged daughter. He has no business spending all his time thinking about that girl down the road.

"What do you figure is the matter?" he asks.

"You know these teen years," says Doris. "A girl gets a spot on her nose and she figures her life is over."

"Why don't I just take my girls out to the movies this evening?" says Reg. "Maybe Howard Johnson's too. Make a night of it."

"That would be nice," says Doris.

Ann feels reckless. She's a little bit drunk to begin with. She recognizes the passenger stretched out on her backseat, soaking wet and shivering, as the boy whose lovemaking she observed, right at this very spot, just two days before. The passenger in the seat beside her, she knows, recently experienced an erection while reading the current issue of *Rolling Stone* outside Felsen's News. One of those Linda Ronstadt nuts probably.

They are neither of them at the George Jones stage of life—pining, suffering, feeling lonely and blue. These boys probably don't go twenty-four hours without screwing some girl or other. They certainly don't bring these girls windmills and garden gloves either. For them sex is simple and uncomplicated, like breathing and eating. If she could be like that she might feel more like a member of the human race. Nobody would be miserable. Nobody would love anybody.

Which would she choose? The one in the front seat—Mark—is more attractive. The one in the back, Virgil, looks wilder. He would probably like to have Led Zeppelin playing, for atmosphere. Of course he has that broken ankle.

She could drop him off and say to the other one, "Let's go back to my place." Or just drive someplace. He probably does it mostly in cars.

She's standing at the edge of a waterfall. Might as well plunge. She has broken every bone in her body anyway.

Now is the moment, Mark thinks. Drop Virgil off at the medical center, then ask this girl do you have any plans? Of course she doesn't.

As for himself, he went over the edge a couple of hours ago. He has now broken into some people's house, stolen three albums, missed work. Soon he will also miss dinner, and his son's bath time.

In a minute, Virgil is thinking, we will be at the medical center. Mark will say, "Think you can manage O.K.?" Then, while he's stretched out on an examining table getting pictures taken of his bones, Mark will be parked by the side of the road somewhere, getting laid. He can just tell. Maybe they'll even go back to her place, and they'll do stuff like take a shower together. She probably knows how to give a massage. The doctor will be telling him, "Keep off that foot," and Mark will be on top of her. Mark has the dope too. Virg will take two aspirins and there they'll be, stoned out of their minds.

She pulls up in front of the emergency entrance and puts the car into neutral. Mark says, "Hey, man, think you can manage O.K.?" "Sure thing," says Virgil. "I guess Sandy and the baby will be wondering what happened to you." That's all it takes.

There's a plate of celery sticks stuffed with cream cheese and walnuts sitting on Mrs. Ramsay's lazy Susan. She has also put out a bowl of party snacks made with Corn Chex and Wheat Chex and peanuts. "Have as much as you like, dear," says Mrs. Ramsay. She's not touching anything herself.

Wanda is not really hungry tonight, after all that Softee Freeze Mr. Pineo gave her. Melissa had some too. He put it on his finger and she licked it off. He thought that was funny. "Why don't we just take off Baby's hat and sweater?" says Mrs. Ramsay. "It's so warm tonight."

Wanda doesn't want to remove the hat, on account of Melissa's bruise. "I think she has a cold," says Wanda. "I'd better just leave this stuff on."

"I once knew a woman whose baby got caught in the rain without a hat on," says Mrs. Ramsay. "The next morning when she went to get it, that baby was dead."

That's terrible.

"There was this other child, she used to play with Dwight sometimes when they were still toddlers. Her mother gave her milk in a glass bottle. One day the baby tripped on a toy car, holding that bottle. Glass shattered all over her face. She had to have nine operations. Today her face is covered with scars. No one ever asks her out on a date."

"Wow," says Wanda. "Jeez."

"That's nothing. There was this woman who took drugs

while she was pregnant. Her baby was born without any face. Eyes, nose, mouth, nothing. She has to wear a little knitted mask all the time. Have some more of this party mix. It will just go to waste otherwise.

"There was this man in Russia. A truckdriver, forty years old. He started feeling sick. Like there was something pressing against his chest is the way he put it.

"So they performed exploratory surgery. Inside his left lung they found the petrified forty-year-old fetus of his twin brother. This embryo had hair on his head, eyes. There was supple fatty tissue around its waist. It had one tooth."

Mrs. Ramsay is not looking into Wanda's eyes as she speaks. She is watching Wanda's mouth, chewing on a stuffed celery stick. Wanda is feeling slightly sick to her stomach, and wishes she hadn't started eating this celery stick, but she has started now, and can't very well spit it out. These things take forever to chew.

"And here is the amazing thing. The reason this man started feeling pain all of a sudden was, this fetus had begun to grow."

Mrs. Ramsay goes to check the pork chops. "We'll just leave you little fellows another ten minutes," she says, returning to her seat.

"So," she says. "I hope you had a very lovely evening with that young man of yours."

Wanda says it's nothing serious.

"Oh, come on now," says Mrs. Ramsay. "I saw that glow in his eyes when he dropped you off."

What was she doing looking out the window? How could she see in the car? What glow?

"It must be hard for a lovely young person like yourself, having to take care of a baby all the time. Sometimes you must get very impatient."

Mrs. Ramsay has seen the bruise. Wanda will have to work it into the conversation about how Melissa fell.

Mrs. Ramsay is ladling soup into Wanda's bowl. Wanda gets up to put Melissa in her infant seat and hangs a string of wooden beads around her neck. Melissa looks like all she wants to do is sleep.

"And money must be a big problem." She passes Wanda a roll.

Wanda says she got a job today. Moonlight Acres. If Mrs. Ramsay would be willing to watch Melissa for her.

"Don't think about us," says Mrs. Ramsay. "We'll be fine."

Wanda's shift is six to midnight. Melissa usually sleeps through most of that time anyway.

"Now here's something fascinating," says Mrs. Ramsay. "I heard about this woman whose tubes were blocked. Her eggs couldn't get down from her ovaries to be fertilized? In the picture she seemed quite obese, I don't know if that was the problem.

"Well, she had this friend. I guess you could say the friend was a loner. Never married. In fact, she was a virgin.

"The friend said she'd have a baby for the other woman, the obese one, using the husband's sperm. Of course it would be adultery if they actually had intercourse. So they went to a doctor to get artificial insemination. The doctor wouldn't do it."

Mrs. Ramsay says the chops are ready. Also, have a baked potato and some asparagus. That's not enough cheese sauce. Take some more.

"So here's what they did. They got some books out of the library and read up on artificial insemination. They figured out just when her eggs would be released and got some sperm.

"Then they put his sperm into a syringe and injected it into the friend. The virgin. And she got pregnant. And now they have the baby and it thinks the obese woman is the mother and the friend lives with them. They're a very happy family."

"Wow," says Wanda. She adds that the chops are very good.

"Have more." Mrs. Ramsay has scraped the cheese

sauce off her asparagus. She gets up and turns on the TV set, which faces the dinner table.

"I just love these Muppets, don't you?" she says. Kermit is saying that Diana Ross is this week's guest host. More Negroes.

"I met one of your young friends yesterday," says Mrs. Ramsay. "She was sitting with her baby outside the Laundromat."

"Oh," says Wanda. "Tara."

"Her baby was sucking on her breast. It was a very beautiful sight. That's what motherhood is all about."

Wanda is going to say that she didn't breast-feed because someone told her that would ruin her boobs. But they're ruined anyway.

"But it is a shame to see a beautiful young person like that having to take care of a baby. She should be out having a good time. She could go dancing."

Wanda is thinking about Jill, sitting in her apartment eating a Mystic Mint and looking at her stomach. "It isn't even the size of my thumbnail," she said. "It isn't even as big as those planarians we cut up in biology."

"And money is such a problem," says Mrs. Ramsay. "How can a young girl possibly come up with the money?" In a minute she will take down *Joy of Cooking*.

Why didn't Wanda think of it before? She can ask Mrs. Ramsay. She is sure Mrs. Ramsay would want to help Jill.

"Do you think you could lend me a hundred dollars?" says Wanda.

So easy. Mrs. Ramsay opens the cookbook to page 200, takes out a hundred-dollar bill. "Here is the paper," she says. "There is more money too. Just sign here."

Right underneath where it says ". . . agree to give up all rights as Mother and admit that I am a slut."

What is going on anyway?

On the TV screen, Fozzie Bear has just asked Diana Ross what you get when you make a soft drink out of acorns. Oaka Cola. Wocka wocka wocka.

*   *   *

Carla gets home before Greg. The first thing she sees is a dead fish lying on the doorstep. The door open. Her teapot lying on the floor. Contraceptive cream smeared on the window. "Fuck you sucker." She screams.

Ann stops at the Grand Union for some honey yogurt and more popcorn. She knows what she will do tonight.

Then she goes home. Turns on the TV set, heats some oil in a pan, melts the butter. By the time the popcorn has popped she will have finished two cups of yogurt. She will save the other one for after, to help her throw up.

She goes to the pantry for the popping corn, reaches up to the top shelf for a bowl. There is a rustling, a little high-pitched cheeping sound and then a frantic fluttering over-head. For a second she thinks there must have been birds nesting here. But it's bats. At least a dozen.

"Let's talk some more about Loretta," says Dr. Poster. "About what you said last week. How she was just asking for it."

Wayne stretches his arms and folds them behind his head, as if he's lying on a beach someplace. This is a trick, of course, designed to get his guard down. Dr. Poster is trying to look as if he agrees that Loretta deserved what happened to her, so Wayne will admit that he did in fact make those teeth marks on her buttocks. But he knows that Dr. Poster could never understand a woman like Loretta, or what it means to have something such as he and Loretta had. Dr. Poster probably makes love to his wife for three minutes every Saturday night. Weekdays they talk about how their stocks are doing and whose turn it is to pick up the kids. Comment on what nice tender steak this is.

Loretta understood. She knew she belonged to him. She

knew she wasn't supposed to talk to anybody else, wasn't supposed to leave their apartment. She was supposed to wait there for him, on her mattress with her cunt ready. Thinking about how it was going to be. That was the deal. He made it worth her while, when he came to her. She was the one who broke the rules.

First she wanted to go to the supermarket. Said he never bought the right kind of oranges. Said he never took advantage of the sales. Didn't like the clothes he bought for her. Said I don't use sanitary napkins, I use Tampax.

Then she wanted a TV. Said how am I supposed to know what's going on in the world? You didn't even tell me Nixon resigned.

What does a person need to know that sort of stuff for, he would like to know. What is more important than the kind of love they had?

Then she wanted that baby. There was not supposed to be any baby. He brought her those pills every day. Even kept track of her cycle on the calendar.

She tricked him. Didn't even tell him. Didn't she know, when you have something like they had, she wouldn't have to tell him. He knew her body that well. Even before she missed her period he could tell there was something in her body that wasn't supposed to be there.

When he realized what had happened, first he thought he would kill himself. That would have been easier for him.

But how could he do that to her? She would never manage. She didn't even know Ed Sullivan died.

Then he thought maybe they could just get rid of the baby. He tried that, with a piece of wire he bought, but even before she began to bleed he knew it would never be the same. In the end she knew it too. She was begging him to do it.

She was just asking for it. That's what he means. Dr. Poster would never understand.

*   *   *

Tara is standing in front of her mirror. She's naked. Tomorrow, she thinks, a man will see my body. She is happy with the way she looks. There's nothing she would change.

Jill sits in the third row at the Merrimack Cinema, watching *Lady and the Tramp*. It was the only movie her mother could find that didn't have any sex. "We'd be footloose and collar-free," says Tramp, who has just asked Lady to run away with him. "It sounds wonderful," says Lady. "But who'd watch over the baby?"

Reg leans toward Jill. Doris has just reminded him that they've got to put some meat on those bones. He is about to say, "How about another box of buttered popcorn?" but then he sees the look on her face.

"Don't worry," he says. "I've seen this before. Everything turns out fine in the end."

Tonight Sandy's mother has prepared Luau Chicken with pineapple chunks, Rice-A-Roni, Chinese Style, and Stouffer's egg rolls. She tries to make it so their weekly family dinners with the kids have some kind of theme. (Everything tinted with green food coloring—even the mashed potatoes—on Saint Patrick's Day. Red, white and blue gelatin salad for patriotic holidays. A salute to some foreign country when it's no special occasion.)

"Aloha," says Sandy's father, George, when he greets them at the door. He gives his daughter a hug, shakes his son-in-law's hand. Sandy's mother, Sylvia, is already rearranging Mark Junior's hair, commenting (though she saw him only yesterday) on how big he's getting.

Mark's mother, Annette, is also here. Since Mark's father was shot down in Vietnam in '69, Sandy's folks have tried to include Annette in most of their family activities, and especially now that their kids have got together. Sylvia had the notion at one time that they might fix Annette up

with George's brother Glenn, whose wife left him the week
before their silver wedding anniversary, but Annette wasn't
interested, said there could never be anyone else after
Gerald. Annette often reminds her son of the ways in which
he differs from his father, who was two inches taller, had a
B.S. degree from the University of Maine, never so much as
dented his car. The truth is, Mark can hardly remember his
father now; he had been overseas eighteen months when he
was killed, and Mark was only seven then. Mark knows his
father chiefly from his mother's accounts, and from them he
knows that unless there's another war, and he dies in it, he
will never have a hope of catching up with the guy.

"Some Red Sox game the other night," says George.
"That was a real bazooka Remy fired off to second, eh?"

"Sure was," says Mark. He missed that play, on account
of Sandy's underpants landing on the TV set, hanging down
over the screen.

"Stanley might get us to the Series yet," says George.
"That was the best velocity I've seen on him all season."
George has not yet fully recovered from the Sox's loss of Luis
Tiant to New York.

"Do you believe this men-talk, girls?" says Sandy's
mother. "Now, who's going to try using chopsticks?"

They have moved to the living room now, and Sylvia is carrying out the tray of Sanka. Mark Junior has finally fallen
asleep in the crib his grandparents set up for him in the spare
bedroom. George has turned on the hi-fi. Annette is just fin-
ishing a story about how, when Mark was a baby, his father
built him a cradle, not from a kit or anything. Entirely by
hand. "If only I hadn't given that cradle away," she says.
"When you're young, you never realize how precious these
things are going to be."

"So how's everything going at the plant?" says George.
Once before, after Annette finished the cradle story, she
began to cry. He's anxious to get onto another subject.

"Fine," says Mark. Sandy says she thinks Mark will get a promotion by Christmas, he's got such a good mechanical mind. And she can tell that Mark Junior has inherited some of his father's talent that way. He's already trying to unscrew the nipple on his bottle. How do you like that?

"I hear your friend Virgil twisted up his ankle down at the falls this morning," says Sylvia. One of the nurses at the medical center is a friend of hers. Word travels fast in this town.

"Bad luck," says George. "Still, I'm glad to see you kids getting out in the fresh air. It makes me sick to see some of these young fellows spending all their time leaning on those darned pinball machines at Rocky's."

"Mark's no different from any of them, George," says Annette. "I've seen this son of mine plenty of times, throwing away his paycheck in that place. I remember when Gerald and I were newlyweds, we'd go to the movies maybe twice a year, and that was a big treat. You kids don't know how easy you have it."

"Guess who I met today," says Sandy. She wishes Mark wouldn't smoke those cigars, knows that her mother will spray the room with air freshener the minute they leave, on account of Mark's Tiparillos.

"This woman from New York City. She used to be an editor of a magazine. She was wearing those new kind of pants that get narrower at the ankles."

"How interesting," says Sylvia.

"I invited her to Mark Junior's five-month birthday party," Sandy says. "Also, there was this great sale on Pampers."

"Smart little wife you've got yourself, son," says Sandy's father. He does not hear Annette's comment about the advantages of cloth diapers.

When Greg comes home, Carla is sitting on the front steps, crying. The only words he can make out are that she wants to go back home. She doesn't like it here. She would feel safer on the worst block in New York City.

Later, after he has looked inside, he points out that all they lost was some grass. Nothing major. It was probably just a bunch of kids.

"We could go back tomorrow," says Carla. Stay with friends, look for another apartment. (With two bedrooms.)

Tomorrow Greg will see Tara again. He will tell Carla later, when she calms down.

The telephone is ringing when Reg and Doris walk in the door. Jill has gone straight upstairs. The evening was not a success. Jill didn't even want an ice cream at HoJo's.

"For you." Doris hands the phone to Reg, looking puzzled.

It's Ann. She's been trying to get him all evening. She sounds hysterical. "All over the house now," she says. "Can't even see out the windows. One got stuck in my hair." It's a little difficult to understand what she is talking about.

He says he will be right down.

Finally Wanda understands. Mrs. Ramsay wants Melissa. She's offering to pay eighteen hundred and twenty-six dollars if Wanda will sign this piece of paper.

"I only hit her one time," Wanda says, starting to cry. She thinks that's what this is all about. Maybe Mrs. Ramsay is going to tell the police. "The other time didn't count. She didn't fall asleep that other time." And the rest isn't Wanda's fault. The way Melissa keeps having the green diarrhea.

"The money was for my friend Jill," she says. "So she could have an abortion. I don't want any money for Melissa. I love her. She's the only thing I have. I'm going to be a good mother."

"Hitting babies. Killing babies. I have heard enough," says Mrs. Ramsay. She's still holding the money in one hand and *Joy of Cooking* in the other. "And I have heard enough of your Negro singers and your dirty boyfriends with just one thing on their minds. Soon you are going to be so fat they won't even be able to find it. I will tell Susan to pray for your soul; that is all I can do. She will not even remember your birthday. I would not be surprised if that formula you give her has caused brain damage. Ice cream parlors. Why don't you just charge for spreading your legs? Then there would be no money problems. You could kill all the babies you wanted to."

Mrs. Ramsay has just remembered the blueberry pie that was in the oven, keeping warm. She takes it out and puts it on a hand-crocheted mat in the middle of the table. Wanda has got up. She's putting on Melissa's jacket, packing her toys in the diaper bag as fast as she can.

"I bet you think I am going to give you a piece of this," says Mrs. Ramsay. "Well, I am not. Not one berry."

Ann is standing in the driveway when Reg drives up in his truck. She's wearing a long blue nightgown and a shawl like an old woman. When his high beams hit her nightgown they light a triangle between her legs. She's holding a fly swatter.

"Show me the scene of the crime," he says. He would expect to be tongue-tied with her and here he is, talking like a detective on TV.

She leads him into the kitchen. No bats at the moment. There's an empty yogurt container on the floor by the record player, another one on top of the stove. Photographs of Elizabeth Taylor at her fattest, plus some other pictures of overweight, mostly obese women taped to the refrigerator. Popcorn all over the floor (she must have forgotten to put the top on the electric fry pan). A cat on the counter, licking a stick

of butter. A whole lot of magazines. Two small barbells and
an exercise mat, one of those rubber belts they advertise in
TV Guide to take inches off your midriff. Another one of those
yellow legal pads covered with writing and cross-outs.

"The worst part is their terrible little faces," she says.
"They have these tiny sharp teeth."

Reg says you've got to remember they're afraid of you
too.

She's heard about these bats they have out West that
suck the blood out of cattle. Whole herds wiped out. She
couldn't sleep, thinking one might land on her neck. (Ann is
also having her period now, though she does not tell Reg
this. Did they smell it, like those grizzly bears that sometimes
attack women campers in Glacier Park? She thinks about
bat wings flapping between her legs, those little teeth scraping against her thighs, little bat fingers tugging at the string
of her Tampax.) "Oh, God," she says.

Reg has poured a cup of milk into a saucepan. Without
needing to ask, he has found where she keeps the honey. Now
he's stirring the honey into the hot milk, putting it in a mug,
washing the spoon.

If he kissed her now that would be all right. If he built a
fire in her bedroom fireplace (the nights are still cool) and
put on a George Jones record, told her he would take care of
her. She does not think about making love, though she
would do it. What she thinks about are his arms around her.
She puts her feet up on the chair.

"My daughter Jill used to have real bad nightmares,"
he says. "I'd get up with her and make hot milk. Sit her on
my knee and tell her stories about her and me, adventures
we'd go on. Never had much imagination. I'd go in my son's
room and look at his Hardy Boys books sometimes when he
was at school, write down ideas. One time Timmy heard me
telling Jill some story and he came in. 'Hey, Dad,' he says,
'you took that out of Hardy Boys, didn't you?' After that I
only told Jill true stories. Fish I caught, times I got a strike in

bowling, that kind of thing. She'd get so bored she went right back to sleep."

Ann says her father used to teach her a poem every night before bed. "Little Lamb, who made thee?" "I wandered lonely as a cloud . . ." She has forgotten most of them now, but there was some line about "nine bean rows will I have there."

Reg says speaking of that, he was thinking maybe they could put in some asparagus for next year. She's got the soil for it. He has to keep talking, because he is beginning to get an erection.

"That sounds good," she says. She's thinking: I am going to eat only fruits and vegetables from now on, with maybe one muffin for breakfast. I would be embarrassed for anybody to see my body, the way it is now. Uncared for.

Her breasts—though she's so young—do not tilt up after all. He can see them through the nightgown, though he's trying not to look. He doesn't mind that they droop though. It touches him. He wants to take his palms and cup one under each breast, support her.

She would like to lean her head on his chest. She likes it that he is not thin—a little overweight, in fact. She likes to think of him, stripped to the waist, unloading beams off a truck. That strong.

Oh, he could make this house tight as a drum. Jack up the sills, mend the roof, caulk around all the windows. He would make built-in cabinets, a chair swing, window boxes. So many little things—new washers in the faucets, a storm door on the porch, flashing along the eaves. Get rid of these bats, of course.

Winter nights—no TV—under a down quilt and a flannel sheet. He doesn't think she'd make him gargle and spray on Right Guard first. Does the woman always close her eyes the whole time?

She thinks about the weight of him on her chest. The creak of the bedsprings, warm breath on her face. I don't want to be alone (Sammi Smith singing). Help me make it through the night.

"Planting time," Reg tells her, "let me till you, let me sow you."

Not really, of course.

There's something about the sight of her son wearing a hat that always makes Sandy want to cry. This morning, because the sun's so bright and Mark Junior is very fair-skinned, she put him in a little white cotton beanie with a button on top and an elastic chin strap, the kind sailors wear. Not when they're in port—when they're swabbing the decks. He is sitting in the front of her shopping cart with a bag of onions on each side of him. Sandy is not going to buy all those onions. They're just for support. Mark Junior can sit up by himself, of course, but when he gets excited, like in the supermarket (so many other babies, and he loves the inflated plastic bananas hanging overhead), he gets a little wobbly. At the moment his hat has slipped down over his left eye and he's not sure what to do about it. An older woman studying the steaks a few feet away has noticed this, and smiles at Sandy. Sandy smiles back but when she does this she feels she has sold her baby down the river. Like when Mark and his friends were over at their apartment one time listening to records and Ronnie Spaulding put this pair of red wax lips on Mark Junior's mouth, so it looked like he was wearing makeup, and Mark said too bad we don't have a camera. Sandy isn't sorry they don't have a picture of that.

Duncan Hines Devil's Food Cake Mix. Sandy will use her special recipe, with four eggs instead of two. The secret ingredient is a package of Jell-O chocolate instant pudding mix and a cup of vegetable oil. The oil makes it very moist.

Frosting mix. Candles. Mark Junior is only five months old, of course, but Sandy has decided she will put candles on the cake. The babies will enjoy that. Also, in spite of what she feels about hats, she's going to buy some. She's sure none of the other mothers will laugh. She just wants this to be like a party in a Kodak ad. Even though her life is nothing like in the magazines.

She sees Jill's mother up ahead by the canned foods. Mrs. Johnson doesn't like her, Sandy knows that. When she finds out about Jill she will probably think it's all Sandy's fault. This isn't fair. Jill's really much wilder than Sandy ever was. Sandy never ran around. All she ever wanted was to get married and have babies.

"How are you, Mrs. Johnson?"

"Same as always," says Doris. "About to have a heart attack from these prices."

Sandy asks Doris if she would like a Land O Lakes butter coupon she cut out. She has two.

"We use margarine," says Doris.

"How's Jill?" says Sandy. She can't think of anything else, and she doesn't know how to end things.

"Well, I don't mind telling you I'm worried about her," says Doris. "The way you kids eat. I'm just now getting her some nutritional supplement powder. She needs more protein."

"I took some of that when I was expecting," says Sandy. What a dope. Why did she have to say that? She can't believe Jill would've told her mother, even though it sounds that way.

"Yes, well," says Doris. "I'd better get a move on before the ice cream melts."

"Mail for you." It's Charles, standing in the doorway, wearing a shirt that says "Would you adopt this child?" He has greasy hair and bad skin. The reason Wayne likes him—speaks to him anyway—is that Charles sells pills. Sometimes grass too, but that's tricky to handle because of the smell. Mostly pills. Half the ward is flying.

Wayne does not get up off the bed. He has been having a bad day, thinking about Loretta. It was a day like this—

just May, but hot, steamy—when he found her. Picked her toll booth only because he needed change for a twenty-dollar bill. Watched her counting out those little stacks of quarters very slowly, as if she was in some tower in a fairy tale instead of the middle of the Mass Pike with twenty cars backed up, waiting. She did not tell him to have a nice day.

He knew right away he had to have her. He took the next exit, Needham, and circled around. It was a twelve-mile drive back to her booth. He gave her another twenty. She looked at him and didn't say anything. Counted out the money very slowly, just like before. He circled back again, making no plans, just feeling sure she would end up in his car.

He had five twenties. Always carried plenty of cash—he doesn't like banks. He didn't even look to see where the money fell when she handed him the change. Just kept shoveling it in. Some bills blew out the window. Who cared?

On the sixth trip he handed her the note. Come with me. He put the car in park, left the motor running, got out and opened the door on the passenger side. He did not look back to see if she was coming. She was there beside him when he drove away. The next twenty cars probably got through free. He drove straight back to his apartment in Manchester, behind one of the old shoe factories. Brought her upstairs, closed the door behind her. Didn't have to lock it. She would never leave.

Charles puts a small stack of envelopes on the mattress beside Wayne's hand. For several minutes Wayne doesn't even look. He's thinking about Loretta's incredibly pale skin. When a person never goes outside and isn't soaking up all that radiation and carbon monoxide, the skin gets almost transparent. Not like those mill workers that just look like they live under a rock somewhere. Wayne kept everything around Loretta very clean. And she was smooth as a baby, from all the lotions he bought her.

He's not sure if he can even sit up, he is so depressed. All his muscles don't help one bit when he feels like this. He rolls over on his side and glances at the pile of papers Charles has laid beside him. Might as well be ashes.

The new issue of *Prevention*. The ABC's of a Pain-Free Back. Feeding the Kids Right (Trying Anyway). How Nutrition Helps Menopause. Nothing much for him this month. He should order some more acidophilus capsules and kelp, and he's almost out of vitamin E. But why bother?

There is a computer-addressed card from CBS Television. The producers of *Sixty Minutes* regret that we cannot answer personally every inquiry we receive. However, we are always pleased to hear from our viewers and hope you will let us know again how you feel about segments on the show. . . . He has got this card a million times before. Mike Wallace will never come here and do an exposé.

A religious pamphlet. Jesus people are always after him. They must figure when a guy's this bad off, we can rope him. People in mental institutions, people in prisons. Those are the sitting ducks for religion. Wayne is not interested.

It's not until he sees the three-by-five card addressed with the post office box number that he remembers his ad. There's just the one response.

This is one person who doesn't think you're crazy.

Of all the things a person might have written and sent to him, that is the one right sentence. It's just like what he put on that piece of paper he handed Loretta on the turnpike, coming just on that day, into that particular steamy booth, read by a woman who was just thinking: In four more hours I can go home and swallow two bottles of sleeping pills. Wayne gets off the bed, onto the floor, and begins doing his push-ups.

Because the bathroom is the only room in her house that has a door, that's where Ann slept last night. All night she could hear the bats scratching on the walls upstairs. They have invaded.

Reg Johnson says this happens in spring sometimes, when they start looking for a place to have their babies. Last May this house was empty. The bats must have some happy memories.

He went up in the crawl space under the roof—something Ann has never done. "Just as well," he said. "Quite a few bats hanging from the rafters, and a good six inches of bat droppings. Not a pretty sight," he said.

So today he will begin stopping up all the holes under the eaves. He'll probably have to patch the roof in quite a few places too. "These critters are so small," he says, "they don't need much more than a pinhole to get in."

She is very lucky to know Reg. None of the exterminators she called this morning, in Manchester and Concord, would consider the job. "I'll get back to you," said the one in Keene. "Nothing worse than bats," they said. "Bat turds carry TB too. Wouldn't touch the stuff with a ten-foot pole."

And right now Reg is up there with a shovel and a box of plastic trash bags and a piece of cotton tied over his nose and mouth like a surgeon, working for three dollars an hour. Ann knows she should be there too, helping him, but she keeps thinking she hears that cheeping sound. This morning when she went out to the kitchen to make the coffee she felt something brush against her leg and she began to scream again. It was only Joey, wanting a Milk-Bone. She had forgotten all about him.

Carla wakes up feeling a little better. Greg has made French toast for breakfast, with real maple syrup, and there's a glass filled with violets on the table. Also, today is Sandy's party for her son. Carla feels proud to have made a friend here in town. She will go shopping this morning for a nice toy. What does a five-month-old baby like to do? These are things she will have to find out.

It's such a beautiful day she thinks she will just walk into town. There was a gift shop next to the drugstore. They probably have music boxes, or maybe a stuffed animal. It will be fun to choose.

"I hired a girl to model for me," says Greg. His back is to her. He's squeezing oranges for juice.

"I thought you were going to be working on abstractions," says Carla. The girl at the Laundromat, she is thinking. He was not just asking directions. Greg hasn't asked Carla to pose for him in years. He has said he isn't interested in figures anymore.

He says he guesses it's being up here in the country. He is feeling less cerebral. More interested in nature.

"You could've asked me to pose," says Carla.

He has another type in mind, he tells her. Also, the girl has a baby. The baby's going to be part of the picture. There's just something about this girl. Hair like corn silk.

Carla's hair is naturally straight too. Just before they left New York she spent fifty dollars on a permanent.

There are quite a few bat bones up here. Reg actually started to put a couple into his shirt pockets before he remembered his kids are past the age now where they bring stuff like this in to school, for science. Timmy is down in Fort Benning. Jill would say, "Oh, gross."

But really, they are kind of beautiful. He has found a tiny skull, the size of a plum pit, with a complete set of teeth. He would like to show Ann. Wonders if it would just upset her.

He shakes another shovelful of bat droppings into the trash bag and there's a flutter of wings. A baby bat not much bigger than a lima bean is flopping around in the dust. Only for a second; then he's dead. So they're beginning to reproduce now. He'll have to work fast.

"See, it was the fan belt," says Mark. He's sitting on an imitation-leather chair opposite Mr. Terrill, personnel manager

of the plant, who has called him in because yesterday was
the fourth time in three weeks that Mark was late to work.

"I was way the heck out in the sticks, fishing," he says.
He's hoping Mr. Terrill is a trout fisherman. "Just heading
back to go to work when the damn car quit on me. No phone
booths around. I had to hitchhike into town." He starts to
reach for a cigarette and decides that is a bad idea. He runs
his hand down his pants leg instead. Sandy has mended the
hole on the knee with a piece of denim shaped like a heart.

The personnel manager says he is sorry. This facility
just can't absorb repeat absenteeism on the part of its em-
ployees. He's sure Mark understands. It wouldn't be fair to
everyone who punches in on time. He thinks Mark will be
happier elsewhere.

Mark says it won't happen again. Mr. Terrill says he's
sure it won't. Mark has been terminated. He puts out his
hand. Mark's supposed to shake it.

Mark just sits there, staring at the photograph on Mr.
Terrill's desk. Three very fat children sitting around a
Christmas tree. Girls in look-alike red velvet skirts and
matching vests with green felt holly leaves stuck on just
about where their breasts would come. A set of very fancy-
looking golf clubs leaned up against all the other presents.
This guy's not into fishing.

"So if you'll just stop over in payroll."

There is one of those gadgets on Mr. Terrill's desk, a
wooden stand with six metal balls suspended from it, and
when you pull up the metal ball on one end and let it drop,
the metal ball on the other end swings up. Mark imagines
that he sees them swinging. His son would enjoy a toy like
that.

"I have nothing left to say." Mr. Terrill gets up. Mark
knows he should get up now too. He's thinking: Today is
Mark Junior's five-month birthday. It still takes him by surprise sometimes that he's a father.

He told Sandy he'd bring home a bottle of pink champagne.

*   *   *

Mrs. Ramsay had really hoped to avoid litigation. She knows, from the Dustin Hoffman movie, what heartbreak that can bring. But the mother did not sign the paper. Mrs. Ramsay will just have to take her to court.

She will need photographs, of course. Pictures of the mother and her boyfriends. Evidently she hits Baby too. Involved with some kind of abortion ring. Nothing would surprise Mrs. Ramsay now.

She just has to bind off this last row and the pink duck sweater will be finished. So feminine. She will go look for that other young mother today and explain her problem. She is sure a lovely girl like that, who feeds her baby only good pure mother's milk, will understand. Mrs. Ramsay smiles and turns on the set with her remote control.

Oh, Dinah, what a fool Burt was to leave you. At least he finally had the good sense to break off his engagement to that Sally Field. That will teach her to make fun of nuns.

Greg arrives at the Laundromat ten minutes early, but Tara and Sunshine are already there, sitting on the steps. He recognizes the dress she's wearing as one that was hanging outside the Just-like-nu Shop the day he bought the present for Carla. It's bright orange, one of those synthetic fabrics Carla hates, a style that's meant to be tight. On Tara it falls loose. She's wearing her hair in a bun on top of her head. The baby has a kind of topknot hairdo too. When Tara gets into the car he can smell perfume. Also that milky aroma babies have. Sunshine has just spit up very slightly on the orange outfit.

He's so happy. He would like to give Tara a hug. He would like to buy her another outfit, a nice one, and take the bobby pins out of her hair. He would like to hold the baby.

"I should be back by three," she says. "A friend of mine is having a party."

Greg says that's fine. It's hard holding a pose more than a couple of hours anyway. They can take it slow.

He asks what kind of art she likes. Does she have a favorite painter?

Well, there are quite a few. There's a man named Paul Klee who has a very wild imagination. She has a wild imagination too, so she likes that. "You wouldn't believe some of the things I dream," she says.

He would like to ask, but he decides to wait.

Other artworks she likes: there was this tapestry of a princess and a unicorn. She saw it printed on a greeting card. She also likes Paul Gauguin and Henri Rousseau and Pablo Picasso. And there is a female painter who used to do pictures of mothers and children a lot. Tara thinks she's dead now. She likes that woman.

"Mary Cassatt," says Greg. He wishes he could take her to the Museum of Modern Art. He thinks about all the hours he's spent there, giving lectures on the water lilies and *Guernica* to his students at Walker. Explaining why their six-year-old cousin could not have done *Les Demoiselles d'Avignon*. They always like the Roy Lichtenstein cartoon painting best. They always want to go to the gift shop first.

They're silent for a mile or so, except for once when Sunshine sneezes. Greg thinks this is incredible. It's just like an adult sneeze in miniature.

"I sometimes paint pictures too," says Tara. "That used to be my favorite subject."

What sort of pictures?

"Oh, crazy things, from my imagination. When I was pregnant I did this picture of what the world might look like from inside me. To my baby."

Greg says that sounds like an interesting idea.

"I used to draw dolphins a lot. I always liked dolphins."

Greg says he feels that way about bears.

"Now mostly I draw pictures of Sunshine. Only sometimes I pretend that she's older, and I make her with teeth and long hair. I try to imagine what she might look like."

"You probably looked a lot like her when you were a baby."

"I wasn't nearly this cute," says Tara. "I was premature. I had to live in an incubator for seven weeks. My parents had to take out a loan for sixteen hundred dollars. I only weighed two pounds two ounces. That's why I'm thin like this."

"It looks nice," says Greg. "It looks just right."

They are at the house now. Greg jumps out to open the door on Tara's side. He hasn't done that since high school. She reaches in the back for a diaper bag. He'd like to say, "Let me carry the baby."

"Are these all your records?"

Greg says, "Yes, what would you like to hear?"

"Do you have that song James Taylor and Carly Simon sing that goes 'devoted to you'?"

He puts it on, tells her the Everly Brothers recorded that one, back when he was a kid.

"How about some coffee? Lemonade?"

She says no thank you. She's standing in the middle of the room with the baby on her shoulder, looking at everything.

"It's beautiful here," she says. "I'd like to live in a room just like this."

Greg is setting up a chair for her, putting a pillow on the seat. He's careful to place the chair so the sun won't be in her eyes.

"What am I supposed to do now?"

"I don't want you to feel uncomfortable," he says. He is sweating himself. "If you would be uncomfortable you could just put on one of—one of my friend's T-shirts.

"But my idea was to do a nude. You nursing your baby. Only if you don't feel uncomfortable.

"You should know, to a painter, a nude figure is no different from a bowl of fruit in a still life. I guess it's just like how a doctor would feel."

He's not really telling the truth. He is longing for her to take off that orange dress. He imagines his hand pulling the zipper down, her feet stepping out of her underpants. He's thirty years old and he's in a sweat to think of this sixteen-year-old girl sitting naked before him, nursing her baby.

"Listen." He is going to tell her it's all right. She can just put on a T-shirt. He wants to take good care of her. Probably no one else does.

But she has already pulled the dress over her head. Now she's folding it, setting it beside her chair. She takes off her underpants and sets them on top of the dress. They're the kind that come right up to the waist, not the bikini style.

"Sunshine too?" She's completely naked now, holding Sunshine in the little frilly dress. Her breasts are so small he wonders how she can have anything there for the baby.

"If she won't be cold."

"I'll just leave her diapers on." She sits down with Sunshine resting against her skin. That must feel good.

"Like this?"

He moves toward Tara, bends over and touches her leg as if she were marble.

Sunshine is sucking now, and wrapping her fingers around Tara's other breast. Greg notices now that Tara has tied a pink bow around the baby's topknot.

"Really just one change," says Greg. He pulls three bobby pins out of Tara's hair, very gently so he won't pull her hair. It falls onto her shoulders.

She's alone in a room with a man. She has no clothes on. She is not embarrassed.

Carla is trying to decide between a panda bear and a seal. They're both cute. What she likes about the seal is the way he isn't smiling. He looks like a seal whose mother has just been slaughtered by seal hunters. Probably most people would like the panda better. She'll get the bear for Sandy's baby. She'll get the seal for herself.

She wishes she had told Greg this morning. When he

said, "But this girl is another type. She has a baby." She should have told him then.

Carla never used to believe the stories women told, about knowing the instant their child was conceived. She didn't feel that way the other time, never thought of what was conceived the other time as being a child. But now she has no doubt. She's one and a half days pregnant.

Jill has just thrown up again. It's called morning sickness but she has it all day long. She goes through two packs of Pep-O-Mint Life Savers a day, just to get rid of the bad taste in her mouth.

One thing's for sure. Her absolute least favorite place in the world to spend this afternoon is in a roomful of babies and mothers. She will just call Sandy tomorrow and explain. Right now all she wants to do is go back to bed.

Wanda wishes she was smarter. She is sure there is something she should do now, about Mrs. Ramsay, but she doesn't know what. Mrs. Ramsay said so many things last night that Wanda can hardly remember any of them. She just knows she has to be a very good mother now, or Mrs. Ramsay will get the police after her. She always thought Mrs. Ramsay liked her. She thought Mrs. Ramsay was sort of like a mother to her. Now she understands that Mrs. Ramsay does not like her after all.

She also understands that Mrs. Ramsay thinks she's fat. She didn't know she was that bad. Mr. Pineo, yesterday, didn't seem to mind. He said he liked to see a girl with curves on her. Of course she does not like Mr. Pineo. He wants to do some very weird things. She wishes she had said no about the chocolate sauce. That was gross.

Well, she is not going to eat any birthday cake at Sandy's party. Or just a thin slice. And she's going to be a good mother. She will put Melissa in a party dress and tights. Maybe it's too hot for tights. But the only clean socks she has don't match the party dress. All the other babies will be looking perfect. It isn't that hot anyway.

She gets dressed up too. Actually, she looks pretty nice. She puts on some lip gloss. Something funny happens then. For a second, or not even that long, she forgets that Melissa's just a baby. She thinks: Now I've got to put on Melissa's lip gloss. Then of course she realizes that Melissa doesn't wear lip gloss.

She thinks about Dwight. It's really too bad he went away. She liked him much better than any of the others she has dated since then. In fact she was in love, she thinks. She wishes he was here now and they were married, or just going to Sandy's party together. She would tell him what happened with the lip gloss. That's the sort of thing she never has anybody to tell. She would like the old ladies who come up to look at Melissa in stores to say, "Oh, I see she has her father's eyes."

She wishes she hadn't let Mr. Pineo do that thing with the chocolate sauce.

A present for Mark Junior. She has forgotten a present.

Also, she has split the underarm seam of her shirt. Also, Melissa just wet through her party tights.

Why did you do that, you idiot? I just changed you. Why are you always wetting all over the place? I'm sick of it.

She's holding the baby, not close up against her, but out in the air. She's shaking the baby. Melissa's head is wobbling all over the place, and she won't even cry. Wanda keeps shaking her.

Her guests aren't due for an hour yet, but Sandy is ready. She has hung blue and yellow streamers from the kitchen light—twisted, the way they did it for her junior prom—and there's a bunch of balloons hanging down the middle, right over the cake. The cake says: "We love you, Mark Jr." She will keep it out of sight until she lights the candles. Sandy just wanted to see what it looked like on the table, before putting it back in the refrigerator.

She has covered the table with a paper Holly Hobbie tablecloth and matching paper plates and napkins. Of course Holly Hobbie is more for a girl, but that was all they had left at Felsen's News, and besides, all the guests are female. Sandy has put their party hats on their plates and little baskets full of jelly beans and Sweetarts next to them. Sandy knows the babies won't be able to eat the jelly beans, although she gave Mark Junior a Sweetart just now, and it dissolved on his tongue. He made a very cute face. The jelly beans are more for the mothers.

They're going to have pink champagne. Mark will bring it when he comes home. He's putting in some overtime today. But he promised to be back in time for a toast.

Sandy was hoping the portrait of her and Mark Junior would have been ready today, but when she checked at the K-Mart they told her they'd mail it in a couple of days. It probably won't be that great anyway.

Mark Junior is wearing his New York Wets shirt again and a pair of tiny little sneakers that look like the kind joggers wear. They cost too much, of course, but Sandy couldn't resist. She'll tell Mark they were on sale.

She couldn't decide what to put on herself. The woman from New York, Carla, is coming to the party, and Sandy doesn't want to look like a hick. She decided her white frilly dress is too immature. So she has put on jeans and a shirt, with a chain around her neck. Safer to be casual.

The others will be impressed that she knows Carla. Sandy will work it into the conversation that Carla used to have a job at a magazine. She hopes they don't say anything dumb.

She tries to imagine what it would have been like if she had come up with the money for a portfolio and gone to modeling school. If someone had discovered her, like Margaux Hemingway, just sitting in a restaurant. Although she has the impression it was an expensive restaurant, and of course Margaux Hemingway already had a relative who was a famous writer. She read a book by him once. *The Old Man and the Sea.* She skipped all the fishing parts.

But if she had gone to New York or Boston and a modeling agency had liked her, she would have rented an apartment. She knows just what kind of furniture she would want. Those modular units you can rearrange and make into a conversation pit for parties, or a regular sofa-loveseat combination, or even a bed. How would she meet anyone, living in a city? Probably it would be like in *Scruples,* where the model falls in love with one of the photographers who takes her picture. She ends up going to Hollywood and getting hooked on drugs. It's a miserable life. Money does not buy happiness. A person's best bet is staying home and building a family. Look at Margaux Hemingway. She ended up getting a divorce.

Sandy feels guilty that she was even thinking about that other life. She is very lucky to have Mark. He takes good care of her. He never had much chance to sow his wild oats. It's understandable if he wants to go out to Rocky's and play Space Invaders sometimes. Why shouldn't he go fishing with Virgil? He brings home the bacon, doesn't he?

The thing about a champagne drunk is, it doesn't last long, but while it lasts, far out. Normally Mark would prefer beer. But this stuff isn't half bad.

He's sitting on the bank of the Contoocook River, out behind the plant where he works. Used to work. He has sixty-three dollars in his pocket, from his last paycheck. The rest went for the champagne. Which is mostly gone now.

He's thinking about his son, who is five months old today. He's remembering the day Mark Junior was born. Sandy thinks the reason he ran out of the delivery room was the blood. She always blames him for that. She says he ruined the bonding.

It wasn't the blood at all. He has seen plenty of blood and guts, deer hunting. What he couldn't stand was the look on Sandy's face. She didn't even look like Sandy anymore. She could have been his mother, could've been his grandmother. Could've been a man, in fact. Mark had never seen anyone in that much pain, working that hard before. It made him feel like a jerk, that it was his wife, and not he, working so hard. Nothing he ever did in his whole life mattered, compared to that. And since then, it's as if she knows that too. He used to think she was so delicate and fragile. Now he knows that is just a trick. She humors him, like he's a little boy. She knows, and someday his son will know, that when it came down to it, Sandy was the strong one. Mark just stood out in the hall throwing up.

He wants to be a good father. When Mark Junior is older, they will go fishing together. Mark will teach him how to tie flies. They will sleep out in the woods, just the two of them. In the morning Mark will build a fire and they'll cook sausages and hash browns. Mark will tell his son what it was like when he was a little boy and he went camping with his dad. (He doesn't remember this exactly, but he knows they did, from all his mother's stories about what a terrific father he had.)

A terrific father does not smoke marijuana, that's for sure. Especially not marijuana he stole out of somebody else's house. He doesn't steal records and think about balling Linda Ronstadt. Mark tries to picture his dad fantasizing about Patti Page and Teresa Brewer. Sure.

This is good grass. He didn't mean to smoke any. He was just going to give the bag to Virg. But it's good stuff.

He read in *Rolling Stone* the other day that the Grateful Dead are going to give a concert on top of Mount McKinley at summer solstice. Mark picked up a hitchhiker one time who had seen the Dead live. The guy said this amazing thing happens at their concerts. Everybody in the crowd—twenty, thirty thousand people—everyone is thinking the exact same thoughts. Coexperience, he called it. The other great thing, he said, is that their music actually causes negative ions. At first Mark thought that was a bad thing, but the guy explained it's the other way around. Positive ions are what cause stagnation. Pollution. Negative ions refresh the air. Like, a thunderstorm is full of supercharged negative ions. If you could get the Dead to play in the middle of Los Angeles during one of those really bad smog periods, and you got all those thirty thousand people there listening and coexperiencing, the negative ions would actually break up the smog.

The girl with the red car. What is she doing in that house all alone, listening to redneck music? If he had been this stoned when he got in her car yesterday, and they didn't have Virgil along, he would've balled her. Sandy's crazy friend Jill. There's another one for you. Virgil told him one time they did it three times in a single afternoon.

Mark would screw her five times. She would be begging him to stop. "Can't stop now," he says. "I'm full of negative ions."

Screwing Linda Ronstadt on top of Mount McKinley while the Dead play "Sugar Magnolia." Is it cold in Alaska, even at summer solstice? They are wrapped in furs. They don't even need to light up a joint; all you have to do is breathe.

Linda Ronstadt has never had a baby, for Christ's sake. Why is everyone he knows having babies?

Wanda can't stand it anymore, the way all Melissa does is sleep. If she would've cried, Wanda would've stopped sooner. What drives Wanda crazy is the way Melissa goes all limp and stares at her, like she is the mother and not the baby, and she's saying: "Now don't you feel guilty? See how I suffer? But do I object? Do I complain?"

She has got to get out of this apartment. No way is she going to Sandy's party, with Melissa like this. She will step out for some air, maybe some French fries at Rocky's. Melissa sure isn't going anyplace.

"Long time no see." It's Ronnie Spaulding, leaning on the pinball machine. He didn't act so buddy-buddy when he dropped her off the other night. Maybe he was just in a rush.

"Hi."

"So where've you been keeping yourself? I was looking for you."

She has a telephone. There is such a thing as knocking on the door.

"Want to take a drive?"

They will do just about as much driving as they did bowling. Wanda knows.

"My baby's upstairs, sleeping."

"So we'll make it fast. The kid will sleep another twenty minutes, right?" He strokes her hair. Puts his head against hers. Sticks his tongue in her ear. He probably read about that somewhere.

Greg has never done a picture like this. It could almost go on the front of a Mother's Day card. Actually, Greg isn't drawing in a sentimental way. This is just what Tara looks like.

Since that first conversation they've said very little. She has just been sitting here with Sunshine in her arms and he's standing at his worktable, sketching. Every once in a while he gets up to change the record. He has tried to pick music she would like, and although she has not said anything, he thinks she does like it. Sometimes she sings along with the chorus, very softly, once she's learned it. All the lyrics have been sounding significant to her. Emmylou Harris, at the moment. "If I could only win your love." Their eyes meet a lot.

She gets up to go to the bathroom. "Would you mind taking Sun?"

Of course not. He hopes she won't cry. Not that it

would bother him. He just wants Sunshine to like him.

She wrinkles her brow for a second, moves her mouth sort of like a guppy. She is looking for Tara's nipple. She accepts that it's not around.

Tara closes the door behind her. He can hear her peeing. Everything about her is dear to him.

Water running. She comes out with her arms wrapped around her breasts, the rest of her exposed. Pubic hair so pale it's almost invisible. No bathing suit marks, no sign of last summer's tan. (Does she know how to swim? He can teach her.) Bright red polish on her toenails. A small scar on her right knee, an old one. A little tuft of hair at the base of her spine. Just like the baby.

He had never thought to wonder before who the father is. He can't picture Tara with anyone but him. He wants to ask her: What happened? Who was he? How could he ever leave you?

Carla hadn't meant to walk so far. It was just so beautiful down by the river. Somebody should buy one of those old abandoned mills and restore it. You could turn it into a great restaurant. Or studios.

There's a couple—the girl is naked—making out in a car parked outside one of the mills. A young guy sitting on the grass by the river, smoking a joint. She thinks of that painting by Manet. *Déjeuner sur l'herbe*. All that's missing are the parasols.

She takes the stuffed seal out of the bag to look again. She puts it next to her cheek, trying to imagine what it feels like to be a baby. What it feels like to be a mother. Of course she will breast-feed. She will get some of those little Portuguese booties they sell in that shop in SoHo that look like Mary Janes with red-and-white-striped socks attached. Greg will do a painting that looks like mountains. Only it will be Carla. Her breasts, her belly.

*　*　*

This time Ronnie wanted Wanda to take all her clothes off. She was a little embarrassed, on account of not having started her diet yet, but she's also pleased, that he would be interested. And he has parked the car way out behind one of the mills that was closed down ages ago. No one will see.

He wanted her on top. He said "Press your ass up against the window. Let me see your boobs." He is not even trying to get inside. He just wants her to do all this stuff.

He has checked his watch three times. He must be worried that Melissa might wake up and need her. Wanda knows Melissa won't wake up for a long time yet. "Suck my cock," he says. Well, O.K.

Two-thirty. Ronnie checks his wrist again to make sure. That was when the dame was supposed to be here.

A real space shot. Bright-orange hair and one earring. She was carrying this bag full of yarn, with one piece hanging down and dragging along the ground. Called him young man. Said just a minute there young man. I would like a word with you.

Crazy talk, that she needs pictures of this particular slut spreading her legs, due to pending litigation. Something about Dustin Hoffman. I think you know the particular slut to whom I refer. I need Polaroids of her disgusting body committing sexual acts.

He said, "I'm not a photographer. I don't even have a camera."

"Not to worry," she said. "Just be there at two-thirty and make sure she comes up right next to the window."

You can't argue with eighteen hundred and twenty-six bucks.

*　*　*

Carla arrives at Sandy's apartment forty-five minutes late. She hopes she hasn't missed the cake. She would like to see the looks on all the babies' faces when Sandy lights the candles.

It's a minute before Sandy comes to the door. She has been crying. Over her shoulder Carla can see the table, the hats, the balloons, the streamers. No one else is here.

Ann is hoeing up squash hills. She works one shovelful of the cow manure Reg brought her into each hill. It smells good to her. Anything smells good, compared to those bags of bat droppings Reg has been loading onto his truck all morning. He keeps sneezing. She had to get out in the fresh air.

She bought flats of zucchini and acorn squash down at the feed store. They are about two inches high, with three leaves apiece. She sets each one in its hole very gently, so she won't disturb the roots. She pats down the soil and sprinkles water over every plant. She thinks of a recipe she saw once for deep-fried squash blossoms. She'll make that.

She has not even remembered about the card she sent, the ad in the personals column. So she's not prepared when the phone rings. She's out of breath, because she had to run all the way in from the garden and she was afraid that the person might hang up.

"Hello, Ann."

She has to catch her breath. "Is this the exterminator?"

Laughter. There is a lot of laughter on the other end of the line.

"I'm the man from the newspaper. I got your note."

He got her number from Information, of course. She's still gasping for breath.

"I want to thank you," he says. He has a deep voice, like a disk jockey. Only without the jokes. "I could tell right away you understand. You knew what I was talking about."

She's going to tell him that note was a mistake. She's glad he feels that way. But she didn't mean to start anything. This is not her kind of thing. She was just in a strange mood.

"And I think I understand quite a bit about you too," he says. "For instance, I know that you're in great pain."

She can't say anything. She just stands there, holding the phone.

"You're all alone, aren't you? And that's such a waste. There was a man and he hurt you very badly. You think you will never get over it."

She had not given up hope, that's why she gave her name. She keeps hoping that maybe there is a prince out there to rescue her. She was asking for this call.

"I would never hurt you. I would never let anyone hurt you. I would keep you safe in a room. Safe in my arms. I would never let you go. You would never even have to buy sanitary napkins."

She screams. She drops the receiver and runs, with her hands over her face so it won't get her. Another bat.

Of course Charles is supposed to monitor all inmate calls. Forensics in particular. You have to make sure they don't ask for weapons. You're also supposed to be on the alert for statements indicating a suicidal mood. This is a little hard to determine. Most of the conversations he monitors are pretty depressing. At what point does depressed turn into suicidal? He is a little vague on that.

Most of the time this job is boring. A lot of complaints that so-and-so is trying to kill me. They are putting something in my food. As soon as I get out of this place. That type of thing.

Now Wayne, he provides some entertainment. Charles wishes he was that smart. Also that good-looking. The Burt Reynolds type.

Charles has heard that Wayne kept this one woman hypnotized by his powers for three and a half years. A sexual slave, that's what one of the other orderlies said. In the end he murdered her, and he was so smart he got off on insanity. There's nothing insane about that guy. You should see him play chess. Three games at once.

Here's another example. Wayne needs barbiturates. Five, six pills a day. And he doesn't have any money on the outside, and even if he did they wouldn't give him more than a cigarette allowance. So what does he do? He finds himself a real muffin head, a doper, and tells him the uppers Charles sells are laced with a powder that makes you impotent. The guy won't go near Charles now. Only buys from Wayne, at a one hundred percent markup. Wayne finances his habit on the profits.

Now he's making a phone call. Asked the operator to charge this to another number. Probably President Carter. Or Dr. McAlister, the head of the hospital. That's the kind of thing Wayne does.

Wayne's side of the conversation sounds pretty average. Although he's making his voice a little deeper than normal.

Sanitary napkins. What was that about sanitary napkins?

Donahue's guest this afternoon is Dr. Benjamin Spock. Doris wishes it was tomorrow, when Marabel Morgan is scheduled to talk about how cooking can spice up a marriage. She would rather listen to a show about incest or sexual surrogates or elderly abuse even. These political guests are so boring.

"Scientific evidence has shown that watching violence on film and television brutalizes everyone, children and adults alike," says Dr. Spock. "Participation in war does the same thing."

She actually bought his book. Kept it on the shelf by the stove, right next to Betty Crocker, so it would always be handy. Tried to follow everything he said with Timmy and Jill. She could probably recite the chapter on toilet training. Then it turned out he was a leftist. Then he divorced his wife of thirty years and married some thirty-five-year-old divorcee. No wonder Jill is having problems now. That's the last time Doris will believe what some book tells her, unless it's the Bible. Although Marabel Morgan does make pretty good sense.

Doris is worried about Jill. She has not got out of bed all day, except to go to the bathroom. It's three o'clock in the afternoon and she's just lying there listening to the radio through an earphone. Doris almost wishes she could hear that Rod Stewart music blaring through the house, like normal. Jill's room is so quiet it's scary.

Now Dr. Spock is talking about the need for men to share fully in housework and child care. Sure, and Doris and Jill will go out in the woods with chain saws and change the tires on the truck. Next thing you know, everyone will be in one bathroom together. She turns off the set.

Peanut butter and marshmallow fluff sandwiches—Jill always liked those. Doris takes down a jar of Jif and gets out the bread. She will make up a tray. Bring Jill a cup of hot liquid Jell-O. That used to be her special treat when she was little and she had measles or something.

"Honey?" Jill rolls over to face Doris. "I thought you might like a snack."

"Thanks," says Jill. She doesn't look at the tray. Her eyes are all red.

Doris wishes she was better at mother-daughter talks. Like the mother on *Family*. Kristy McNichol tells her everything. What would Kate Lawrence say now?

"Is it that time of the month?" says Doris.

Jill begins to cry. That was not the right thing after all.

"You know what I just realized?" says Doris. "I just realized your prom must be coming up. I was thinking, with my Avon money and all, we could go to the mall, shopping. Maybe get you a store-bought gown for a change." What is she saying? The Avon money is for groceries. What with these prices.

Jill brightens a little. "You mean you'd give me some

money? Like fifty dollars?" She has lifted herself a few inches off the pillow.

"Well, we could see how much they cost."

Jill says she already knows a place. She would need fifty dollars and she will have to borrow the car. She would rather go alone.

Doris puts her hand, which was resting a little uncomfortably on Jill's shoulder, back into her apron pocket. This didn't turn out the way she meant. She has just offered her daughter fifty dollars that she can't afford, and she doesn't feel their relationship is any closer than before. She still doesn't understand Jill's mental problem. She will just have to hope that a new dress does the trick.

Fifty dollars. Doris never spent so much on a dress in her whole life. These kids today, they're spoiled.

That Dr. Spock. It's all his fault.

For a minute there, Mrs. Ramsay thought she was going to die. I am going to have a seizure right here on the spot, she thought, and the only ones who could save me will be those two in the car, and I would rather die than sit in that car which is probably all wet from their disgusting sexual secretions. They will not even notice.

But she did not die. In fact, she shot an entire roll of pictures, and they came out very well, if you can call it that. Mrs. Ramsay can hardly bear to look at them. That thing he did in her mouth, she has never heard of that. She does not know how she will look him in the eye, to give him the money. She hates to think of it, all the money from Harold's model train collection, gone to a perverted young man for putting his organ in a girl's mouth. She is just not going to think about it.

The telephone rings. "Hello, Mrs. Ramsay? It's Jill Johnson, I'm a friend of Wanda's. Is she over there?"

"No," says Mrs. Ramsay. "She is not."

"Could you tell her I was looking for her? Tell her I got

the money, and my appointment is tomorrow morning. She'll understand."

"They must have forgotten, that's all," says Carla. She has put her arms around Sandy, who started crying again when she went to cut a piece of cake. She didn't bother to light the candles. Mark Junior, who missed his three o'clock nap so he'd be awake to greet his guests, is now asleep on the water bed.

"Hats and everything" is all Carla can make out of what Sandy is saying. "I try so hard."

Carla hands Sandy the box with the panda. Sandy says Mark Junior will love it, when he wakes up.

"I knew Jill was feeling sick," says Sandy. But she doesn't understand about Wanda and Tara.

Of course Carla knows where Tara is.

Tara is just stepping into her underpants. She pulls the orange dress over her head so that for a few seconds her face is covered, and there are just her arms wriggling into the sleeves. This frightens Sunshine. "It's O.K.," says Greg, into her ear. "Mommy's right here."

"Thank you," says Tara, reaching for the baby. She does not put her hair back into the bun. She goes to look at Greg's picture.

"This is just a study," he says. "It's going to be part of a much larger painting. Of some people at the falls. I'm going to put you and Sunshine on the rocks."

"It looks just like us," says Tara. "Even my scar."

"I have a lot of work to do yet. If you can come again."

She's free.

The baby is so good. He thought babies were always crying.

"She likes you." Tara looks at Carla's green tennis shoes, sitting next to the bed.

"Did your girlfriend like the dress?" she asks.

Greg feels as if he's been caught shoplifting. "She thought it was great," he says.

Tara says she should get back. What time is it?

She's late. The party started two hours ago.

He drives her there, very slowly, wishing the town were farther away. She has already disappeared into Sandy's building when he realizes he forgot to pay her.

Sandy has begun to feel a little better. Carla told her she never tasted such a moist devil's food cake before. So often they're dry. Mark Junior woke up and when he saw the bear he said something that sounded like "panda," and even though Sandy knows that isn't possible, Carla said, "He must be very precocious."

Carla wanted to hear all about Sandy's pregnancy, which is something Sandy loves to talk about. That was such a happy time for her. She still believed then that all they needed for everything to be perfect was a baby.

"I think I may be pregnant myself," says Carla. This is not the same as telling that Avon woman. She really likes Sandy. Besides, this time it's the truth.

Sandy's excited. In spite of what she knows now—that babies make things much more complicated, that they are bound to be the cause of fights and tears, that having one is like getting on a train, taking a long trip while your husband stays home (and who knows if you ever return?)—in spite of all that, Sandy's always glad to hear about someone having a baby.

It is at just this moment that she hears the knock at her door. "This is my friend Tara and her daughter, Sunshine," she says. "Tara, this is Carla, who has just moved here from New York. Her husband's an artist. She just told me she's going to have a baby."

Carla sits there with the stuffed panda bear in her lap, and one bite of cake left that she has not swallowed. She knows it's not important that this girl is wearing a very ugly synthetic orange dress, that she's skinny, that when President Kennedy was assassinated, she wasn't even born, that she has probably never heard of abstract expressionism. Those are the things that matter if you are like Carla and you weigh your decisions and plan your life and ask yourself, Does this make sense? Is this wise? None of these things matters when a person is standing naked in front of you and she's that beautiful.

Tara stands in the doorway holding Sunshine very tight, almost as if it's her baby that is holding her up. She's thinking about Kalima, rubbing her hands in circles over her enormous belly. She's thinking about Denver, squatting on the floor between Kalima's legs, bending over, giving her an open-mouthed kiss. Holding Mountain against his bare chest and saying, "A man never really knows what it is to love a woman until she's had his child." Tara had been telling herself the green tennis shoes didn't matter, until she saw the person who wore them. Now she knows she will never see Greg again.

These are the things Tara and Carla are thinking. What Sandy's thinking, when the door opens again, and she sees Mark standing there with a bunch of ten-dollar bills in one hand and no pink champagne in the other, is that this is nothing like the birthday parties in the Kodak ads.

Ann's screaming doesn't have Wayne worried. Loretta sometimes screamed too. One time the ropes were so tight one of her hands turned blue, but when he untied her she said, "No, please, I want it that way." Women like pain. They like to be scared, like to cry. Keeps all those hormones from getting atrophied. Who does she want to be, Donna Reed? Erma Bombeck?

She has a nice voice. Younger than he thought. Sounds like early twenties. He thought she'd be one of those old-maid first-grade teachers, getting closer to menopause, thinking if I don't do something drastic soon the only kid I can have will be Mongoloid. What would make a girl in her early twenties feel so desperate she'd answer that ad?

She could be paraplegic, of course. He met one of those once. Paralyzed from the neck down. Car wreck. Thirty-four years old and she lived with her mother. She still had a beautiful face, although the mother cut her hair way too short, almost a crew cut, for easy maintenance. She was hooked to a bag for urine, with a tube up her asshole for shit. Completely dead between the legs, of course. But what she could do with her tongue.

Wayne does not think Ann is a paraplegic though. For one thing, she was out of breath like she'd been running. That could just be from trying to pick up the telephone with some weird combination of limbs like her foot and her elbow, of course. But he thinks she was running.

She was outside. RFD address, she lives in the country. Probably planting a vegetable garden. All the young kids who move here from Massachusetts and New Jersey want gardens. Organic, naturally.

She's not a virgin. He can always tell a virgin by the voice. Something tense and squeaky. This one has had a man, but not lately, and she needs one bad.

Cher looked good when she was pregnant. Who else? Marisa Berenson. Goldie Hawn got fat. That actress on *Eight Is Enough*—they kept her on the show and just pretended her character was pregnant too. She looked puffy and awful and even though she has had her baby now, Jill can tell—from the loose tenty dress she was wearing when she went on Mike Douglas last week—that she doesn't have her shape back yet.

Sandy has lent her a book—*Nine Glorious Months*. Jill looks through the table of contents. There's a section on vomiting, a section called Nipple Secretion. Varicose Veins and the Importance of Support Hose. Should You Wear a Maternity Girdle? The Frequent Urination Problem. Flatulence. Hemorrhoids. The Mask of Pregnancy. (What's that? Jill looks up that section. In the later months red splotches sometimes appear on the face, but they are usually temporary.)

Retardation. Dwarfism. Siamese Twins. Spinabifida. Ancephalic Monsters. Fetal Death.

There's a section of pictures taken during one woman's delivery. Sandy must have looked at these photographs a lot, from the way the plates are so worn, with spots that look like Coke spills. The woman is lying on a delivery table with her legs spread apart and her feet stuck in the stirrups. Her stomach is so big it blocks out her face. Her boobs are really big too, but not hard and sticking up like the stomach. They droop over the sides of her body like a couple of beanbags where all the beans are down at one end. Her nipples—instead of being neat and buttonlike, the way Jill's are—have been stretched to the size of sand dollars. It's hard to look at her vagina, the skin is bulging so tight over the baby's head.

Jill feels like she's about to throw up again. She reaches for the bowl under her bed. When she's finished she goes to her bureau to get a peppermint Life Saver, but the taste is never really gone from her mouth.

It's like the baby knows he's in danger. And he keeps wanting to remind her he's here. It's like he's got to get nine months' worth of wriggling around packed into a couple of hours, because he knows tomorrow he'll be gone.

All Tara wants to do now is go to her house, up the stairs to her room, and close the door. She just wants to be alone with Sunshine so she can think about today. She will go over everything that happened, very slowly. Then when it's over she won't think about him anymore. She will take down the atlas and study the map of the United States, plan her trip. There's absolutely no reason to stay now.

She has almost reached the house when she sees Mrs. Ramsay standing there underneath the sign that says Just-like-nu Shop—Good Used Clothing. She hopes maybe Mrs. Ramsay's just waiting to cross the street. But she stands there with a big shoulder bag over one arm.

"It's finished," says Mrs. Ramsay.

What is she talking about?

Mrs. Ramsay's rummaging in the shoulder bag now. Yarn and knitting markers spill onto the sidewalk. She does not appear to notice.

"The pink duck sweater. It is just your color." She holds the sweater out to Sunshine, who doesn't know how to take an object out of a person's hand yet.

Tara says the sweater is adorable. Mrs. Ramsay must be a very good knitter. (Although there's one place, on the left-hand duck, where the stitches go crazy. The orange beak extends clear out to the buttonholes.)

"I didn't want you to be cold. These spring evenings get chilly."

Tara says she's sure Sunshine will get a lot of use out of the sweater.

"Now I want to talk to your mother," says Mrs. Ramsay.

"She's probably in the house," says Tara.

"Not *your* mother," says Mrs. Ramsay. "Baby's mother. You. I need to talk to you."

"Sure." This is the last thing Tara wants to be doing.

"It's very important. We must have privacy."

Tara says they could come inside. The shop is closed. They can talk there. She leads Mrs. Ramsay in.

"I see you carry very fine-quality merchandise," says Mrs. Ramsay. She is inspecting a pair of used men's work boots.

Tara says thank you.

"Now here is something I like." A purple jumpsuit with a zipper down the front. Two dollars and fifty cents.

"Would you like to try it on?" says Tara.

"No. I already have one like that."

What are they doing here? "Is there something in particular you want?"

"Yes," says Mrs. Ramsay. "I want to save a child's life. I want to keep a girl from murdering her baby."

What does she mean?

"I happen to know. Your friend Jill has a baby inside of her. I don't need to tell you why. And she is planning to kill it. She is going to a clinic where they murder babies. Your friend Wanda thought I would pay for it. That will be the day."

She has taken a dog-eared pamphlet from her shoulder bag. She opens the book to a page with a bookmark in it. She reads out loud, so loud that Tara worries her mother might hear.

" 'Second lunar month. The embryo's nest is now well covered with tissues and roots. The embryo feeds through a primitive umbilical cord and the little body floats in the amniotic sac. Currents of gelatinous cells modify and specialize into the nose and ears, the arms, elbows, fingers, legs, knees, feet and toes. The internal organs are getting ready to function. The embryo is covered with a thin layer of tissue and a transparent layer of skin. The body is one inch long. The heart has begun to beat.' "

Tara doesn't say anything.

"Sex organs. It even has sex organs," says Mrs. Ramsay. "Doesn't that mean anything to your friend?"

Tara is still silent. She's staring down at the spot on the floor were Kalima began her labor. She's thinking about something Denver told her, that one time when he was giving a woman a prenatal exam, a few weeks before her due date, and he put his fingers through her cervix to feel if the head was engaged, he felt a tiny hand curl around his finger, through the sac. She's remembering the day, just around this time last year, when she first felt that fluttering in her stomach. She was three months pregnant then.

"What am I supposed to do about it?" says Tara. The

thought of a baby dying has almost made her cry.

"Stop her," says Mrs. Ramsay, waving her knitting nee-
dle through thin air as though it's a wand.

Reg did not even have to think what to do; there was no
question. When he heard Ann's scream he came running
from the attic, and when he saw her standing there with that
look on her face he put his arms around her and kept them
there. Not just loose and friendly, the way he puts his arms
around Doris's sister when they drive to Worcester for a visit.
He wrapped himself around her like a tourniquet. Because
it's like she was bleeding.

Ever since he met her he has been picturing in his head
what he would do, if he had the courage or the foolishness.
Now, after all those hours—down in the garden, up in the
attic, lying in bed next to Doris, inhaling her Dippity-Do—
it's all unplanned. She has leaned her head on his chest and
he is stroking her hair. He had just about forgotten what a
woman's hair feels like without hairspray on it. Ann's hair
doesn't smell like anything besides hair.

There's nothing so bad about this. He would do the
same for Jill if she'd let him. He is just comforting her is all.

No need to ask what's the matter. He wraps his Ashford
Bowling League jacket around her shoulders and walks out
to the yard, where there are no bats, and a patch of trillium
has just come into bloom underneath the lilacs, that he noticed on his way over this morning. He's holding her hand.

He has seen someone cry this way only three times.
Once was his mother, when he was seventeen and she came
home from Rainbow Girls and he had to tell her "Dad
died." Once was Doris, sitting next to him in his old Ford
truck the next year, when she said she hadn't got the curse
for three months now, did he know what that meant. Once
was Jill, when he had to tell her she couldn't keep her
Christmas bike after all because they were laying men off on
his construction crew. In the end she kept it and he sold his

father's rifle instead. He can never bear to see a person cry this way. Their whole body shaking, their face more like a monkey than a person. It always breaks his heart, and he would do anything to make it stop.

What he does this time is, he turns his hat around backward, sort of like Frankie Fontaine on the old Jackie Gleason show, and he begins to dance. He's singing too—a song his father taught him, that he learned out in Oklahoma, back in the twenties. You have to sing it very fast or it won't be funny. Timmy has never taken the time to learn it right.

"Oh, I got a gal I do, and her name is Slewfoot Sue, she's the chief engineer at the old steam laundry down by the Riverside Zoo. Her form was all she had, she had a shape like a soft-shell crab. And every night she had a tussle with her patent leather bustle, and the boys thought she was really bad."

Ann is laughing, the kind of laughing that's part crying too.

Doris stands a few feet back, holding a plate of egg salad sandwiches.

The thing that has always been hardest for Carla about living with Greg is how little he says. For her the words just keep coming. She dreams in sentences, paragraphs, and when she wakes up, she wants to analyze the dreams. Over breakfast she likes to talk about what happened yesterday, and not simply what appeared to happen, but what was going on under the surface, and what will happen today. Even when she's alone she's saying things: First I will wash the dishes, then get dressed, then go to the cleaners. She makes many telephone calls, and they take much longer than they would have to if the only thing that mattered was getting business attended to. At dinner she likes to reenact some of these conversations for Greg, speculate about the personalities of the speakers, her relationships with them, their true feelings. Even in the darkness, making love, Carla

likes to say things. "I'm longing for you. Come live inside
me, never leave. I'm burning up." It doesn't stop.

But if she were to type up a transcript of everything
Greg said on a particular day (as she has pointed out to him
many times), it would probably be about one page, double
spaced. He likes to eat his breakfast in silence, says he's di-
gesting. He sometimes sings while he paints, but only other
people's words. Put on your red dress, Mama, 'cause we're
going out tonight. If you knew, Peggy Sue. And sometimes
just notes or syllables. At dinner he will say, "This is good,"
or mention that the Knicks won. Sometimes Carla will ask
him, "What are you thinking about?" Why she keeps doing
this is a mystery, because his answer is always the same. Artworks.

Of course sometimes he says something more, and when
he does it's always interesting, and Carla will listen very
carefully. But it's not primarily his words that she loves him
for. Carla can never get over it, that a person like her would
end up in such a nonverbal relationship.

In other ways, though, he's much easier to read, less
complicated, than she is. His face and his body—maybe because there's so little extra flesh on his bones—always give
indication when he is anxious or angry. She almost feels
sometimes that she can see his internal organs; it's that clear.
And when there is a high place over a swimming hole, he
doesn't have to stand there five minutes, deciding whether
it's safe to jump. He can roll into a headstand at any second.
He's always ready for sex, and it always feels good for him.

Carla will never understand why he wanted to be with
her. She has told him a hundred times she's not his type. "If
they lined up a hundred women in a room and asked people
to guess which one was your lover," she has said, "nobody
would guess it was me." Although she makes somewhat better sense for him than she did seven years ago, when they
met. She looks a little more, now, like the girls in the photographs she has seen, in the cigar boxes he keeps from his old
days. There were many of them, mostly artists or dancers.

None, certainly, who owned an expensive black suit and worked at a women's magazine. These women did not read magazines or set their hair or spend fifty dollars getting it to look frizzy. They were also the kind that just jumped off rocks when they wanted to, and did cartwheels. At a concert, when it's suggested that the crowd sing along (if they would go to that kind of concert), they do not look around to see whether anybody else is singing.

Carla has never stopped being proud that he would choose her. When they were first together she wanted everyone to see him, to see how beautiful he was, to see that she wasn't with Michael, the medical student, who appeared to be much more the kind they would have expected for her. She'd lie there on the mattress in his loft, once she had given up her place on East Thirtieth Street, thinking: I live on Duane Street, over a feta cheese factory. I ride the kind of elevator that has ropes you have to pull to go upstairs. I jump out when we get to our floor. There's a shower in the middle of the room. I am loved by a man who is not interested in my opinion of *Cries and Whispers.*"

"What was it about me that first night that made you say you loved me?" she asked him once.

"Oh, you know," he said. "The usual."

Greg is not much on words, but there was more to it than that. He thought she was brave and unfashionable. Still liking Joan Baez. Having those copies of *Family Circle* and the *National Enquirer* open on her kitchen table. Owning a sewing machine. Wearing a full slip. Calling her grandmother every Sunday.

He was touched that in spite of her parents in Ohio and the boyfriend at Johns Hopkins and the fact that she was scared of the subway, she would have done something like tap his shoulder in the museum. That seemed more original than the conceptual artist he knew who showed up at a party with a hole cut in the top of her dress and one breast sticking out, or his girlfriend at the time who had recently spent the night with a Puerto Rican taxi driver, and then told him about it. He was touched by how nervous Carla was that first night, and the way she went into the bathroom and closed the door to put her diaphragm in, even though they had just spent two hours rolling around the floor naked with all the lights on. He liked hearing her quote the opinions of her magazine's pair of sex experts. He liked the way, the night she had brought home a story to edit, by a woman whose daughter had died of leukemia, she cried for an hour. He did not make fun of her the night she changed her clothes six times when he took her to meet his friends Bob and Tina, who belong to an experimental music group in the East Village. Carla did not pretend to understand his paintings. She said one of the bears reminded her of her brother.

He didn't want her to ever change.

Carla would never have thought of herself as the kind of person who would live with a man seven years and not get married, who'd reach the age of twenty-eight and still not have a baby. If she'd married Michael they would probably have a couple by now. Michael used to say it was a good idea for the wife to have her kids while the husband was doing his internship and residency, so she'd have something to occupy her, with him gone so much. And for a while she had really believed she would end up married to Michael.

The reason, she has thought until now, why she isn't married to Greg instead, with one or two of Greg's children sitting on her lap, is that she wanted to be Greg's type and not Michael's. She wanted to be like the girls in the cigar boxes. Not so concerned with getting tied down. Keeping things fluid instead. Ready to jump off a boulder at a moment's notice.

Not that she ever has. She has always had to work very hard at being casual. She realizes now it was pointless to try. She is not the fluid type, and if she doesn't sew curtains, first thing, when she moves into a place, she will spend the next twelve months, until they move again, feeling a vague discomfort every time she looks at a window. Carla realizes suddenly that she doesn't care if she never takes another jazz dancing class. All she wants is to marry Greg and have the baby.

This is what Carla is thinking about as she opens the door and sees him just sitting there, listening to an Emmylou Harris record, holding the sketch pad with the picture of Tara and Sunshine on it.

What Greg is thinking, as he sees Carla walk through the door, is that it makes him terribly sad, and he wishes it were different, but he doesn't love her anymore.

In the fifth-floor TV room, six men in bathrobes are watching TV. Facing the set anyway. You could not exactly say that Rodney Quaid is following the show. Rodney is convinced he has cancer, and whenever there are no orderlies around, like now, he picks at his skin so hard he's covered with sores. At the moment he's working on his left thigh. He says he has found another tumor.

The show is called *That's Incredible.* Wayne has just watched a segment about a man who can dip his hand into molten iron without burning the flesh. The stupid part is, there's no point. When one of the hosts (Fran Tarkenton, getting out of shape, Wayne can tell) asked the man why he does this, the guy said well, why not? Wayne could do something like that too if he wanted—it's all a matter of mental concentration, he knows—but there would be a reason. Because my woman let me down. She knew she was supposed to stay on her mattress, and she went out. Because there is a girl alone in a house in Ashford, New Hampshire, who doesn't understand yet that I'm the only man in the world for her. Something along those lines.

Now another one of the hosts—that singer, John Davidson—is telling about this female police detective who can reconstruct an entire crime on the basis of the blood spatters. The detective is telling about a man whose death was ruled a suicide and then six years later she went back and examined the bloodstains on the pillowcase and the drips on the floor. She figured out what the angle of the gun had to be, and that the man could never have held it that way himself. They nailed his girlfriend. "Jesus," says Artie LeFleur, "that's incredible." He says this every time a commercial comes on.

"Yeah, Artie, we know," says Wayne. "That's the point of the show."

John Davidson is talking about another police detective now. How they found these two dead bodies in Nebraska, so decomposed you couldn't even tell if the bigger one was a man or a woman. The other one was a child, they knew that. So they did this skull reconstruction and a police artist made a sculpture, based on that, of what the older person's face looked like, and they ran a picture of the sculpture in some newspapers and a man recognized it as his wife, who had been missing, with their kid, for almost a year. "That's incredible," says John Davidson, smiling. He is talking about this grisly murder, this decomposed child, and he's got a grin on his face, clear back to his molars. What Dr. Poster would call an inappropriate response.

"If that was my wife that got murdered, I sure wouldn't want them to show her face on TV like that," says Artie LeFleur. "It's nobody's business."

"Yeah," says a new guy, who won't tell the others his name. "But they might give him the sculpture for consolation. Like a keepsake."

Wayne has had enough of this. He wanted to stick around for the Ann-Margret special, but he can't take these crazies tonight. Rodney Quaid has begun to ooze blood. ("Aha," says the police detective. "From the way the drips fell I can ascertain that they were caused by a paranoid psychotic suffering from the delusion that he had terminal lymph cancer, picking at his scabs.") Wayne gets up and goes to his room. Forget about Ann-Margret.

He doesn't really want to watch a sexy woman right now anyway. Normally that's the whole point. He sits there for an hour, very still in his chair, soaking it all up, and then he goes back to his room and jerks off. Some of the others don't even bother to wait, they do it right there in the TV room, with their hands underneath their blue hospital bathrobes. That's not Wayne's style. Sex is private.

But he isn't going to jerk off tonight or tomorrow. Or ever, until he is out of this place, and then it will be the real thing. Now that he has a goal, he's going to save it all up. Like Muhammad Ali in training camp. Celibate until the big moment, in the ring.

Doris and Reg have not spoken about this afternoon. In the truck on the way home (the girl offered her a cup of tea but Doris said no thank you), she said, "Darn, I forgot the sandwiches."

Reg said, "Do you want me to go back for them?" Doris said, "Don't bother. I just thought you might like a bite to eat. She could be a nice-looking girl if she'd take off a few pounds."

"She was a little upset," Reg said. "Bats."

He spent the rest of the afternoon out back, splitting wood. Now he is having his Tuna Helper and potatoes in front of the tube. It's a Red Sox night.

"How's it going, Baldy?" says Jill. She's wearing her pink uniform from Sal's with the two top buttons undone, on her way to work. She sits herself down on the arm of Reg's La-Z-Boy. The score is Boston 4, Detroit 2. Jill takes a sip of Reg's beer, leans one arm on his shoulder. She used to call him Baldy when she was younger.

"Since when do you drink this junk?" he says.

"I've been corrupted."

"Better not let your mother hear that kind of talk."

Carlton Fisk is at bat. New Hampshire boy. Reg's favorite of the Sox.

"I bet you could have been a baseball player," says Jill. "You've got the build."

"Water boy maybe." Jill is not wearing a bra. Reg notices that she has filled out, remembers what Doris's breasts used to look like, high and full. He turns back to the game.

"What did you used to think you'd be, when you were growing up?" says Jill. Something about the way she sits, the casual spread of her thighs—all of a sudden he knows she's not a virgin.

"I don't know. In those days you didn't have too many big ideas."

"There must've been something." Jill takes another long sip of his beer, licks the side of her mouth with her tongue.

"Farmer, I guess."

"That was your whole dream?"

More: black soil, no rocks in it, plenty of earthworms. Southern exposure, maybe a pond, for irrigation. Berry patches. An asparagus bed.

"What about you?"

She says she would like to be a stewardess maybe. You get to fly free, see the world.

"Not that it'll happen," she says. The two of them are silent for a few innings.

"Daddy," she says. "Do you believe there are things a person can do, that if they do them they go to hell?"

She's sure it's just temporary, momentary—the way every once in a while you'll be writing a letter and forget how to spell some word like "said"—but all of a sudden Ann can't remember what it was about Rupert that she loved. She has been grieving for so long all she can remember is grieving.

She knows some things they used to do, of course: going down to the garden at suppertime to pick vegetables for salad, setting up tray tables side by side facing the TV when they watched old movies, dancing the fox-trot Saturday nights when Lawrence Welk came on. Nothing very remarkable—nothing that would make a person, hearing about the two of them, think: Wow, what an incredibly beautiful relationship.

Actually, the awful memories are much clearer now: A drive to Massachusetts for Parents' Day at Trina's school, one of the teachers telling her after the fifth-graders' production of *Pygmalion*, "You must be very proud of your little sister." Smashing every one of his Early Girl tomatoes against the side of the house. Shutting herself in his closet after one of their fights, sitting on a pile of his shirts that had been building up for about three weeks, and that she kept meaning to wash, thinking he would open the door and put his arms around her, hearing him running the water instead, his spoon against the honey pot (making tea), and then the sound of typewriter keys. He just went about his business, and in the end she had to get up, open the door, squinting at the brightness of their room, go back to reading her magazine.

What does she want anyway? Rupert was always asking her that. "I need peace," he said. "I'm too old for this kind of thing."

Ann can't imagine wanting peace more than anything. "If that's how you feel, why don't you just go live in a funeral parlor," she told him. What Ann needs is a feeling in her chest sort of like the violin parts of a really sad country song. "Stand on My Own Two Knees," or "She Should Belong to Me." She needs someone who would make her throw herself into a snowbank. She can't imagine being in love and not crying.

Her high school boyfriend, Jeff, for instance. She will never meet someone that nice again, and he was crazy about her too. He used to write these poems and arrange it so one of the secretaries in the principal's office would deliver them to her in the middle of Latin class. He gave her great presents: a purple finch in a Mexican birdcage, a jasmine plant, a handmade Indian belt with her name spelled out in beads. He always had good ideas for things to do—roller skating, before it got so popular, a free introductory plane ride at a flight school. They had their portrait made by a computer, with their faces made into a pattern of X's and O's. He knew a dozen out-of-the-way places to go swimming—always had towels and a blanket in the trunk of his car. They weren't eighteen yet, so he kept six-packs stashed in hiding places all through the woods, and even though they were never cold, and it wouldn't have been that hard just to get somebody to buy for them, it was always exciting, digging up the beer.

But she always knew she would leave him. There was something about their relationship that just wasn't momentous enough. She didn't ache when he was gone or feel her hands getting damp when he came to pick her up. Sitting beside him in the front seat of his old Rambler, she might just as well have been curled up on the sofa at home, it was that comfortable. The closest they ever got to the kind of feelings people sing about on the radio was the night she told him she wanted to break up. They both cried. Ann could have stopped the tears a little sooner than she did, but she remembers thinking it felt sort of good.

A couple of months after she moved out of Rupert's house—during one of her worst eating bouts—she went to Nashville. She just got in the car and started driving, sleeping at the sleaziest motels she could find along the way, living on piña coladas and Rice Krispies. Ann thought of her trip as a kind of pilgrimage to the Heartbreak and Misery Capital of the nation. She made no effort to be friendly with the desk clerk at the Hall of Fame Motel or the other tourists on the sightseeing bus that took her past Webb Pierce's guitar-shaped swimming pool and the ASCAP fountain. She bought a pair of blue cowboy boots and seventy-five dollars' worth of records at Ernest Tubb's music store. She slept until noon most days, bought food at a grocery store on the highway and brought it back to her room, ate with the TV on, or the radio tuned to country, which was all you could get anyway. At night she'd take a cab to one of the clubs along Music Alley, stay till closing and take another cab back to the Hall of Fame.

On the fourth night she went to the Possum Holler because George Jones was singing that night. One of the country music magazines she'd bought and read in her room said George was drinking himself to death. He'd lost about thirty pounds, looked eighty years old. Ann—though she never loses weight when she feels like that—believed she understood.

Partly because of all the piña coladas she had that night, her memory of what happened is fuzzy. She was sitting listening to the music, sipping her drink. She remembers the look of George Jones's neck—stringy and tense, with his head thrown back like a man at the guillotine. She remembers him introducing a woman in the front row as his girlfriend, giving her a long, wet kiss in front of everyone, people whistling, and one man yelling, "Where's Tammy tonight, George?" Over in one corner two men got into a fight and somebody threw them out. Then she felt a hand reach over from the next table and touch hers, a very large hand wrap around hers, that was so cold. The odd thing was, she didn't even turn her head to see who was doing this. She kept staring straight ahead. But she didn't push the hand away.

Their hands stayed that way for about six songs. At one point Ann got something in her eye and wanted to brush it out, but she would have had to use the hand he was holding so she just blinked a lot instead. When she was finished with her piña colada the barmaid brought her another, and when Ann said, "I didn't order that," the woman explained it came from the man at the next table.

That's when she turned to look at him. An Indian, nearly seven feet tall, not fat but enormous. He wore his hair in a braid down his back and he was dressed in black leather. There were two men sitting with him, ordinary-looking men, ordinary size, and they were all acting as if there was nothing odd about this Indian carrying on a conversation while his left hand was stretched out and resting on the next table, holding on to the right hand of a total stranger.

He turned his head toward her very slowly, in such a way that his chin remained perfectly parallel to the floor the whole time. Then he turned back to his friends. He did not let go of her hand.

After the third drink she thought she would go. She remembered a boy she knew once in college explaining to her about this way a person could shake hands, with the middle finger touching the other person's palm in this certain way that meant you wanted to make love. She did not put her middle finger in that position, but she thought about Helen Keller, experiencing her whole life, practically, with her hands. She felt a little like that, as if about ninety things had happened between her and the Indian without either of them saying one word. She thought it would be appropriate, leaving, to just take her hand away and put it back in her pocket and not say good-bye. But she was not all that surprised, when she got outside, to feel him looming behind her. "I'm Randy Burning Tree," he said. "I will drive you home."

He had a white Cadillac with leather seats and a tape player, quadraphonic sound. When he clicked on the tape she realized—without having heard him say anything but those two sentences—that this was him singing. The top of his head touched the interior roof of the car.

She has told herself that all she meant was to get a ride back to the motel. All those cabs and drinks, she was almost out of money. But when they got to the motel and he kissed her, she kissed him back.

"I will walk you to the door," he said. It took him a minute getting out of the car, he was so big.

When they got to the door of the elevator, Ann said, "Well, good-bye."

"I will take you to your room," he said, just as the elevator door opened, and he stepped in.

She thinks that was the moment when she stopped feeling drunk and dreamy and began to feel scared. He stopped the door from closing with his foot. Black cowboy boots.

She pushed number four. Not her floor. Her hand in her pocket was fingering the key to room 207.

She has this memory of careening wildly in the elevator, pushing buttons, lurching to a stop, stepping out, stepping in, like that character in *The French Connection* who keeps getting in and out of subway cars trying to lose two killers. It couldn't have been that way exactly—elevators are never that fast—but she does remember knocking on some doors that weren't hers, reaching her hand out to push *L,* his hand stopping her.

At room 207 finally. Key in the lock, opening the door, thinking for a second: I was crazy, imagining things, he only wanted to make sure I was all right. Inside the room then, facing him as he stood in the threshold, like the ending of a kind of date she hasn't had since high school, where you say thank you, I had a lovely time, and close the door.

Only then his huge leg was in the doorway so she couldn't close it. Then it wasn't only his leg. Then he was ripping off her panty hose, pushing the country music magazines and the bag from Ernest Tubb's off the bed and there were Rice Krispies everywhere (she could hear the crunch as he pushed her down) and he had unzipped the black leather pants, and there was an enormous erect penis in her face.

She remembers only one thing after that. When it was over, and she was just lying there, he walked over to the mirror and took out his contact lenses. He wet them with spit and put them back in his eyes and then he left.

When she was home again and her period didn't come,

she thought she might be pregnant, thought about having an enormous Indian baby and not knowing what tribe it belonged to. A couple of days later she woke up covered with blood and knew that once again nothing was going to change.

Of course now Wanda can't ask Mrs. Ramsay to watch Melissa while she works at Moonlight Acres. It's a little embarrassing to ask Sandy, since she didn't show up at the birthday party. Wanda is just going to explain that Melissa wasn't feeling well. Which is true.

She's standing at their door, Sandy and Mark's. Looking at the sign that says "Love Nest," thinking: Sandy's so lucky. Ronnie Spaulding has asked Wanda out two times now. But she has a feeling he may just be using her. She can't picture her and Ronnie living in an apartment together with a Love Nest sign on the door.

Low voices inside. The radio playing. Somebody turns it up suddenly, so it's really loud. "I will if I want to." "You're so immature I feel like I have two babies to look after." "Well, then maybe you'll be happy to get rid of me."

They must not hear her knocking.

"I didn't mean it like that." Sandy.

Mark saying something about Alaska. Her parents. Want me to be just like them. Live a little. Stuck.

Wanda is about to go when the door opens. It's Mark, leaving. Sandy stands behind him with the baby in her arms.

"Well, it looks like the Mothers Club is all set for a meeting," he says. "I'd just be in the way. What do I know?" He's out of there.

Sandy and Wanda face each other, not saying anything. Mark Junior is saying tuna, tuna, tuna.

Wanda can't think of anything, except that if she doesn't leave now she will be late for her first night on the job. "I was wondering if you could watch Melissa," she says. "She'll probably just sleep."

*   *   *

Jill doesn't understand how it can be that after throwing up four times a day for a solid week (everything except the Saltines), when she put on her uniform to go to work, it was tight. Even her mother noticed, said thank goodness you're finally putting a few pounds back on. Well, tomorrow at this time the whole mess will be over with. She wonders if you go right back to normal after an abortion or if your body still thinks it's pregnant for a while. The woman from the clinic she talked to on the phone today told her she'd have bad cramps for a few hours, and bleeding like a normal period. "No intercourse for two weeks afterwards," she said. Well, Jill is in no mood anyway. Virgil can stick it in a tree as far as she's concerned.

Mark comes in, alone. Jill is going to make some excuse about missing Sandy's party, but then she sees he's too stoned to care. He puts a quarter in the jukebox, selects "Blue Bayou." He sits at the counter, spins around several times on the stool, the way little kids do. He takes a packet out of the sugar dispenser and studies what's written on the back. Sal got these sugars cheap—ten gross—because they were printed up for the Bicentennial.

" 'August 17, 1807. Robert Fulton left New York City on the first practical steamboat trip. Arrived Albany in thirty-two hours,' " he says. Jill smiles.

"Do you know what you want?" she says. She hands Mark a menu.

He stares at her as if he is remembering the way she looked with her shirt off, bouncing around his living room doing her pregnant dance.

He is still studying sugar packets. " 'Seventeen ninety-three. Eli Whitney invented the cotton gin, reviving Southern slavery.' I always wondered why they made such a big deal about the cotton gin," he says. "Far out."

"I'll be back when you're ready," says Jill. She has just seen Virgil come in and she wants to be busy. He sits down on the stool next to Mark's. He's carrying a cane.

Jill puts some more coffee in the filter and checks her reflection in the stainless steel of the machine. "Blue Bayou" clicks on again.

"You want to sign my cast?" says Virgil. Jill isn't sure who he's saying this to. She hands him a menu, even though she knows what he will get. He always gets a cheeseburger.

"So you want to?" He taps her shoulder with the cane. As if everything's like normal.

Jill is not even going to ask how he hurt his ankle, which isn't in a cast at all, just an Ace bandage. Jill puts out a knife and fork. "How's Sandy and the baby?" she says to Mark.

"Just one happy little family," he says.

"What happened to the rest of the dope?" Virgil says. He's talking to Mark now.

"Smoked it. I want a doughnut. With jelly in the middle. What do you call that kind?"

"A jelly doughnut. Coffee?"

Virgil says there was twice that much in the bag.

"Well, man, it's gone." Mark goes over to the jukebox, chooses the same song again. Someone at the other end of the counter makes a booing noise.

"So what time do you get off?" Virgil says to Jill.

"None of your business," she says. Now, if Mark asked her to go for a drive that might be different. It would be adultery, of course, like on *Dallas.* He is so cute. Jill tosses her hair so the highlights show. But Mark is walking toward the door and doesn't even leave a tip.

"Come on, how about it?" says Virgil.

Sperm virus, Jill is thinking. One hundred and thirty-five dollars down the tubes, and I am going to have to figure out how to get a fifty-dollar prom gown to show my mother without spending fifty dollars. She sweeps her sponge across Virgil's end of the counter as if he's invisible.

*   *   *

Johnny Carson has just signed a new three-year contract with NBC for five million dollars a year. Doris read about it in the paper. That is a good topic.

"Johnny isn't leaving the show after all," she says. Reg is lying in bed next to her, but she knows he isn't asleep. The monologue has just ended.

"That's good," says Reg. He doesn't open his eyes.

"You can be sure *his* wife doesn't spend her time looking for Red Dot Specials at the Grand Union," she says. Reg is silent.

"Ed must be relieved. If Johnny had gone, he'd be out on the street."

Reg says that's true.

"Although of course he'd still have those Budweiser commercials."

"Right."

"Will you look at Jim Garner?" she says. That is Johnny's first guest. "Is he ever looking terrible. I guess he's depressed on account of his divorce." Over the years, Johnny and Ed have also left their old wives for younger women, Doris knows.

Johnny asks Jim why he quit *Rockford Files.* Jim says he just couldn't keep up with the physical demands anymore. He might do another series sometime if it didn't call for so much running.

Johnny asks Jim how his golf game is coming. "Not so good," says Jim. "Used to be a lot better when I was younger."

"We are none of us getting any younger, Jim," says Doris. Reg reaches to turn off the light on his side.

"Hitting the hay?" says Doris. "Well, I guess I will too." She gets up to turn off the set and goes to the bathroom.

No curlers tonight. A squirt of the new Avon fragrance, Foxfire.

She pulls back the covers. She puts her hand on his chest, stroking his hair. Marabel Morgan would want her to say something about how manly he is. "You have a manly chest," she says.

He's pretty tired, he says.

She lets her nightgown ride up so her rear end rubs against his leg. She puts his hand on her thigh. She has never been this forward.

She's found the opening in his shorts. She puts her hand inside. Nothing happening.

"Just let your inhibitions run wild," she whispers. She heard that on one of Jill's Rod Stewart records.

Slowly she can feel his penis stiffening. He lifts himself up and lowers himself down on top of her. She spreads her legs.

In her room, with the door closed, Mrs. Farley is typing. She says some of the words out loud as she thinks of them. "Don't you even wonder what it looks like? Well, I'm going to tell you. It looks more like my daughter than your son. But my daughter does not have blue eyes. I have never trusted a person with blue eyes."

College boy. Impregnator.

Tara is going to shut her eyes, that's all. She will run a bath for her and Sunshine, try to remember that song Denver and Kalima sang. "My only sunshine. You make me happy when times are blue. You'll never know, dear."

She unpins Sunshine's diaper. Hardly damp at all. She lays Sun on the bathmat and locks the door. Then she pulls off her dress and pants. She holds Sunshine up against her bare skin, the way she did this morning, for the artist. She steps into the water, which is only lukewarm, the way the baby likes it. She sits down.

Sunshine's body goes rigid when she hits the water, then relaxes gradually as Tara rubs her back. She lies belly-down on her mother's stomach with her head resting on one of Tara's breasts, an inch above the waterline. A few strands of her hair—the longest parts, at the back of her neck—are wet and clinging to her skin. Her head rolls to the side just enough that she gets a little water in her mouth. She sputters a little. Tara pats her on the back. She's calm again, almost floating.

Tara has heard that newborn babies can actually swim. By the time they get to Sunshine's age they've almost forgotten. Tara herself has never gone in the water deeper than her knees. She doesn't even own a bathing suit. But they say if you tossed a newborn baby into the water it would swim. How did they ever find that out? Who would try?

Tara soaps up a washcloth. Sunshine is not really dirty, of course. She's never anything but clean. Tara just likes washing her, checking every inch.

What is Tara's favorite part? The delicate chin. Sunshine's little shell ears. Kalima's children, even the little boy, had pierced ears. Tara thinks Sun would look nice with little gold studs in her ears. But it's her body, Tara decided. What if when she grew up she decided she didn't want pierced ears, and it made her mad that I decided to do it without asking her? Like cutting someone's hair off while they're asleep. She will wait on the earrings.

Such a round belly Sunshine has. Tara feels proud that a baby fed on nothing but her milk could be so healthy. Her legs have these deep folds in the thighs where the skin is a shade lighter. So chubby the skin there never sees the light of day. That's one of Tara's favorite parts. Also the little monkey toes—long, almost like fingers. Sterling Lewis must have toes like that. Strange that she doesn't even know. And the blue eyes—her mother's right about that. Nothing else about Sterling Lewis was exceptional, but he had beautiful blue eyes.

"I am thinking tonight of my blue eyes, who is sailing far over the sea." Line from one of the songs the artist played for her today. It was on a record by a whole family that performed together with guitars and banjos and even an Autoharp. What was the Autoharp player's name? Maybelle. Mother Maybelle Carter. She played the Autoharp nothing like Tara's old music teacher.

Imagine having a whole family that played instruments like that, knew all those songs. On Sunday afternoons, instead of ironing blouses with the television tuned to *Bowling for Dollars* or making up crazy letters to people, imagine sitting around the living room singing harmony.

When she asked the artist if he'd play that song again, the one about blue eyes, he said, "I'll give you the record."

"I don't have a record player," she said. "But I'm saving up for an Autoharp."

He liked Sunshine. When she came out of the bathroom he was kissing her toes. "I was just looking," he said, embarrassed.

"I can't believe you had a baby," he said. "You're so small."

She told him how they thought she'd need to have a Caesarean, but in the end she opened up.

He took out this book he had of African art. All these wood carvings of pregnant women, women with long dangling breasts, squatting women with babies coming out. Beautiful, huh?

She wanted to tell him her stomach looked like that too when she was pregnant. Stretched so tight her belly button popped out, and she had to keep a quarter taped over it. She would've liked to pose for him when she was pregnant.

"It's the same expression a woman has on her face when she's making love," he said. He was looking at one of the African sculptures.

That was the one time Tara felt uncomfortable. She doesn't know what expression that is. She doesn't really know what it feels like to make love. Can't imagine.

If the artist hadn't been married, she would've explained to him how she had to get Sunshine out of this house, her mother was giving out such bad vibrations. He would say, "You can come live here." He would have built a railing around the sleeping loft, so they wouldn't need to worry about Sunshine. They would put her crib beside the bed.

She would sleep beside him the very first night. Naked probably. She doesn't even know what his body would look like. All she has seen is a couple of statues.

She would tell him that. He would say I understand, that's all right. I used to be a teacher. He would explain everything he was doing. She would watch carefully so the next time she'd know. He would kiss her the way Denver kissed Kalima to make the baby come out faster. That must open you up. Then it probably won't hurt so much, the way it did with Sterling Lewis. Is that why the African wood carving had that expression on her face? Does it always hurt?

"You'll be tight as a virgin again when we're done with this," the intern said when he was stitching her up. Then he patted her bottom.

So tight you get a look on your face like the wood carving. Is that the point?

She is sure the artist would have known a very gentle way.

But his wife is going to have a baby. Soon it will be her looking like an African sculpture, and when he needs someone to nurse a baby for a picture he can ask her. He will kiss his own baby's toes, and they will be toes that look like his. A year from now if you asked him, Remember that girl and her baby? he will say, What girl, what baby? The only baby that will matter will be his. Once you have your baby, nothing else matters.

Right now, for instance, Sandy may be upset about Mark coming home drunk. The artist and his wife (his friend? Why did he call her his friend?) may be having some kind of troubles. (He did not look at Tara as if she were a bowl of fruit in a still life. She's sure of that.) Tara may be living in a house full of bad vibrations, with a mother who, at this moment, is banging on the bathroom door saying, "Nothing but grief, do you hear me?" But the main thing is, all of these people have their baby, or they're going to have their baby. That makes everything else seem small.

Jill is going to have an abortion, Mrs. Ramsay said. Virgil must have said he doesn't want to get married. Maybe her parents found out and got mad.

Her fetus is eight weeks, maybe nine weeks old now. Eyes forming. Hands, feet. Sexual organs. Its little heart has begun to beat, Mrs. Ramsay said.

"Damned children," Mrs. Farley is saying. "I wish I'd had my hysterectomy seventeen years ago when it might have done me some good."

I'm going to save Jill's baby, Tara is thinking. That's what matters now.

There is, for once, no need for Carla to ask Greg what he's thinking. His drawing of the girl and her baby makes it pretty clear.

"How was the birthday party?" he says. He's sitting with his back to the door, looking at the falls, when she comes in, carrying the bag with the stuffed seal inside.

"Most of the guests didn't show up," says Carla. "The girl's husband came home drunk. Her baby slept through the whole thing."

" 'Bright moments. Bright moments,' " Greg sings. It's the lyric from a jazz song he loves. One entire side of an album with only those words, repeated over and over.

He doesn't say anything about Tara modeling for him, and Carla doesn't ask. She always thought if she saw him with that look on his face because of another woman, she would just take her clothes out of the drawers and pack up her dishes. Now it seems to her she was foolish to think it had to be all or nothing. She would rather be one of the women in the supermarket buying baby food than one of those young girls who can only take her hands off her boyfriend long enough to put a jar of artichoke hearts in their cart.

That kind of passion never lasts anyway. Better go with the long-term investment. Carla will just wait this out.

It's as if Melissa has a leak in her somewhere. She keeps draining. When Mark Junior has a bowel movement you can hear a muffled machine gun noise coming from his bottom, and when Sandy takes his diaper off there will usually be three hard pellets lying there, like eggs in a nest. There never seems to be a moment like that when Melissa moves her bowels. This funny streaky green liquid just keeps dribbling out her rear end, so she's never really clean but never all that messy. Her body, in Sandy's arms, feels like somebody let the air out. No muscle tone. She is the only baby Sandy's ever seen that doesn't curl her hand around your finger.

Still there's something cute about her. Not the way she looks, for sure, with her old-looking gray face and that bright pink birthmark on her forehead and her large unmatched ears that stick straight out like handles. Sandy's mother-in-law keeps telling her Mark Junior should go on a diet, he is so plump (and the number of fat cells a person grows in the first year of life is the number he will have forever), but Sandy would rather have a baby with a few extra pounds on him than one like Melissa, where you can feel every rib.

One funny thing is, she's just three months old but she already has a tooth. And even her one tooth isn't quite right. It's coming in all slanted so it cuts into her bottom lip a little, which makes her look like she's been in a fight and lost.

Still it feels sort of nice to cuddle her, especially considering the mood Sandy's in, after the fight with Mark. And Mark Junior has never wanted too much hugging and kissing. He wants to keep moving. Even when he was a tiny baby he used to wrinkle up his nose and sneeze if you'd nuzzle up against him for too long. But Melissa seems happy just lying in Sandy's arms. She isn't smiling exactly (it's almost like her muscles aren't strung tight enough), but her eyes are open, and even though there's a cloudy film over them, Sandy's sure Melissa's really looking at her. A few minutes ago, when Sandy set Mark Junior down on the floor with his Ivory Snow study board, and he started yelling, the way he always does, and waving his fist at the baby in the picture, Melissa made a little noise too, like she wanted to play. But then her eyelids dropped down again and this little trickle of drool came down her chin and she didn't make any more noises. Like she remembered all of a sudden how tired she was.

Ann has begun to learn the bats' timetable. During the day they mostly sleep, or at least rest. Then right around dusk they begin swooping down from the eaves, bumping around in the attic, crashing against the windows. Why they do this she doesn't understand. The ones inside want to get out. The ones outside try to get in. The worst part is the sound of their toenails scraping against the panes.

They do that for about an hour and then they're quiet again. Until about 1 a.m., when they begin to shriek. It's two-thirty now and they have just stopped.

The odd thing is, Ann was almost calm, listening to them. Even though there must have been a hundred bats scratching against the attic walls, flapping against the windows. Even though her neighbor's wife found her today in her neighbor's arms. Even though that TV show about the blood spatters is the kind that usually gives her nightmares.

Now she's sitting in her rocking chair with a glass of Kahlúa, listening to Dolly Parton at full volume. She's still wearing her bath towel, and she has covered her body with powder. She has one hand under the towel. She is watching Simon asleep on the floor. It looks as if he's dreaming of chasing a weasel. Every minute or so he makes a little snorting noise and moves his legs as if he was running.

She should be upset by what that man said to her. She should have called her friend Patsy in Brattleboro and said,

Can I come stay with you for a few days? She should have told him, If you ever call me again I will report you to the police.

But she is just sitting here, rocking. Thinking: Things will not just be this way forever. Something's going to happen. It doesn't even matter what.

Of course this wasn't the first time that Val's mother has grounded her. When she found out the sleep-over party at Casey's house on Long Island was coed, and Casey was a boy, that was one time. When she came home early from the ballet because Baryshnikov wasn't dancing that night after all, and she found Val fixing piña coladas with the special rum she brings back every New Year's from Haiti, that was another. Also, when Val's geometry teacher called to say, "I'm surprised you signed Val's report card, with that F I gave her." And Val's mother said, "F—what F? I thought it was a B." Val was grounded for two weeks for that, and she couldn't even listen to records. Her mother threatened to have the phone in Val's room disconnected too, but she never went through with it.

This time all that happened was Val said she'd be home by one, and then she didn't get back until three. Well, just a little after. It's hard finding a cab at that hour. Anyway, Val's mother must be pretty dense to think she'd make it home by one, when the movie only started at midnight. It was called *Eraserhead,* about this guy whose head is shaped like an eraser. Much better than *Rocky Horror Show.* There was one girl in the audience who had smeared vomit all over her hair. People said it was vomit anyway. Val had a feeling maybe it was just that instant papier-mâché they used one time in art class.

The real pisser about being grounded at this particular moment is her friend Zoe's parents are flying out to L.A. this weekend and Zoe has finally figured out where her father keeps his video cassette of *Story of O.* She's going to have a party with all the coolest guys, and it will probably turn into an orgy. Zoe has been on a diet for a week, in case they play strip poker.

Of course there's nothing to stop Val from going anyway. Her mother (who's out shopping at the moment) doesn't have her chained up or anything. She could just take off after therapy or something. Only she'd have to come home sometime (her records are here, among other things). And when she did, the shit would really hit the fan. No point going through the entire summer with no clothing allowance, all because of a party. If she's going to have to make do with her old horrible bikini, at least she should have a really fantastic time first.

Too much stress. One of these days she is going to get an ulcer, and will her mother ever be sorry. Val could use a vacation. Someplace where there aren't any hassles.

That's when it hits her: she'll go visit her art teacher, Mr. Hansen. Greg. She even has his new address in New Hampshire printed in the back of her yearbook, because the Walker School believes in fostering ongoing student-teacher relationships. They keep telling you: don't lose touch. Let us know how things are going. Well, she will do better than that. Zoe won't believe it when Val tells her. And Mr. Hansen is very cute.

So what she does is, she empties a bottle of aspirin into the toilet and flushes them down, leaves the empty bottle in her mother's medicine chest, where she is sure to go for it when she finds Val gone. Nothing too obvious—just enough to leave her feeling worried.

Then she takes eighty dollars out of the blue Tupperware box her mother keeps in the freezer. She stuffs the money in her overnight case, along with a couple of tops and her diaphragm and her curling iron (she's growing out her bangs, and they're at that impossible length). She changes her shirt three times, also takes off her jeans when she decides not to wear underpants. Then she locks up the apartment, lurches past the doorman (in case her mother talks to him later and says, "Did you notice anything about my daughter?") and hails a cab. She gets out at the Ninety-second Street entrance to the FDR Drive. Slings her overnight bag over her shoulder (regretting having chosen the one with YSL printed all over it) and sticks out her thumb.

It is a little after midnight when the idea comes to him. It's always like this, with Wayne's best plans. He will just be lying on his bed or sitting looking out the window and then a voice inside his head tells him exactly what to do. "Wayne," says the voice, "that woman in the toll booth is meant to be yours." "Wayne, that baby inside her has to go." "Wayne, there is a girl named Ann sitting alone in a house and she is just waiting for you. Now I am going to tell you how to get there." It must have been this way for Joan of Arc. Maybe David Berkowitz too.

He slips on his paper slippers. (Regrettable that he has no regular shoes. He will go barefoot before he puts on those Hush Puppies Charles wears.) He pulls his T-shirt over his head, checks his hair in the mirror. There's nothing he needs to take, except the picture of Loretta.

Charles sits at the orderlies' station, eating cheese puffs and a Twinkie. There is a biography of Bruce Springsteen open on the table, but Charles is not reading. Wayne guesses he is probably stoned. So much the better.

"Nice evening," says Wayne. Charles drops his cheese puff.

"Catching up on your reading, I see," says Wayne.

Charles says Bruce Springsteen comes from my same town in New Jersey. He's older though. You know you aren't supposed to be out on the ward this time of night.

"You know what you aren't supposed to be doing?" says Wayne. He can hear that young kid down the hall, banging his head against the wall again.

Charles says, "Huh?" He relaxes a little. Now Wayne's going to give one of his health food lectures about how cheese puffs just pollute your body, tell him do you know what the inside of your large intestine must look like?

"I'm talking about pills," says Wayne. "I'm talking about all those little red pills in that lunchbox of yours. Wondering what Dr. McAlister would say."

Charles sags back in his chair. There is no point trying to fight whatever is coming now. He will simply sit here and wait to see what Wayne has in mind. More free dope probably. Well, Charles will not even wait for Wayne to ask. He reaches into his pocket.

"Do you think I want more of that poison?" says Wayne. "Why do you think I took it in the first place? I've just been gathering the information, that's all. Compiling data, as Dr. Poster would say. Names, dates, transactions. In case someone might be interested."

Charles just sits there. Even if he weren't so stoned, he wouldn't know what to do now. Might as well ask Wayne. He will know.

"But suppose," says Wayne, "that the person who had all this data escaped? Suppose he wasn't around to tell Dr. McAlister?"

Charles does not have to point out that there are two guards downstairs, and another one patrolling the grounds. He already understands that of course Wayne will take his uniform and ID. The only question left is what to tell them in the morning, when they find him sitting here wearing Wayne's pajamas. He will lose his job, naturally. But that's better than a drug charge.

He is stripped down now, except for his shorts. Even at a time like this, he feels embarrassed to have Wayne see his body. Wayne is in such good shape.

"You know what you need?" says Wayne, zipping up Charles's white pants, which are too short, of course. "Brewer's yeast. And stay away from that refined sugar. It'll kill you."

*   *   *

Mrs. Ramsay's idea was, she would give the mother one more chance. Show her a couple of the photographs, say do you really want me to give this to a judge? Even Perry Mason couldn't win this case for you. So just sign the paper and give Baby to me. Or don't sign the paper. Just put Baby in my arms, and remember there are more photographs where these come from.

But the mother was not home. And then who should she see but the other girl, the one with the little boy, sitting on the steps of the apartment building across from the Laundromat with the little boy in her arms and Baby Susan in the stroller next to her.

Baby Susan did not look well. She was an odd color, and her head kept rolling around. The little boy—Mark is his name—was holding a rattle and smiling. And Baby Susan was just sitting there with her mouth open and her eyes shut. The girl, Baby Mark's mother, did not seem to be paying attention. She appeared to have been crying, in fact. Maybe she had just heard the news about Michael Landon and his wife getting a divorce. Mrs. Ramsay has been upset about that all day. That, combined with talking to the girl who is going to the clinic where they kill babies, and taking the disgusting photographs, and having to speak with that young man and give him the eighteen hundred and twenty-six dollars, and reading in the *Star* that the character of Linc Tyler is about to be written out of *All My Children*. So many bad things, Mrs. Ramsay's head was spinning.

But she knew she had to get that baby right away. "Why don't I just take Baby home with me," she said to Baby Mark's mother. "I am the grandmother, you know. I will let Baby's mother know that she's with me." The girl looked as if she wasn't even paying attention.

"Oh," she said. "Sure. I just changed her, but she wasn't even wet." Muttered something about maybe the baby's a little dehydrated. Then Mrs. Ramsay wheeled the stroller down the street. It was that simple.

Of course, when the mother comes to pick up Baby,

they will not be there. Mrs. Ramsay has finished loading up
the car with everything she needs. She will go to that place
in New York City where they have the breast-feeding machines for adoptive mothers first. Then she and Baby Susan
will visit Disney World in Orlando. She will take a picture of
Susan and Mickey Mouse together, with her new Polaroid
camera. She has heard that everything at Disney World is
very clean.

There is just one more thing she has to do first.

It has been a rougher trip than Val expected. First she had
to wait almost two hours for a ride and she wished she'd
worn something besides her Hawaiian print shirt, which is
short-sleeved and very punk, but not all that warm after
sundown.

The first man that picked her up was around her father's age, and not fat but kind of saggy. Going to a convention in Bridgeport. Said he sold industrial cleaning fluids.
Going to a cleaning fluid convention evidently.

He kept wanting to talk about sex. How much things
had changed from back in his day. How it used to be the
only girls that would do it were the kind that you'd have to
worry about giving you a disease. Kept talking about the Pill
like it was big news and he was so hip. When the truth is,
most of Val's friends have IUD's or diaphragms. Val thinks
the Pill is very sixties.

The man said he'd heard girls were getting so aggressive
these days that all these young boys were suffering from im-
potence. Wished the girls would just back off. Also, they
were so used to getting it all, they didn't know any of the
preliminaries anymore. The man said he heard they were
giving this course at some Princeton fraternity on how to
make out. "If that's what they're studying now at college, I
would be a Ph.D.," he said. "If I was only young." He said
that three times.

Nothing happened with him, but she was still glad

when they got to Bridgeport. "Am I supposed to do something or what?" said the man just before he let her out of the car.

Val said, "No, you aren't supposed to do anything." Unbelievable.

The next guy was really obese. So fat he spilled over the bucket seat and the stick shift dug into his leg. Val had to squeeze right up against the car door to keep from pushing up against him. That would have really grossed her out.

He stopped at two different Howard Johnsons on the Connecticut Turnpike. He insisted on buying her a sundae like his at the second one, and when she left three quarters of it sitting there, he said, "We can't let this go to waste now, can we?" and ate it all in about two bites. He said, "Have you ever tasted Baskin-Robbins' Chocolate Almond? That's the best flavor in the United States."

When they got to Rocky Hill he said gee, he could use some Tendersweet clams right about now. That was the limit. Val said she'd just stay on the highway and find another ride.

It was a couple that picked her up at Rocky Hill. In their fifties maybe. Val is never sure about the ages of old people.

Anyway, the woman looked like a real grandmother type. In fact, she was a grandmother. She took all these pictures out of her wallet, of her grandchildren. Called them grandkids. She said, "We have one just about your age. Fifteen, right? Sixteen? Does your mother know you're out hitchhiking like this? It's not safe, you know. You never know whom you are going to meet.

"Isn't she a lovely young girl, Perley?" the woman said. Perley was the man's name.

"Yes, indeed, Mother," Perley said.

"So young and innocent," said the woman. "So much to learn."

Perley said that's true.

"Show her your photographs," said the woman. "I bet

she would find them very educational." Then she asked Val if she would like to see more photographs. Val said sure.

Even after some of the movies she has seen with Warren Hackett, and that wild party he took her to that his stepfather gave for a British new wave band whose records he produced, even after that, Val wasn't prepared for Perley's photographs. He kept them in the same type of picture holder the woman used for her grandkids. Only these were pictures of naked little girls, around junior high school age. Sometimes there were little boys in the pictures too. Sometimes there were old men like Perley.

"Wouldn't you like Perley to show you how to do those things?" said the woman. "He would be pleased as Punch, and I wouldn't mind one bit."

That was when Val said, "Please let me out of the car."

She was scared that they wouldn't, but Perley just said, "Well, surely, although Mother is going to fret about you, out on the highway this time of night." Val got out of there so fast she forgot her overnight bag with the eighty dollars in it.

She doesn't know where she is now, but she remembers, around the time Perley put his hand on her knee, seeing a sign that said Welcome to New Hampshire. There was a bridge they passed under, with the words painted on it: "I Love you Sally McDermott." It was about then that Mother said, "Don't mind me. I like to watch."

It's probably about two o'clock in the morning now. Val's arms are covered with goose bumps and there hasn't been a car on the road for twenty minutes. She has begun to cry, and the ridiculous thought has struck her that she wishes her mother was here.

Several things went wrong for Wanda tonight. First Mr. Pineo said her uniform was too long, hem it. And Wanda knows if she does, the customers will be able to see right up her legs when she reaches into the potato chip bin. "If I wanted some granny serving my ice cream I'd put up a help-wanted notice at the old folks' home," said Mr. Pineo.

Then Ronnie Spaulding came by for some fried chicken, and Sharon Lovett was with him, all over him. Nancy, the waitress who brought their order, said Ronnie was handing out free beers all over the place and telling people he hit the jackpot. The sweepstakes maybe. It must've just happened. He didn't mention a thing about any jackpot this afternoon. And tonight he didn't even say hi to Wanda.

A man came by with a bunch of little boys on some baseball team. They all wanted ice cream, and they kept changing their minds every two seconds. Two of the boys started squirting ketchup at each other, and a big blob landed on Wanda in a very embarrassing place. The man who was supposed to be in charge of the boys didn't even get mad at them. One kid in particular—Wanda just wanted to shake him.

They all have a million things they want. Hold the onions. Extra napkins. No ice in the water. I like my burgers pink inside. Do you have a cherry—ha ha—for my sundae. They throw their straws on the ground and butt out their cigarettes in the oozed-over mustard. They want their change in dimes, for the dryer. Where's the bathroom? My kid just bit off the bottom of his cone and it's dripping all over the place. Can I have another one?

Then they don't leave a tip.

After they closed up and Nancy had finished cleaning her station and gone home, Mr. Pineo said to her how about a little something. Now he is going to expect it all the time. He put his hand on her ass like he owned her. Wanda said, "I've got to pick up my daughter at a friend's house."

"You don't know what you're missing," he said. She could imagine.

Her feet are so sore. She should've got a bigger size shoes. Wanda feels like she's even gained weight in her feet.

It's a half-mile walk to Sandy's. Even though the evening has cooled off, Wanda is sweating. She can't wait to take off her bra and panty hose, fix herself a bowl of macaroni. She's really looking forward to seeing Melissa too. Six hours is the longest Wanda has ever been away from her. She'll give her a big hug and tell her she's sorry for getting mad. She won't do that anymore. Tomorrow she's going down to Zayre and get the Fisher-Price musical Ferris wheel.

Sandy is sitting there at the kitchen table, crying. The party streamers are still up, also the balloons. "Mark hasn't come back," she says when Wanda comes in. "He said he feels trapped and old. He said he wished he was in Alaska. He got fired."

Wanda feels bad for Sandy. She's really sorry to hear this. But right now she also wants to get Melissa and go home.

"Oh," says Sandy. "I thought you knew. Melissa's grandmother came and got her."

At 3 a.m.—Ann has finally fallen asleep—the telephone rings. She has been lying on the living room couch, on account of the bat in her bedroom, so she picks it up on the first ring.

"You can go ahead now," says the operator. Then she hears coins clicking in a pay phone.

"I hope I didn't offend you before." It is the the deep-voiced man from the ad, of course.

"But you and I are both beyond being delicate about things, aren't we? Why should we pretend? I just knew from your voice, from that card you sent, that you've had enough of dealing with the world. And I wanted to say I'll take care of everything. You've been taking care of things by yourself for too long now, haven't you?"

"Yes," says Ann. She feels very tired. She's also drunk on Kahlúa.

"And you need a man."

"Yes," says Ann. That's also true. She is half asleep.

"And I'm hungry for your love," he says. "I've got such a lot of love. I'm going to give it to you."

Ann thinks she has heard those words somewhere in a song.

"Put on your pretty summer dress," he says. "I want to make love to you, yes, yes. The healing has begun."

It occurs to her that she doesn't know his name.

"It isn't important," he says. She hadn't even asked him.

"Just be there waiting for me," he says. "I'm coming for you soon. All you need to do is wait for me."

She doesn't have to do anything but wait. She can just lie here on the couch.

"Just be ready for me," he says. "Just leave the door open, that's all."

She knows there is no need to give him directions. He will find her.

"I will take care of everything," he says. "You won't believe how strong I am.

"Total devotion," he says. "That's the only thing."

Mark has been driving for a couple of hours but now he has no particular destination in mind. He is not even going in the direction of Alaska, in fact. He isn't wearing warm enough clothes.

Vermont. "I love you Sally McDermott." The words have been painted on this bridge ever since Mark can remember. The poor sucker who put them there is probably married with five kids now, and Sally McDermott most likely weighs two hundred pounds. Every time her husband drives under this bridge he must feel like a class A dope, thinking love would last as long as a coat of spray paint.

Or passion anyway—the hots—or whatever you call the feeling Mark used to get nights in the backseat, with Sandy and a six-pack. Winter afternoons, junior year, a basketball between his fingertips, poised for a foul shot—concentrating, focusing on that place inside the hoop, but also thinking: She's in the bleachers, she's watching. Telling her: "You're my dream girl, you're all I'll ever need." All those things they sing about on the radio, that he believed.

Gone now, except something they don't sing about. Just feeling safe, and comfortable. Knowing nothing wonderful will happen, but nothing terrible either. Fit together, one into the other, like two spoons in a silverware drawer. "Honey, I'm home." Two eggs every morning and a drawerful of clean socks, walking down Main Street, not hand in hand, but swinging a child between the two of them. A cup of cocoa on a cold night, and a handmade Christmas stocking with your name on it in sequins.

He has known all along, of course, that he would turn back, and now he does it. Pulls a U-turn in the middle of the highway—his last adventure for the evening, he thinks. Only up ahead, just beyond the Sally McDermott bridge, is a scrawny girl in a short-sleeved shirt and platform shoes and her thumb sticking out. No suitcase, no jacket. A person could wait all night for an eastbound car on this section of road.

Mark looks in the rearview mirror and smooths back his hair, reaches for a cigarette. He brakes, leans over to open the door on her side.

"Am I glad you stopped," she says, jumping in. She looks about fifteen. The hairs on her arms are standing up and her teeth are chattering. Mark has never seen a girl with a tattoo before. On her earlobe.

All the house lights are turned off when Mrs. Ramsay pulls up to the Just-like-nu Shop. But she is sure Tara will understand once she hears the plan. Mrs. Ramsay could see, when she told Tara about the other girl and the clinic, that Tara was as upset as she is to think of the girl murdering her baby.

She pounds on the door. A light comes on. The door opens.

"What is it?" Tara has opened the door only partway.

"I have to talk to you."

"We just did a few hours ago. If my mother wakes up she'll kill me."

"I have figured out my plan now. I want you to help me."

"Couldn't we talk another time? Maybe tomorrow."

"Tomorrow will be too late. I will be gone. I am driving south. Taking my granddaughter on a vacation."

Driving south. Driving away. Maybe she'll pass through Georgia. This is Tara's chance to get away.

She's packed in fifteen minutes. She wraps Sunshine in a towel and ties a knitted cap over her head. The baby doesn't even wake up.

For a second there, Doris had this look on her face as if Reg was strangling her. He has never seen her look like that before, while they're having sex. Normally she just closes her eyes and purses her lips, as if she's thinking about how much things cost.

But for a minute she looked like she was dying, and Reg had the thought that he killed her and now he was going down the road, to Ann. Then Doris came out of it and she began to cry in this funny squeaky way that sounded like Jill when she was little. Reg put his arms around her then. "Don't cry, honey," he says. "It's all right."

"Don't leave me," says Doris.

"Why would I do a thing like that?" says Reg. He pats her, the same way he pets Chester, their cocker spaniel.

Tomorrow morning, early, he's thinking, he will take down his rifle. He is going down to the girl's house. He's going to shoot those damn bats.

The girl's name is Val. ("As in Valium," she said.) She has seen the Rolling Stones live. Also the B52's and the Eagles and Blondie. She was going to see the Who, but then all those people got killed at that concert in Cincinnati and her mother grounded her. She saw Peter Townshend at Bloomingdale's once though. He's not as tall as you'd think.

Mark feels like one of the Beverly Hillbillies, sitting on the gold terry-cloth seat covers of his Valiant and talking to her. She's four years younger than him but she knows so much. She goes to a private school called Walker. There's a girl in her class who grows mushrooms in her locker that are supposed to be hallucinogenic. There's an entire drawer in the lost and found filled with nothing but cocaine spoons.

He turns on the radio, hoping for some really heavy rock. All he can get is a French-Canadian station and country. He tries the dial. "Hey, turn it back," she says. "That's perfect. I feel like I'm in an episode of *Happy Days*. Time Warp City."

Mark doesn't know what she's talking about but he thinks she may be making fun of him. He wishes he still had that bag of New York dope.

"So what do people do around here for thrills?" she says. "Go to Clint Eastwood film festivals? Have a contest to see who has the most Kenny Rogers albums?" The song that's playing is "Lucille." You picked a fine time to leave me.

"Get high, listen to the Dead. You know," he says. He's not about to mention trout fishing.

"I bet all the girls marry their high school sweetheart and have ten kids by the time they're eighteen and live happily ever after, right?"

"I guess some do."

" 'Bingo Every Thursday Night,' " she says. They have just passed a Moose lodge. "Bowling. I bet that's big."

"Where I live," says Mark, "we have this miniature golf course. That's where everyone goes parking Saturday nights. There and the dump." He feels proud when she laughs at that.

"A girl I know got laid by this gas station attendant in

Vermont who lived near her parents' summer place," says
Val. "Actually, it was a real hot and heavy romance. He
wanted to get married. The whole bit. Of course she was
going to Vassar in the fall."

"What happened?" says Mark.

"Gee, I don't know. She majored in women's studies, I
think."

Some guy on the country station is singing "Would you
lay with me in a field of stone?" If I could just get some decent music, Mark is thinking, I might get somewhere with
this girl.

"I bet you have a boyfriend," he says. "Cute kid like
you."

"Commitment to one person is a drag," she says. "Ricky
Nelson–type stuff. I see different guys."

"Older, probably."

"All ages. One time this twelve-year-old brother of a
friend of mine tried to lay me. Got a hard-on and everything,
if you can picture it. But I'm not into corrupting the young."

"How old do you think I am?"

"Twenty-four, twenty-five?"

Mark is pleased about that. He lights up one of his
Tiparillos.

"Do you have any boyfriends like me?"

"Not exactly," she says. She has picked up the tune of
the song now and is singing along. Would you bathe with me
in the stream of life?

"Hey," she says. "Any lakes or stuff around here?"

"Sure," he says. "Why?"

"We could go skinny dipping."

"We'd freeze," he says.

"What are you, scared?"

Mark Junior can always sense when something is wrong. It's
one of the reasons why Sandy knows he must be exception-
ally intelligent. The night Mark came home with a stereo

cassette player for the Valiant, for instance, and that money was meant for Sandy's washing machine fund. Sandy didn't even raise her voice at Mark that time—just made him promise to return it—but Mark Junior knew something was wrong. He got diarrhea and he wouldn't go to sleep until eleven-thirty. There was another time when Sandy mentioned to Mark how she was thinking maybe they should have their second child soon, so their kids could be friends, and before Mark Junior gets so old that a new baby would be traumatic for him. Sandy knew Mark was going to argue—was even prepared for him to yell. But what he did was, he went into their bedroom and came out with the blue tie he got for their wedding looped around his neck, holding one end up in the air, with his head drooped to one side. "You want to put me in a noose, don't you," he said. Not loud. Mark Junior began to scream that time too. Also when Mark and Sandy make love, even if they do it in the other room, with the door closed. Mark Junior never cries when they're doing it. But when it's over, and the two of them are lying there, he almost always wakes up. He makes this odd noise like someone just stabbed him and then he fusses for a minute and finally he goes back to sleep. "They have a name for that," Mark said once. "Some type of complex where little boys wish their father would drop dead so they could make it with their mother. You'd like that too, wouldn't you?"

Of course that was crazy. Sometimes when she's kissing Mark Junior though, it's true that Sandy forgets just for a second that he's her baby and not her husband. One time she put her tongue in his mouth and he started sucking it, just like his bottle. She couldn't believe how strong his mouth was. And sometimes she lies on the water bed, naked, after her shower, with Mark Junior lying on her stomach. She will look at him and think: You came out of me. She will rest her chin on the top of his head, just where the soft spot is, where—when he was smaller—she could see the skin rise and fall with his pulse. One of the books she has says there's a special gland there, on the top of the baby's head, that gives off a particular smell that makes the mother want to cuddle it. It's true, Mark Junior's head smells wonderful even without shampoo.

That's the spot she's kissing right now. Mark Junior has been crying off and on all night, ever since Mark left, and Sandy's sure Mark's leaving is the reason. It didn't even help, having Wanda's baby over. Normally he loves having other babies around, but tonight he didn't even seem to notice. Just kept screaming. He'd stop for a few minutes, gulping, catching his breath. Then he'd start up again. He did that for five hours nearly.

It's midnight now, and he has finally quieted down. Sandy has put on the *Heart Like a Wheel* album and Mark Junior is in her arms and they're dancing. Sandy's singing along, pretending she's Linda Ronstadt. Or just some singer in a band. She never does this when Mark's around—he says she has a terrible voice. But with the record turned up you can't tell, she just blends in. At the dark end of the street. Just you and me. Those are the words.

When Sandy and Mark slow dance (they haven't done this in a long time now), Sandy's always tense, worried that she will step on his feet. Their movements are choppy. Mostly they just go back and forth in the same spot. Mark's hands make a sweat mark on her dress. Sandy looks at the floor. Even though they're only dancing in the first place because Sandy has begged Mark, she's usually glad when the song's over and they can go sit down.

The nice thing about dancing with Mark Junior in her arms is, Sandy's never out of step. She feels the way Ginger Rogers must have felt in those old Fed Astaire movies. Or the girl in *Saturday Night Fever,* John Travolta's partner. So totally in tune with Mark Junior it's like they're one person. She has one arm around his back and one arm outstretched, holding his hand. She leads, of course. The two of them are spinning, twirling, sweeping all around the room, and they never bump into anything. When Sandy dips, Mark Junior makes a contented little sighing sound. They don't stop for one whole side of a record, and even then, only long enough to change sides. She sings into his ear, and he must like it because when she stops he begins to cry again. *My love for you is like a sinking ship and my heart is on that ship out in midocean.*

They park the Valiant just below the falls and walk up to the swimming hole, because Mark doesn't want the people in the cottage—the artist with the fancy stereo—to see them. The lights aren't on in the house, but he can hear music playing. The water is really crashing down on the rocks tonight too, from yesterday's rain.

"Too much," says Val, when they get close enough to see the water. She's still wearing her high-heeled sandals, so it takes her a long time to climb down the rocks. Some kind of phosphorescent moss is glowing underneath one of the rocks.

"I don't know about this," says Mark. "The water's still pretty cold."

"One time when I was in Norway," she says, "I met this guy who had his own personal sauna. We lay in it until we couldn't stand the heat anymore and then we ran outside naked and jumped in the snow. Then we screwed, right there in the snow. It's supposed to be great for your skin."

She's unbuckling her sandal strap now. Mark is trying to remember some of the pictures in *More Joy of Sex*.

"This is unreal," says Val. "Somebody's playing one of my favorite albums." Van Morrison is saying *meet me down by the pylons. I've got something I want to give you.*

"Maybe we shouldn't be here," says Mark. The moon is nearly full. That's all he needs, for the artist to look out the window and paint the two of them into his picture. Recognize him from there, fishing with Virgil. Say, "You wouldn't know about those three ounces of dope, would you? And my two vintage Beatles albums and Jackson Browne, *Running on*

Empty?" They are probably still lying under the pine needles, maybe ten feet away.

Val is not paying attention. She has already taken off her clothes. (Mark wonders how she managed to get a tan even on her rear end.) She is standing naked on one of the higher rocks. "Van Morrison is so good I can't believe it," she says. Then she dives in.

Mark does not feel much like taking his clothes off. He's thinking about Sandy, wondering what she did after he left. Call her mother? Complain about him to her friend? Probably not. She wants everyone to think their life is perfect.

Sunrise in a couple of hours. The girl will be hungry. He will have to drive her through town. Someone—one of those girlfriends of Sandy's that's always hanging around downtown—will see him with her.

How is he supposed to get an erection when the water is so cold? His cock will just shrivel up.

The girl swims like Mark Spitz, naturally. Mark has never really learned how to do any stroke other than dog-paddle.

For dinner tonight Carla made stuffed grape leaves and lemon soup—one of Greg's favorite meals—and they had fresh strawberries with whipped cream for dessert. Greg went to get some grass for a joint and then he remembered that of course those kids who broke in took it. Carla has already decided to stay away from all drugs anyway until after the baby's born. And then she will be breast-feeding anyway. She may never touch the stuff again. She doesn't plan to be one of those mothers who gets high with their children sitting right there in the room. In fact, she doesn't want Greg to do that either. She has begun to understand—though she's still nine months away from being a parent—why it is that people with children are often so conservative.

So he's drinking wine instead, and she has made herself a glass of Perrier with a lime. Greg is sitting at his worktable, sketching out a plan for when to plant his vegetables. A copy of *Crockett's Victory Garden* is open beside him. Carla flips through cookbooks, looking up recipes that call for rhubarb because they have some growing in the yard. She has put the newest Van Morrison album on.

"Are you going to do a painting of that girl?" she says.

"I have a whole scene in mind," he says. "A tableau, sort of. She and her baby are part of it."

"What's the rest?"

"Some boys fishing below the falls," he says. "This house." He's not sure. He and Carla might be part of it too.

Carla asks why it is after all this time working with wire and nails and acrylic compound and coffee grounds, that he would want to paint a realistic scene again.

"There's something powerful about this spot," he says. "I feel as if a lot converges here. It's the kind of place where things happen."

Carla does not want anything else to happen. She would like to be safe at home in New York again, shopping for a well-designed crib. "I'll tell you one thing you don't know about this spot," says Carla. She hadn't intended to say this now. She was saving it.

"We conceived a baby here."

Mrs. Ramsay is hunched over the steering wheel of her dead husband's 1964 Eldorado. One reason she drives like this is that she's nearsighted and doesn't believe in wearing glasses, so it's hard for her to read the road signs. Another reason is that she hasn't driven in three years, and she's a little rusty. The car hasn't been registered either, so it's just as well that they're driving at night.

Tara sits beside her. Sunshine is in Tara's lap. (She knows this isn't safe, especially the way Mrs. Ramsay drives. The first city they get to, Tara is going to ask Mrs. Ramsay to stop so she can buy a car seat. She has forty-three dollars with her, from the till in the Just-like-nu Shop. She will worry later about what to do when that's gone.)

Melissa-Susan lies in the back. Mrs. Ramsay took the top drawer out of her oak buffet, and that's what Melissa-Susan is lying in. She's wrapped up in a hand-crocheted lace tablecloth that Mrs. Ramsay got for a wedding present. Tara was thinking, when Mrs. Ramsay wrapped her up in that, what a shame it would be if the baby got the tablecloth dirty. Mrs. Ramsay doesn't seem to be worried about that.

The car is so full you can't see out the rearview mirror. There is an eight-piece place setting of the Harvest Gold china they were giving away with purchases over five dollars at the Grand Union a couple of years back, and the dishes are not very well protected, so they're clattering quite a bit. There are Mrs. Ramsay's TV and a twelve-volume set of the *Golden How and Why Encyclopedia.* There are two African violet plants and a pressure cooker, a plaster cast of the *Praying Hands,* a beach umbrella, Mrs. Ramsay's Barbie Doll collection (one is the 1962 version, with a bubble cut and the Dinner at Eight evening gown). There is a framed photograph of Mrs. Ramsay's son Dwight in his Cub Scout uniform, an autographed copy of Lawrence Welk's autobiography, *Wunnerful, Wunnerful,* four boxes of 20 Mule Team Borax. The reason for that is they don't make Borax the way they used to anymore, back when Ronald Reagan was the host of *Death Valley Days.* Mrs. Ramsay happens to know they mix in chalk dust now. She found out just before they started doing it, so she bought enough of the old kind to last her.

Those are just a few of the things Mrs. Ramsay is taking with her to Disney World. Tara is not taking much: just a few outfits for her and Sunshine, the rainbow quilt she's making, Sunshine's stuffed panda bear and the plastic clip they put on her umbilical cord at the hospital. Tara keeps that because she has no pictures of Sunshine as a newborn. It is her only keepsake from that time.

They will stay overnight at a motel in Concord. Tara has never been to a motel before. Mrs. Ramsay says she has one thing to do there in the morning and then they will head south. She also mentioned something about stopping to talk to a breast-feeding consultant in New York City. Tara isn't clear what that was all about. Also, Tara doesn't understand why Mrs. Ramsay keeps calling Melissa "Susan." It must be her middle name.

Tara has begun to understand that Mrs. Ramsay is a little odd. But it's hard for her to gauge, because her own mother is odd, and people have always said that Tara is odd too. Most people would say Denver and Kalima were odd, and Tara thought they were wonderful. People probably called Pablo Picasso odd when he started doing those cubist paintings. On the other hand, nobody calls Sterling Lewis odd, and he has a five-month-old baby daughter who lives just down the street from him—or did—that he never even wanted to see.

"Now, there's a sensible person," says Mrs. Ramsay. They have just passed a man walking along the highway, heading in the direction they're coming from. Tara doesn't know what Mrs. Ramsay means.

"His feet, for goodness' sake. He wasn't wearing any shoes on his feet. He knows his feet have to breathe."

Though it is a good distance from Concord to Ashford, Wayne does not intend to hitchhike. This is not because there will be a police report out on him soon. Wayne knows the police here are fools. They will put up roadblocks and stake out bus stations, but they would never think to look for him walking along the highway, barefoot. The reason Wayne prefers to walk is, he doesn't want to make small talk just now. He has to store his energy, keep his concentration.

The girl is waiting for him, lying on her couch. Like him, she has been waiting a very long time. She understands that he isn't crazy. She knows that there are worse things than dying. Like living, when total devotion has died. When the passion is all withered up. That is what Wayne has had to do. He spared Loretta that.

They kept it going longer than he ever thought possible. For three years almost, it was as if they lived on top of a mountain—right at the brink of the precipice. Most people don't have ten minutes like that. The unluckiest ones have about ten minutes and then they lose it, and they have to spend the next fifty years trying to figure out what happened, get it back, finally knowing they never will. Reading the newspaper, going to McDonald's, watching TV shows. Breathing, shitting, fucking. Like some zoo gorilla with one thin memory somewhere inside his skull of life in the jungle.

Wayne has not forgotten his real life, his days with Loretta.

Those days are the reason he can do two hundred push-ups without feeling any pain, the reason why he knows he could put his hand in molten iron; his whole body, for that matter. Because he has already survived those three years, and nothing else he can think of would require any more of a person, their body or their mind.

The most obvious thing to do with Loretta was fuck. For the first six months he didn't let himself do it. There she was, lying naked on that mattress with her legs spread open, her cunt dripping, crying, after a few weeks of it, "Come into me, I can't stand it anymore." He was hard all the time—even in his sleep. It was like having a migraine in his groin. He would pound himself against the wall for relief, but there wasn't any.

He wouldn't let her touch him those months. Her arms kept reaching up, falling back when she remembered she wasn't supposed to, her hands flopping around like fish on a riverbank. "I've got to just feel your skin against my hand," she said. Finally he had to tie her arms down.

He touched her, though. Every inch. He spent one

whole night massaging her feet. He shaved her head so he could know her skull, just the way he knew her stomach and her breasts and her ears and her teeth, her tongue, the lines on her palms, the veins in her wrists. It got so he could just graze her eyelid and she'd come, if he left her waiting long enough for it. He knew all her places. Even today, five years since they buried her, Wayne could draw a map of her body. An atlas.

One night he came back and told her, "Now I'm ready." First he gave her a bath, so hot that tears ran down her cheeks. She knew by then not to say anything. Not after what he'd been through. She was just grateful.

He scrubbed her with a wire brush. Then he laid her out and dried her like a newborn baby. "Now?" she said. "Now?"

Finally she was ready and he entered her. Her muscles practically sucked him in, tugged at his cock, wouldn't release it. All those months holding the semen in, he was ready to explode. But he stayed inside her, didn't let go until the sun came up.

One whole year he kept her blindfolded. He'd read something Stevie Wonder said about how your sense of touch becomes refined when you can't see. It was true. She never had orgasms, before or after, like the ones she had the year she was blind. She cried when he told her he was taking the bandages off her eyes.

They invented a language. He read twins do that sometimes, when they're children. He never said to her, this word means this, or I want to make up words with you. He just started saying things and she started answering him. They had words for things that don't even exist in English.

Toward the end it was hardest. She was getting more restless—wanting to wear clothes, to get a TV set. Wanting to go out, those last months. That was when he had to stay up all night, thinking of things to do. It was like trying to find a cure for cancer. Not even a cure; he knew the case was terminal, always knew this couldn't last. It was just a matter of trying to keep what they had going as long as he could.

Once, that last month, she said to him, "Couldn't we get married? Move to a different apartment. I'd get a job and we'd make friends, have kids. We could be like other people."

After all he had shown her, she wanted to be like other people. That was the most depressing thing. He knew then there was no more point in prolonging it. Time to finish.

He thought he would just kill himself. If she believed—after everything that had happened—that she could live like other people, let her try it. Then he found out about the baby and that changed everything.

He had the one weak moment. Coming home—it was February, and down below zero—and finding that even though the superintendent had turned their heat off, she was still naked, the way he wanted her to be. Not pacing around, the way she had been those last few weeks, but lying on her mattress with her hands on her belly. He knew to look at her that she must have been sick.

"I was wrong wanting things to change," she said. Now she'd be good. Now she'd do everything he told her to. She only wanted one thing.

"That's the one thing you can't have," he said. He had spent three days in the state library studying medical books, figuring out the best way to get rid of a baby. Even though he knew getting rid of the baby wouldn't be enough. He was weak enough to hope.

He worked like a watchmaker, inserting the wire. No problem dilating her cervix, of course. She couldn't close herself to him if she wanted. But then when he began scraping her uterus, probing the wire deeper and deeper to make sure he'd dislodged it, she started bleeding. At first just a trickle, like her period, so he wasn't worried. Then streams of blood, deep red, soaking the mattress, spreading into a bigger and bigger stain underneath her. She was pale to begin with, of course, from never going outside. Her skin tone just changed to bluish. Pulse got very slow. She was so weak she could hardly talk. Didn't need to. He knew she was thinking: Kill me now please. So he did.

And now there is someone else waiting for him to take care of her. Someone else who understands that life in the zoo is not worth living after life in the jungle. If he were stronger—younger maybe, not so tired, because he is still strong—Wayne would try it again. Find another apartment in some other old mill building, get another mattress, another set of black window shades. Take her there, try for a few more months of shutting everything out except their two bodies. But the hospital has taken a lot out of him—even with the vitamins and the exercising. What he said to Charles about drugs being poison—that was true too. His concentration isn't as sharp as it used to be. It's too late for him to be her lover.

"Is this the exterminator?" That's what she asked him on the phone. Well, yes, he will tell her. Yes, I am.

Mrs. Ramsay is not home, of course. Wanda came straight over here from Sandy's, but she did not expect to find Mrs. Ramsay and Melissa, and she was right. The door is locked but the lights are on in the dining room. Wanda can see, from the window on the porch, that some of Mrs. Ramsay's things are gone. (The TV for one. There is the remote control machine, sitting on one of the chair pillows, connected to nothing.) The top drawer of Mrs. Ramsay's buffet is missing, and some photographs have been laid out in a line on the table. Hard to tell what the subject was—just a lot of large pink shapes.

What to do? Wanda thinks that taking someone's baby, even if it's your grandchild, must be against the law. But what if you hit that baby, and now all she does is have diarrhea and sleep? If Wanda told the police and they found Mrs. Ramsay, she would tell them about that.

Wanda has that feeling in her stomach like when she has just eaten a pizza and three Milky Way bars, wishing she could throw up and it would all go away. She just stands there in her Moonlight Acres uniform with the ketchup spatters on the front, her face pressed up to the window, watching the glass fog up.

"You're probably wondering where I got my scar," says Mrs. Ramsay. She is sitting naked except for her underpants on the mint-green motel bedspread facing Tara, rubbing vitamin E oil into her breasts. Tara has been focusing on a painting of a covered bridge that hangs over the TV set.

"After Dwight was born," she says, "Harold didn't want to do it anymore. He had this problem with his weenie, if you want to know the truth.

"Which was fine by me, only I wished I could have a little baby girl. What's the use of knowing the detached rosette chain stitch if you never have a little girl to make dresses for?

"So I prayed to God to give me a baby. I waited, and then what do you think? My stomach starts getting bigger. Mrs. Smith stops paying her monthly visits. Harold gets pretty disturbed, because the situation with his weenie is still the same, you understand. I explain to him: I did not commit any sins to get this baby. This is like Mary and Jesus.

"You have never seen needlework like I did that winter. A tiny cable-knit cardigan. A little lattice-smocked bathrobe. Argyle booties. A crewel-embroidered bunting. You name it.

"In my sixth month, the doctor says, 'I don't understand this. There is no kicking.' 'This is a well-mannered little girl,' I say. 'That's all.' 'But I can't get a heartbeat either,' he says.

"In my seventh month, I get pains like you can't imagine. They open me up—Caesarean. And you know what's in there? A mole. Hydatiform mole, it's called; looks like a bunch of grapes. They think I am out cold for this, but I am not. I hear everything—doctors and nurses coming from all over the hospital to see. Two of them fighting over who gets to keep it. Lots of jokes.

"And here is what my doctor does, just before he sews me up. He puts one hand on each side of my incision and he makes my skin move like it's the mouth on a puppet. He makes this puppet mouth ask one of the nurses what she's doing Friday night. She gets very excited and tells the doctor she's free. 'Too bad,' he says. (This is still my stomach he's playing around with.) 'Because I'll be all tied up.' Then he gives me the stitches, and this is where he gave them to me. After I got home I took all the little dresses to the dump."

It literally takes Mark's breath away, the water is that cold. "I don't know how the trout stand this," he says.

"Trout?" says Val. "You mean there are fish in this brook?" Then she sort of goes crazy, screaming, splashing all over the place, pulling herself up on a rock. Mark's pants and the Hawaiian shirt fall into the water, float downstream.

"Get my shirt," she yells. Mark is downstream, standing naked on the shore near the shallower water. He steps out on a fallen log, reaching. Misses, falls in. The shirt is gone.

"What a bummer," says Val. "That was my best top."

All they have left to wear are Val's jeans and the terry-cloth seat cover from Mark's car. They get inside and Mark turns on the heater. Val sits way on her side. Her nipples are all wrinkled up from the cold. "You sure look like an idiot, wearing that seat cover," she says. Mark guesses he is not going to make it with her after all.

"How can you be sure?" says Greg. "If it's only been a couple of days."

"My breasts feel different. I feel all this blood pumping to my uterus. It's just very clear to me."

He is silent, peeling the paper off a conté crayon.

"So how do you feel about it?" she says.

"I have to think. I need some time."

He has never needed time before, to know how he feels.

"You want it, don't you?"

"Did you hear a car start? What's a car doing out here in the middle of the night?"

Wanda is standing on Sandy's doorstep again. She wouldn't have come up if she hadn't seen the light on. In fact, through the window from the street, it looked to Wanda as if Sandy was dancing. She turned the music off when Wanda knocked. Now she has opened the door. Mark Junior is asleep in her arms with one fist wrapped around a piece of her hair.

"I need help," says Wanda. Up to now she has held it in, but when she sees Sandy with her baby, she begins to cry so hard that at first Sandy can't make out what she's saying. "Mrs. Ramsay took Melissa. We've got to find her."

The sound of her parents screwing woke Jill up. (Was that her mother crying? Hard to picture.) Now she can't get back to sleep, thinking about tomorrow. She is thinking of the fetus diagrams in her biology book, the little fish faces and the tiny curled spines, the transparent skin with the bones showing through. She wonders if it will be big enough to see. What do they do with it after they take it out?

Bring sanitary napkins, size super, they said. There will be bleeding. Jill has not used sanitary napkins since the first year she had her period, when she was thirteen. It happened during math class—a wet feeling in her pants, a trickle down her leg when she went up to the board. Her friend Debbie took her to the girls' room and showed her what to do. "Now you can be a mother," Debbie said. Did they ever laugh.

She will leave around seven, explain that she'll get breakfast at McDonald's so she can be at the mall when it

opens. Later she will tell her mother that one of her friends is
altering the dress for her.

She wishes she didn't have to go alone.

No matter how many kids she has someday, she will
never name any of them Patrick.

The records are stacked high next to the stereo—all Dolly
Parton. Ann hasn't been putting them back in the jackets tonight. She has not mopped up the spilled Kahlúa either, or
drained the tub. There's a pool of wax on the windowsill,
under one of the candlesticks. The dog has not been fed.

Ann is pacing the floor. Back and forth over the Orien-
tal rug a thousand times, leaving a little trail of bath powder.
Sometimes she will say the words to the songs along with
Dolly. I hold an armful of nothing close to my side. The days
come and go, they mean nothing to me. I want you to be the
last one to touch me. I will always love you.

The sky has begun to lighten. Sun's coming up. Ann
goes to the door, steps outside, looking down the road. The
air is heavy with the smell of lilacs. The black flies hover
around her. She can tell it's going to be hot. She goes back
in, leaving the door ajar.

Mount Saint Helens has erupted again. Volcanic ash is falling as far as Wyoming. In Spokane, day looks like night. The
Columbia River is about to wash out three towns. That's
what the newscaster on the *Today* show says. It is a black-
and-white set. Budget motel.

"Rise and shine," says Mrs. Ramsay. Tara is curled up
in one of the two twin beds with her arms around Sunshine.
They only got here four hours ago. She wishes she could
sleep some more.

"Could we stay here a little longer?" says Tara. "If I get
Sunshine up now she'll be fussy all day." Melissa-Susan lies
in her drawer, not moving.

"We have to hurry," says Mrs. Ramsay. "We have to stop them before they kill any more babies."

Carla dreams of a baby on the rocks. He is propped up in an infant seat, kicking a piece of grass with his foot. All around him the water is swirling. Where's the mother? Is she crazy?

He is smiling, straining at the little safety belt that holds him in. He lifts his head up, leans forward. He has never been able to do that before. A butterfly lands just beyond his toe. He would like to hold it. Stretch.

There she is, in the water. Shampooing her hair. Bubbles drip all down her neck, onto her breasts. She is naked. There is a man with her—a boy really—scrubbing her back. "Not there," she says. She's laughing.

The sun's in his eyes. He doesn't like that. "Uh," he says. "Huh. Huh. Uh. Bub. Bub. Bub."

She can't hear; the radio's turned up too loud. "What do you think this is, a James Bond movie?" she says.

Kicking harder now. Butterfly gone. She hasn't changed his diaper in a long time. His skin is beginning to turn pink. Toe on moss. Head forward. Hands reaching. Bub. Bub. Bub.

"I should check the baby," she says. They kiss again.

Seat forward. He lands on his face against the rock, too stunned to cry. Water crashes down, lifts him up. He's spinning, swirling, upside down. Moving so fast. Where is the air? It's like being born again.

"The baby," she screams. "The baby's in the water."

Head on rock. Bubbles.

Here is what Wayne did, once Loretta's heart stopped beating. First he cut the nails on her toes and her fingers. When she was alive he kept them long, filed very sharp, so he could feel her fingers digging into his back, his thighs, his biceps, her toes running up and down his calves, while they made love. Feeling is the important thing. Not necessarily feeling comfortable.

He knew some places where he didn't want to put the clippings. In the wastebasket, for instance, for some eager beaver police sergeant to hit on. Down the drain. So he swallowed them—felt them scratching deep inside his throat, one of the few places where he had never felt her before. He took the longest fingernail and carved a deep X in his forearm, deep enough to draw blood. He sharpened a pencil with his penknife and sprinkled the lead dust into the cut. He still has the silver-colored scar.

Then he clipped a little curl of her pubic hair. He didn't wash the blood off, because that would have taken away her smell. He made it into a ring (her hair was that long, that thick; you could braid it) and he wore the ring all through the trial. The prosecutor would be up there leaning on the jury box, saying, "What we have here is an animal. No respect for human life," and Wayne could sit listening, with his head leaned against his hand, his ring finger, just inhaling her.

After he got what he needed, he had to clean things up. Not with any plan about getting rid of the evidence, staying free. His life was over anyway. He just wanted to protect their privacy—his and Loretta's. Certain things are private.

So he cut up her mattress. This takes a long time when you're using nail scissors. Somewhere in all the blood was a clot he thought maybe was the fetus. He put that back up inside her—she would like that.

The mattress pieces—he stuffed them in four green plastic garbage bags and drove out to the highway, scattering them in little bits over a fifteen-mile stretch near where he had met her, watching out for cops, because there was a fifty-dollar fine for littering.

Then he went to Jordan Marsh to buy her an outfit. He never liked getting her clothes while she was alive—liked her naked, let her have a few pieces of men's long underwear just because the room got cold, winters. But he wanted her dead body dressed just like anybody else, so they would never know.

It was the first time he'd gone into a store like that. There was a woman standing right by the door demonstrating a new line of umbrellas and another one that tried to squirt some men's cologne on his arm. "Where can I buy a dress?" he said. "Also some shoes, and some underwear."

She told him so many different departments he couldn't keep track, drifted off.

Way in back, on the third floor, he found the pink chenille bathrobe. "It doesn't matter what size," he said. "I don't need a bag."

Underpants. He rubbed seven different pairs against his cheek, studied the way they made the crotch. "Are you interested in bikini style?" said the girl. No, Loretta would not like that. He chose the plainest kind. White, one hundred percent cotton, elastic on the waist and reinforced crotch panel. A white cotton brassiere. "What size?" she said.

He put his hands on the glass display case, spreading his fingers to just the size of her two breasts, making them curve out just in the shape of Loretta. "Like that," he said.

"Oh. Thirty-six B."

Then he bought her some pink bedroom slippers with rhinestone clips, and rhinestone earrings. He bought her a fourteen-carat gold ring and a natural-bristle hairbrush from England. The one thing he would not buy, even now that it didn't really matter, was makeup. How could you paint that face?

He carried the packages up the steps to their apartment and laid them next to her. He carried her to the bathroom, scrubbed her all over, until their smells were gone. He shampooed her hair and blew on it very softly while it was drying, to make it fluffy. Then he brushed and brushed. Then he eased the brassiere over her arms, fitted her breasts into the cups. He started to hook the brassiere in back and then he turned her over again to kiss her one more time in that place just above her nipples.

Her skin was colder than usual and her legs were getting stiff. He put the shoes on slowly, and the robe, screwed on the earrings and fitted on the ring, leaving the underpants until last. Then it was time and he put her feet through the leg holes. He had to take off the slippers and put them on again. He slid the panties up her legs.

Done. A few hairs sticking out the sides of the double-reinforced crotch panel, that was all. A single dot of blood. He turned her on her side and buried his face in her buttocks. That's when the policemen broke down the door.

"All I can say is, you'd just better not come home with one of those strapless numbers," says Doris. She still doesn't understand why Jill wouldn't want her to come along on the shopping trip. People have always said what a smart shopper Doris is.

"Believe me, you'll be much more popular with the boys if you leave a little something to the imagination," says Doris. She has suddenly noticed that her daughter's filling out on top. Jill had better not have any ideas about some low-cut Raquel Welch number, that's all.

"I'll only look at the turtlenecked prom gowns, O.K.?" says Jill.

"You don't need to get fresh with me, young lady. Don't forget where that fifty dollars in your purse came from."

"O.K., O.K.," says Jill. She is heading for the door.

"Aren't you even going to get something to eat?"

"I'll stop somewhere on the way." Jill puts her hand out for the car keys.

"I'll never get over it," says Doris. "It seems like only yesterday we were sending you off to first grade. I keep wondering, what happened to my little girl?"

*   *   *

Sandy says Mrs. Ramsay probably just went to some friend's house with Melissa. Maybe she's going through menopause or something. That's supposed to make you act a little weird. Sandy says she has a friend with a car. They can ask Carla if she would just drive them around town, looking for an old green Cadillac. While they are at it they can look for Mark's Valiant too. It's seven-thirty. Carla is probably up by now.

Greg has to see Tara again. He can't wait until noon, the way he said. He will go over to her house, explain that they have to talk. The truth is, that's the one thing he doesn't feel a need to do. But just having her in his car again, sitting beside him on the seat (what kind of hairdo will the baby wear today?) might make things clearer. Carla is still asleep. He will just leave a note.

Nothing good on the radio. Just a lot of stuff about that volcano that keeps erupting. In the local news, escaped mental patient, believed dangerous. Jill isn't really paying attention.

She needs gas, pulls into Speedway. A man taps on her window; she rolls it down. "Five dollars' worth of regular," she says. Why is he barefoot?

"Say," he says after he has put the nozzle in her tank. "There's someone I'm trying to find. I wonder if you'd know where she lives." He tells the name. "She lives alone," he says.

"I think that's the girl my father does odd jobs for," Jill says. She gives him the directions and a five-dollar bill.

By the time the station attendant wakes up, Wayne is a half mile down the road.

Mark was so beat he slept right through past sunrise. It must be half-past eight now, and he's sitting here in broad daylight with a girl he just met, wearing nothing but a seat cover. Val is curled up in the backseat with her arms crossed over her breasts. Asleep, she looks like a little kid.

At least his pants will be dry enough to put on now. He puts his feet in the legs and steps outside the car to pull them up. That's what he's doing—standing in the dirt with his pants around his ankles and his ass in the breeze—when he sees his wife coming down the road with their son in her arms.

At first Tara thought they were just stopping here so Mrs. Ramsay could drop off some of her pamphlets. It seemed unusual that an abortion clinic would agree to distribute a pamphlet called "I Am Your Fetus," but she thought maybe it's like the TV stations giving equal time to all the presidential candidates. She understood that something funny was going on when Mrs. Ramsay told her to walk up to the reception desk with Sunshine and then keel over on the floor, saying, "Get me a doctor." The real reason she was willing to go up to the reception desk was because Melissa-Susan, out in the car, has been looking so strange, and when she said that to Mrs. Ramsay, said maybe they should stop by the hospital, ask if there was a pediatrician who could take a look at her, Mrs. Ramsay said, "All she needs is a good dose of my milk."

When Mrs. Ramsay said that, it suddenly occurred to Tara that she might be more than just odd, that Wanda might not have been told about their vacation plans, that they might not really be headed for Disney World, or if they were, it might not be a good idea for Tara and Sunshine to come along. That business about passing through Jupiter, Florida, to say hello to her old friend Burt Reynolds—that was definitely not true. All this Tara understood. What she did not understand was that while she was trying to explain to the woman at the reception desk about Melissa's funny green diarrhea, while the plump-looking girl sat on the Danish modern sofa reading *Mademoiselle* and those identical twin girls crawling around on the floor reached for their mother's urine sample, while the boy in the leather jacket clicked away on his rosary beads and the doctor was saying, "I am not a pediatrician but if this is a real emergency"— while all this was happening, Mrs. Ramsay was sprinkling gasoline in the operating room and lighting a match. The first Tara heard of any such goings on was when the other nurse ran out, yelling, "Call the fire department. There's a crazy woman trying to burn the building down." There was so much confusion then that Tara just slipped away without anybody noticing.

Jill has chosen not to have an anesthetic. That way she can get out of here in two hours, be at Jordan Marsh by noon, stuff a prom gown in the shopping bag she brought along, drive home in time for work.

She's lying on a paper-covered table waiting for the doctor to come. She's wearing a white hospital gown, open at the back. The paper crackles when she shifts her buttocks. She slides one heel in the stirrups, remembers a pony ride she took once—her father holding the reins—at the Hopkinton fair. There's a poster of koala bears taped to the ceiling. A Muzak version of "I Am the Walrus" drifts in from the hall. A nurse rushes through, setting out a row of metal implements. Get all your ingredients ready before you start, her mother says. The secret to good cooking.

"Doctor will be with you in a moment," she says. She pats Jill on the foot. A new song comes on—heavily orchestrated Joni Mitchell. Jill closes her eyes.

She hears the door open again, the clatter of bottles, metal, hitting the floor, a crash. The reason she doesn't open her eyes is, she doesn't want to remember the doctor's face, see it in her dreams. She especially doesn't want to see what comes out when it's over. She is going to think about the day she and Virgil went to Weirs beach and got tickets for the Water Slide. She is going to think about that until they've

wheeled her out of this room and the worst of the cramps are
over. Putting on her bikini now. Standing at the top of the
slide, looking down, and the man punching her ticket.
There's water splashing against her back and she is shooting
along the aqua tube. Chlorine in her eyes but she doesn't
mind. Gliding around a curve, speeding up, nearing the pool
at the bottom and then hitting water. Up for air, Virgil beside her. One of her breasts has popped out of her bikini top,
but no one else notices. "Lose a tit?" he says. They kiss.

   Gasoline smell, a popping, crackling sound. Jill opens
her eyes and sees a face she knows but can't place. Red-
headed woman throwing lit matches on the floor, somebody
yelling, "Run."

   For a second she forgets where she is, and then she is
down off the table, jumping over a burning spot, racing
down the hall. Not until she's out the door and standing on
cool grass does she realize she left her best-broken-in pair of
jeans on the chair inside, and the back of her hospital gown
is flapping in the breeze.

"Gone," says Mrs. Farley. "Forty-three dollars' worth gone,
if you want to know. She and the little bastard left sometime
in the night. No note or anything."

   He will never find Tara, Greg knows. She would never
come back to a place like this.

   "You have any kids?" says Mrs. Farley, who did not
take the time to put on her prosthetic brassiere before answering the door, so that her chest is not simply flat but
actually caved in. "Take my advice," she says. "Don't."

Doris doesn't bother taking out her curlers this time. Not for
that frizzy-haired hippie down the road who only bought
one jar of moisturizer, and not even the twelve-ounce. She
can just go the way she is, and when the woman offers her a
cup of tea she will know enough to say no thank you.

"I'm just stepping out to make an Avon delivery," she calles to Reg, who is rustling around in the den. "Back in a jiffy."

"Take your time," he says.

Doris may have been fooled, but Reg is not. He remembers the way his wife looked when she was expecting Jill and Timmy, knows the sound of a woman retching into the toilet bowl at dawn. Something's different about Jill's face too. She's pregnant, all right.

He also figures where she must have gone today, why she came into the den last night and put her arms around his neck the way she hasn't since she was about ten. She sat through two innings of the Red Sox game with him and didn't even notice when Yaz hit a homer. Then she asked if he could give her twenty dollars, and please not to tell Mom.

His life hasn't turned out anything like how he thought. He has a wife who says, "Zinnias? Can I eat zinnias?" and a son whose big dream is meeting Charo on a USO tour. The worst problem his daughter ever had in her life, she doesn't tell him about. And no wonder. He's a forty-five-year-old man who lies awake at night fantasizing about a moony girl who sits around all day listening to records. Made-up songs about tragedies that never really happened. Cutworms got her squash plants and she hasn't even noticed.

It seems appropriate that a man in his situation should be taking down his .22-caliber rifle, loading it, so he can blow the brains out of a few blind animals that don't weigh much more than hummingbirds.

There's a flower bed in front of the Women's Health Clinic—salvia, planted to form an O with a tail on it, that symbol for woman that Tara remembers from old Ben Casey reruns. One of the firemen is standing right in the middle of this flower bed, and some of the water from his hose is dripping down in the dirt, making mud. A nurse runs past him, carrying file folders and a typewriter. Another fireman staggers out the door of the building with a large black machine, a long tube attached. That must be what they hook you up to.

Tara stands just behind the police barricade. She knows she should probably be upset, but she isn't. She feels a little like she did in Sterling Lewis's father's den that night, as he was easing her underpants down her legs. A little like when she was lying on the delivery table at the Concord Hospital watching Sunshine shoot out between her legs; a little like when Denver stood at the door of the Just-like-nu Shop, just before taking off for Georgia, and he reached his hand into her shirt and squeezed her breast in just the right way to make milk come out on his fingers. And he raised his hand to his mouth and licked it. Tara feels, now too, as if she's floating about three feet off the ground, watching everything happen, bobbing along in a slow-moving brook maybe, heading toward open sea. Not like there's anything to do about it; just being carried along. Like this is all a movie or a TV show. She isn't thinking about what she will do next. She's just waiting until she does it.

The firemen are shooting water into the flames now. There's a police car out in front, with the blue light flashing. Two policemen are leading Mrs. Ramsay toward the cruiser—more like escorts to a ball than policemen. It looks as if Mrs. Ramsay might melt into the ground if they let go of her arms. She's screaming something about having to feed her baby.

"Sure, sure," says one of the policemen. A third officer has gone over to inspect Mrs. Ramsay's car, parked cockeyed across the street. A doctor from the clinic is peering in the windows. He collects vintage Cadillacs.

"She's right," the policeman yells back to the others. "There is a baby in here."

"I wouldn't worry about feedings now if I were you," says the doctor to Mrs. Ramsay. "That baby's dead."

*   *   *

Pamphlet (opened to page one): "I Am Your Fetus. The moment I was conceived, the whole Universe shifted to make room for me. I am a pure and unsoiled entity, closer to God than I will ever be again. When I am born it will be like the birth of Jesus. For that one moment I will be holy. Please don't flush me down the toilet."

Carla wakes up feeling nauseated. Greg's side of the bed is empty. She climbs down the ladder, heading for the bathroom. In the middle of the living room (Greg must have been up late, working on this) is the painting of Packers Falls. A tableau, he called it. The boys fishing, the naked girl and her baby. Above them all, walking over the bridge, is a mask-faced woman pushing a baby carriage. Not one of those umbrella strollers most people use. This is the kind of pram an English nanny would push through a park. And in the background, caught in the center of a whirlpool, there is a man with his mouth open and his arms in the air. He's drowning.

Greg drives back to the cottage, gripping the wheel. He knows some things now. He will not be planting winter squash and pumpkins, for instance. He and Carla will be back in the city by the time they'd be ready to harvest. He should be hitting the Renaissance right about then, assuming Walker takes him back. They will find an apartment in a safer neighborhood and take natural childbirth classes. They will get married, have the wedding somewhere interesting and amusing, like on the Staten Island ferry. Just a few of their friends. Afterwards they'll go back to the new apartment. Maybe Carla will make her couscous.

It would get very cold here in the winter anyway.

*   *   *

Tara thinks about Melissa's clothes hanging, soon, on the racks at the Just-like-nu Shop (where Wanda got them in the first place), and other pregnant women fingering the terry cloth, checking to see if the snappers still work, washing them in Ivory and folding them away, ready for new babies. She thinks about Sunshine taking her first steps, saying apple, kitty, book, riding the school bus, going on a date, and Melissa frozen in everybody's minds (if they remember her at all) at three and a half months, with a red mark on her forehead, and diarrhea. Crazily, she thinks about something she read once, that every girl baby is born with her complete lifetime supply of eggs tucked into tiny baby ovaries. And how Melissa's will just stay there.

Wanda buying a child psychology book, showing Sandy and Tara a folder she keeps, of Ann Landers's advice on child raising. Got to be firm, spare the rod and spoil the child. Saying, I won't ever understand how you get a screaming baby to stop.

Tara thinks about Wanda's stretch marks. How she will always have them. She thinks about Melissa, dead in Mrs. Ramsay's car. The expression, *leaving your mark.*

Of course Tara cries. She also thinks about how lucky she is, that Sunshine is here and gurgling in her arms, that her toes curl, her fingernails grow, her face gets red and screws up when she cries, she wets. Of course she knows that Mrs. Ramsay won't be driving south now, but also, she knows she doesn't need Mrs. Ramsay to take care of her. She's a mother, not a child. She can take care of things. All she needs to do now is get the two of them to Georgia, where the babies are safe.

A crowd has gathered by Mrs. Ramsay's car now, and a lot of rumors are going around: that what they found inside was a six-month-old aborted fetus, that the mother was a nun, she took drugs, the baby was deformed, there was a whole roomful of others like this one in the clinic, in bottles. Some people are saying "Where?" Latecomers are pushing to get a better view.

Tara stands on the grass a few feet back, holding Sunshine very tight. She's thinking about a time last fall, when she and Wanda were both pregnant and sitting on the steps by the Laundromat. One of the last warm days. Putting their hands on each other's stomach to feel the kicks. A lump the size of a walnut sticking out very plainly under Wanda's sweater. Melissa's foot. Wanda talking about how their kids could be best friends, ride the school bus together.

She remembers the first time she saw Melissa, a few days after Wanda brought her home from the hospital. Wanda must have put baby powder on Melissa's red birthmark. She looked sort of dusty.

Also, her eyes were always getting stuck shut. She'd wake up and try to lift up her eyelids and there'd be this stuff caked on her short pale lashes, so she could only open her eyes partway. It turned out to be blocked tear ducts. The pediatrician said they'd clear up on their own by six months.

Tara pictures someone—Wanda?—picking the flecks of dried tears off Melissa's lashes now, putting her in a final fresh diaper. Cloth?

She thinks about Wanda telling her one time (at the Laundromat again, only it was late winter now, and they had their babies, and wash to do) about an article she read, this woman that got paid $20,000 to have a baby for some woman that couldn't have one. Nice woman, college education. Not that Wanda would ever give any baby of hers away. Still, it made you think. Having Melissa meant she had something worth $20,000. "I never had anything valuable before," she said.

Because she can't imagine what to do now, Jill is not doing anything. She's just hanging around on the sidewalk watching the firemen reel in their hoses, watching the clinic nurses load equipment into somebody's car. One of them walks past carrying a scale model of a pelvis. Another one is saying, "What are we supposed to do with ten cases of waterlogged maxi-pads?" Somebody has put a sheet over the dead baby. They've taken away the red-haired woman screaming something about syphilis.

"Have you got any pains?" Jill turns around to see Tara standing there, holding her baby and an airline flight bag. Small world.

"Because there's this place in Georgia where they have all these midwives and babies. A spiritual community. Everything's natural." Tara unbuttons her shirt and guides Sunshine's mouth onto her left nipple.

"I was just thinking, we could go there together."

Jill stares past Tara for a second. They are putting the baby's body in an ambulance. What looks like an empty bureau drawer is just sitting in the middle of the sidewalk. A woman bends to examine it—you can see her trying to decide if it's worth lugging home—and then moves on.

"They have this man there named Denver that kisses you while your baby's coming out, so it won't hurt."

And Virgil thinks he's so cool, with his three alternate positions and that pair of jockey shorts that says "Home of the Whopper." Imagine what they do in a commune.

"They grow all their own food, no chemicals. At Christmas they make this giant fruitcake and there's a candlelight ceremony that lasts until sunrise. Everybody singing. The babies there hardly ever get colds."

What if she just never went home? Her father would call the hospitals, drive around all night in his pickup, looking for her. All her mother would worry about is the car.

When the baby's born she will send a letter. Just a postcard maybe: You have a grandson. He looks like you, Daddy—bald.

And then one morning her mother turns on the Phil Donahue show. She doesn't even look up from her ironing until Donahue says here's our other guest, an unwed mother from a spiritual community in Georgia, and it's Jill. Forget about strapless dresses: hers is unbuttoned to the waist and wide open. She's nursing her baby on national television.

"What did your parents do wrong?" says a woman in the studio audience. (Those women on Donahue are always worrying about how to keep their kids from turning .into drug addicts and lesbians.)

"My dad's O.K.," she will say. "My mother was a real tight-ass."

"Why do you think you had such an easy labor?" Donahue asks her.

French kissing.

"They have this bus they drive around in," Tara's saying now. "And they're always singing." She has taken a wraparound Indian skirt out of the flight bag for Jill to put on over the hospital gown. She has set Sunshine down on the grass, and one of Mrs. Ramsay's pamphlets lies beside her, with the pages flapping.

"So," says Tara. "You want to come?"

Jill thinks about her father for a second—imagines that she's sitting on his lap again and he's telling her not to worry, he'll make everything O.K., she'll always be his little girl. Then she thinks about her mother.

"We could take my car," says Jill. Nobody even sees them go.

Val is always a wreck in the morning. She's not used to waking up this early, and certainly not the way she had to wake up just now. One minute she's asleep in the guy's car, having this terrific dream that they made her lead singer of Pink Floyd, and the next thing she knows, the guy is practically throwing her out of the car and saying, "I've got to split, man." And there's this little kid screaming his head off, and two chicks, one fat and one thin, getting into the front seat. No good morning or anything. And now she's out in the middle of nowhere with her tits bare and the heel broken off one of her sandals—starving, among other things.

There is something sticking up through the leaves over by the water. She goes to look. Wild! A Jackson Browne album and two old Beatles. That's one good thing anyway.

So she does what she always does when she can't think of anything else. She sits down and reads the liner notes.

Greg is just rounding the last curve when he sees the girl sitting there. Skinny back, tiny bare breasts. She's holding something but it's not the baby. A book maybe, or a picture.

In another second of course he knows it's not Tara after all. This girl is nothing like Tara. He parks the car, gets out. She looks up, tilts her head sideways for a moment, then comes toward him. She makes no effort to cover herself.

"Mr. Hansen?" she says. "Don't you know who I am? It's Valerie from art class. Remember, I did that oil painting of my foot for spring term? This is so cosmic."

Even before her house comes into view, Wayne can smell the lilacs. The scent is almost too sweet, like having your face pressed tight up against some old grandma's bosom at Christmastime. But it's nice hearing birds for a change. And it will be good to put his feet on that grass, after twenty miles of gravel.

Loretta's last spring (he knew by then it was probably her last) he drove all over Manchester, looking for the best lilac bush. He waited until after dark, after all the house lights went out. Then he went into the people's yard and chopped it down, right at the base. It was more a tree than a bush actually. He could just barely haul it into the back of his truck. It was a real bitch to carry up three flights of stairs.

He had to break off some of the branches to get it in the door of their apartment. There were little purple flowers shedding all over the place. He dragged it into the middle of the room. Loretta was lying on her mattress, her eyes closed, but not asleep.

"You want to see the lilacs blooming—well, here they are," he said. Almost nothing made her cry by that point, but when he lay down next to her there were tears on her cheeks. She never said a word.

Mark and Sandy drop Wanda off at Rocky's, then go home. Mark says nothing because he can't think of what to say. Sandy says nothing because if they can just manage to never talk about this, they can go on like it never happened.

There's a newspaper on the doorstep: ten more dead from the volcano, ninety-eight still missing. There's a circular announcing this week's specials at the Grand Union. There's an envelope from a photographer's studio.

In the picture, Sandy and Mark Junior sit in front of a snow-capped peak, not a cloud in the sky. Sandy's eyes are closed, blinking, and her head is tilted a little to one side, the way they said to do in the brochure from the modeling school. One hand is raised (brushing a piece of hair out of her face). The other hand is wrapped around Mark Junior's stomach. You can tell how tight she's holding him by the way the fabric of his shirt is all pulled up, so his belly button shows. Sandy's not exactly smiling but her mouth is turned up. She has just said cheese.

Mark Junior is looking right into the camera. One of his arms is raised too, but in a fist, like some protestor. The other arm is a little blurry (it must have been moving). He's wearing his baseball cap.

But here is the amazing thing. He is not crying after all. His skin is not red and his mouth is not screwed up. He's smiling. He looks like an angel.

Of course her dog doesn't bark at Wayne. They never do. This one licks his bare feet as he comes up the walk and follows him onto the porch. There's a bowl of granola on the table. Wayne takes a handful and starts chewing. He looks out toward the field at a little wooden windmill, a man swinging an ax up and down and up. Stiff breeze.

The door is not quite shut. No sound comes from inside the house except the noise a record player makes when the amplifier's turned on but the record's over. "I'm here," he says, stepping in.

A few hundred yards back, Reg Johnson walks slowly toward the house, a rifle in his hands.

A NOTE ON THE TYPE

The text of this book was set, via computer-driven cathode-ray tube, in a film version of a type face called Baskerville. The face is a facsimile reproduction of types cast from molds made for John Baskerville (1706–75) from his designs. Baskerville's original face was one of the forerunners of the type style known as "modern face" to printers—a "modern" of the period A.D. 1800.

This book was composed by American–Stratford Graphic Services, Inc., Brattleboro, Vermont.

Design by Dorothy Schmiderer